Shattered Dreams

Betrayed by Love, Book 2

HD KELLEY

Green Way
PUBLISHING

ISBN: 0692655506
ISBN-13: 978-0-69265-550-4

PUBLISHED BY GREEN WAY PUBLISHING
www.greenwaypublishing.com

Disclaimer:
This book is not suitable for younger readers. There is strong language, adult situations, and some violence.

DEDICATION

For all those who believe in second chances.
Love will find a way.
Enjoy!

Shattered Dreams

Author Warning:

Dear Reader,

    As a reader myself, I know how important it is to be aware of sensitive issues that could trigger painful memories for some. Shattered Dreams is a love story born out of betrayal. The path to love for Spencer and Ashlan didn't come easy. In order to tell their story, I had to touch on some of those 'hot button' issues. While neither the book nor I glorify or excuse infidelity, domestic abuse, or alcoholism, all three themes were explored in order to tell their story.

    Life isn't always fair. Sometimes things happen that are beyond our control that can flip our lives upside down. Picking up the pieces afterwards isn't always easy. In fact, it takes great courage and strength. It was my intention with Shattered Dreams to show the inner strength and courage found, not in forgetting, but in forgiveness.

    To anyone who has been hurt by love, I hope you find the strength to move on so **you** too can find your happily ever after.

Sincerely,
HD Kelley

Spoiler Alert!
Shattered Dreams is book two in the Betrayed by Love series. If you have not read book one, *Scattered Thoughts,* prepare to have the ending spoiled.

Chapter One
Spencer

Nothing excited me more than the smell of leather intermingled with sex, a heady mix that had my cock pulsing with need. Maybe it was the excitement of what would come. Pain, pleasure, the control it was sure to bring. *God, I love this place.* Esoteric, a private BDSM club in Chicago, was one of the few places I could be myself. No one understood me the way the members there did. We all shared a special type of bond, a brotherhood at its finest. To the outside world, we were seen as deviants, our lifestyle of kinky sex and dominance often misunderstood. But inside the club things were different. There was no judgement. Only respect, no matter what your sexual fetish. Dominance just happened to be mine.

Wuh- psssh! The crack of my whip filled the air, followed by the most delicious scream, a sound that penetrated the depths of my soul. My nostrils flared as the smells of the club imprinted on my mind. How the hell was I going to survive two weeks away from this place?

The spotlight shone down on Ashlan, the submissive I was playing with. Actually, she was the *only* submissive I'd played with in months. Bound by the leather cuffs at her wrists and ankles, her arms pulled high above her head, her legs held spread eagle to the floor, she was completely at my mercy. I itched to touch every inch of her sexy-as-sin body—and I would—just as soon as she gave me what I'd asked for.

My whip connected with her skin once more, raising another gorgeous welt. I hadn't struck her hard enough to draw blood—Ashlan's hard limits didn't allow permanent marks—but even if she hadn't thought to exclude the edgier play herself, I would have. She had enough scars on the inside to deal with. She sure as hell didn't need any on the outside.

Another flick of my wrist sent the leather tail flying, connecting with her hip bone. That one would leave a bruise. Ash wouldn't object though, which was exactly why I had to make sure she promised she wouldn't scene with anyone else.

I'd seen Ash playing with a couple of the less experienced Doms when she first joined the club, and I never once saw her say no. She'd slip into that subspace and take whatever was dished out without an ounce of regard for her own safety. How was I supposed to leave her for two weeks without knowing she'd be safe?

Six months ago, one particularly rough motherfucker got a two-fisted reminder about the importance of control when I saw the marks he'd left on Ashlan's perfect olive skin. Of course, after the ass kicking I gave that sonofabitch, I got a lesson of my own—from Master Dane, one of the club's owners. He was half a step away from banning me from the club when I bared my soul to him.

Seeing Ash like that broke something inside me. She wasn't thinking about her own well-being, and I couldn't sit back and let her get hurt. Whatever demon she was up against had stolen the fight right out of her, and it was my job to get it back. Luckily for me, Dane agreed.

I'd spent the last six months dialing down the intensity with Ash. The fact that I was leaving for two weeks left an uneasy feeling in the pit of my stomach. The mere thought of her playing with another Dom while I was away left a taste in my mouth too horrible to think about, especially considering she didn't always play inside the safety of the club. The effects of the last time she played without me still lingered. The subtle flinch when I drew back my shoulders, the way her legs trembled anytime she even saw the cane. It was more than enough to send my inner Dom into protective mode. Ash was mine, even if she wasn't ready to admit it.

Tonight I'd make sure she remembered that.

Three more lashes, twenty-four in total, and Ashlan was right where I wanted her. Her heavy breathing told me she was on the edge of that cliff. One more kiss from my whip, and she'd get the release she so desperately craved. I'd give it to her too. I'd remind her of the pleasure only I could give her—after she said the words I wanted to hear.

I fisted my hand in her hair and tugged, leaving her head no choice but to follow. Kissing my way up her elongated necked, I whispered in her ear. "Tell me what you need, sunshine."

"More pain, sir," she answered immediately, but then again, that was always her answer.

"Not until you say it."

"Please, sir," she begged. "You know I can't. Please don't make me."

She could beg all she wanted. Ash knew what I wanted to hear and, if she wanted that orgasm she was chasing, she'd have to promise to save herself for me while I was gone. Ash needed pain in a way even I didn't fully understand and I couldn't have some other Dom taking advantage of that again.

I dropped my hand between her thighs, shoving two fingers deep inside her dripping wet canal. Her legs began to shake as I rubbed my fingers back and forth across that sensitive spot inside her. "Say it, Ash."

"I can't, sir," she said, panting.

Wrong answer.

Faster and faster, I pumped my fingers, the palm of my hand hitting her swollen clit with every thrust.

"Ahhhhhhh!"

She was so close but, without the pain she craved, she'd never fall off the wave she was riding.

Just as Ash's inner walls began to spasm, I withdrew my fingers. The hitch in her breath said she was less than pleased, but she'd left me no choice. I couldn't go away unless I knew she'd be safe. With Ash's level of submission, not even her hard limits would protect her from the emotional scars an inexperienced Dom could leave. And *that's* what I was afraid of.

For the next two weeks I would be trapped on my father-in-law's ranch. Night after night, forced to continue the charade I'd been living. Two whole weeks away from Ashlan and the kink we both craved; night after night left to worry if she was being safe, unless she agreed she wouldn't play while I was gone.

The whip clanged against the metal cart when I let it go. I turned to face Ash. The lift of her chin, the defiance in her stare, told me everything I needed to know. She was trying to bait me into giving her the pain she was after. That little game of hers had worked with other Doms, but it would never work on me, especially not when there was so much at stake.

"Please, sir," she begged. "I need more pain."

My cock twitched every time she called me *sir*. The way the word rolled off her tongue had me practically begging to hear it again. Holding back was pure hell, but what choice did I have?

My fingers worked quickly to unfasten the cuffs on Ash's ankles. "I've already told you, sunshine. I want to hear you say it. Your body is mine. *Only* mine."

"Please, sir."

Sir. There it was again. My swollen cock pressed hard against the zipper of my leather pants, those metal teeth digging into my sensitive flesh. Who the hell thought putting a zipper right over your cock was a good idea? Clearly, they'd never had a hard-on with their pants on.

I unfastened the button on my waistband and then carefully moved the zipper down to free my erection before those sharp teeth did permanent damage to my manhood.

Ash's pussy glistened in the spotlight, evidence of her arousal covering her inner thighs. Digging my fingers into her firm ass, I pulled her close, my tongue connecting with the hot, wet folds between her legs. Damn, she tasted good, a combination of salty and sweet that was hers alone.

Swirling my tongue around her clit had her gasping for air. When my teeth closed around that sensitive nub, I had her right where I wanted her. "Whose body is this, Ash?"

"Yours, sir," she said between breaths. "Only yours."

Hell yeah! That's what I'd been waiting for. Finally, I could give her the pain she craved.

• • • • •

Ashlan

When Spencer bit down on my clit, the world around me faded: the stage, the crowd, my practically naked body on full display. At that moment I would have promised him anything. Slave to the needs of my body, my desires had overridden any fears. All sense of reason was lost with that one bite. I wanted this release. I *needed* it--more than the air in my lungs.

Spencer pushed his fingers further inside me, the walls of my canal already starting to tighten around him. By the time his teeth closed around that sensitive nub again, I was teetering over the edge of the cliff. One command from my Dom and I'd fall faster than I'd ever fallen before.

"Come for me," Master Spence finally said. That's all it took. Three little words and I was soaring—the highest of all highs—floating weightless through the sky in a direct path to the clouds, every nerve in my body alight with a pleasure only pain could bring.

Spencer's thick cock pushed past my opening, bringing me back to where I was: bound to a Saint Andrews cross on the main stage. He inched his way in, my body fighting against the fullness of his erection. "Ahhhh," I cried out, loud and uninhibited. While playing on the stage wasn't something I was used to, not even the crowd of people watching us could quiet the sounds of my pleasure. That was in the hands of Master Spence.

With my leg wrapped around his waist, Spencer thrust his hips again, the head of his cock slamming up against my cervix.

"Ahhhhh," I screamed, louder than I'd ever screamed before. The vibrations in my throat so empowering, I couldn't help but scream again. A wave of pleasure rippled down my spine, arching my back in its wake. One leg tightened around Spencer's arm, the other around his waist. "Oh, God, yesssss!"

"That's right, sunshine." He pumped harder, faster. "Let me hear you."

Another thrust of his hips had me begging for release. "Please, sir."

"Scream it, Ash. Let everyone hear that you're mine when you come for me." One more thrust. "Now!"

Just like that, the room around me disappeared. Cradled by fluffy white clouds, I was free. Nothing could hurt me now.

"Welcome back," Spencer said when my eyes finally met his again.

An involuntary smile spread across my face. "Mmmm," was all I could manage, my brain still too mushy to form actual words.

Spencer's arms tightened around me, the ultra-soft Giza cotton of the club's signature robe against my back was a sure sign he'd taken me to aftercare. I'd been so lost in my orgasm that I hadn't noticed the robe before then. I hadn't even noticed when he removed the cuffs from my wrists or when he wrapped me in his arms...

His arms.

Fluffy white robe.

Those weren't clouds cradling me as I floated towards Heaven. They were the arms of Spencer James.

Chapter Two
Spencer

Spending Christmas at the Jones' ranch wouldn't be all that bad, at least, that's what I'd been telling myself. Getting on that plane to leave Chicago was harder than I thought it'd be after Ash's promise. I felt like an asshole for demanding she save herself for me, knowing I might not be able to offer her the same in return.

That knot in the pit of my stomach was a small price to pay for knowing Ash would be safe. Besides, being married complicated things. Ash and I both knew that. We also knew that what Izzy and I did in the bedroom was *nothing* like what she and I did. Maybe that's why I hadn't seen my life at the club as cheating. Until I found Ashlan.

Before Ash, what I'd done at Esoteric was just sex. I didn't have any emotional attachments inside club walls. My first scene with Ashlan—from the very first time I touched her beautiful, creamy skin—I realized how wrong I'd been. There hadn't been any emotional connections before because I hadn't met the right sub. As soon as realization dawned, I knew I had to end things with Izzy. She deserved better than to continue living with my lies.

God knows, cheating on my wife was never my intention. Actually, it was something I swore I'd never do. I made a vow to myself long before I stood beside Izzy at the altar. After seeing what my dad's affair did to my mom, I sure as hell wasn't going to be that kind of husband.

Fucking alcohol.

One too many drinks and a spur of the moment decision walked my ass into my first BDSM club with Valerie, my wife's best friend. I had no idea the draw to control—to bring pleasure through pain, to trust completely, to earn a woman's submission... I had no idea that draw would be so strong. That night at the club Val opened my eyes to a world I'd only fantasized about before then.

One night, that's all it'd taken to forget the promise I made to myself and destroy the sanctity of my marriage. And that wasn't even the worst part. I was too big a coward to even tell Izzy what Val and I had done. I wanted to come clean. So many times I'd tried to tell her what we'd done, about that part of my life I'd kept hidden for all this time, about the need so deep inside me not even the vow I made before God and a church full of our closest friends and family had been able to stop me from answering its call.

As it turned out, that same force driving my need to tie women up and whip them until they came, was also preventing me from ending things with my wife. I'd betrayed her. And when she learned the truth, I'd hurt her then too. And I fucking hated hurting Izzy. God knows she deserved so much more than I could ever give her.

Izzy and I had been in love when we married, not the kind of all-consuming love I thought I'd feel when I met *the one*. You know, the kind of love that knocked you off your feet and made you feel complete. Izzy didn't love me like that, either. A truth she held in her eyes no matter how much she pretended otherwise.

We'd married in haste shortly after I took her to an orchestra in Miami. Valerie had tagged along for the trip. We'd all gone out for drinks after the concert. One thing led to another and before I knew what was happening we were all three back in our hotel room, naked.

Guilt over what happened that night overcame all my senses. I'd taken Izzy's innocence. That part of herself she'd been saving for the man of her dreams, the man she was going to spend the rest of her life with. In my mind, it didn't matter that Izzy had offered herself to me that night, begged me even. The second I found out she'd been high on ecstasy I knew I had to marry her.

Something had to give, that was for damn sure. All that sneaking around had put a serious strain on my emotions. More and more I found myself reaching for a bottle of Jack to settle my nerves. If I didn't come clean soon, I'd have a whole new problem to deal with.

"Flight attendants, prepare for landing," the captain's voice said over the speaker. And there it was, out of time...two whole weeks in the middle of nowhere, surrounded by nothing but mountains and snow and cows...*Thank fuck Pot is legal or I might lose my damn mind.*

"Dad, are you awake?" Anna, my seventeen year-old daughter asked, shaking me gently. "You need to put your seatbelt on. We're about to land."

Realization began to set in.

This is really happening.

Doing the best to hide the frown that crossed my face, I leaned down and buckled my seatbelt. Fourteen days. Two fucking weeks of pretending things were fine between me and Izzy when I knew the truth. A truth I needed to tell her. I would too, after the first of the year. It would only be worse for Izzy if I broke the news before the trip she'd spent weeks planning, especially considering that would be our last Christmas before the kids left for college, off preparing for their own lives.

What's done is done. A fact I reminded myself of daily. Nothing I did now would change the past. All I could do was try to minimize the hurt Izzy was sure to feel. Being out in the middle of nowhere, in the dead of winter, and the only thing we'd have to keep us busy for the next two weeks was each other. And that's what worried me the most about keeping my secret until after we got home. Nineteen years of marriage had blinded Izzy to my bullshit, but her father would see right through it.

• • • • •

Ashlan

Two weeks. How the hell was I going to make it that long without the release I needed, that reminder I was still alive? Spencer had no idea what he was asking me to do. He didn't even have the slightest inkling I depended on the club for survival, that without the gentle reminder of a Dom I was doomed. That's the way things had to be. The less he knew about my life outside the club the better, for both our sakes.

It's not like I wanted to play with anyone else, but even a bad Dom would be better than going without. I trusted Spencer more than I'd ever trusted anyone. He always knew exactly what I needed, and he never disappointed. He respected me—mind, body, and soul. More importantly, he respected my limits, unlike that bastard I was married to.

No one at Esoteric knew I was married, especially Spencer. Well, no one except my friend, Valerie. Thanks to the new identity she helped me get, none of the hellish details of my past made their way onto my club application. If anyone there were to find out I was married to Diego Rivera, the largest distributor of cocaine and heroin on the entire West Coast, I'd get a one-way ticket back to California.

And if Diego were to find out about my life at the club, that trip would be in a body bag. No way in hell would Diego let me or Spencer live if he knew what we did inside Esoteric.

Turns out, pretty much everyone knew Diego's history, everyone but me anyway. I had no idea he was a well-known drug lord until I'd willingly put his ring on my finger. Twenty-five with a master's in psychology, but dumber than a box of rocks.

I was so naïve back then. My father had never allowed me to have a boyfriend. No one had ever sent me flowers or bought me expensive jewelry or taken me to Spain. Swept off my feet by the attention Diego lavished upon me, I'd been too stupid to see the wolf inside him, too blinded by his charm to see that the second I became his everything between us would change.

Diego owned me. A fact he regularly reminded me of with his fists. He wanted me all to himself, isolated and totally dependent—only I was much too stubborn for that.

Cursed with a piece of shit addict for a father, pain had always been part of my life. That's just how things were for me. Dear old dad would be gone for days, and when he did finally come home—high as a kite on God only knows what—all hell would break loose. He was mean and cruel. Pure evil reincarnated. No one in his line of sight was safe, not his wife or the dog or even his three year-old daughter.

After the childhood I endured, I swore to myself I'd never be that weak little girl again. Diego could break my body, but he'd never squash my soul. I'd face his shit for two lifetimes before I let that narcissistic bastard break me down that far.

BDSM, the lifestyle, that's what saved me. It connected me to that space inside my head where the pain no longer existed. In that world obedience was a sign of strength, and submissives had all the power. Esoteric had become my escape, a place where I could hide away from the hate Diego rained down on me. Inside those walls Ashlan Rivera didn't exist. There was no Diego or stupid mistakes or broken bones. More importantly, there was no fear. At the hands of my Dom, pain was always for my pleasure, one thing Diego never cared about.

What Spencer and I had at the club, that's what kept me grounded. More importantly, Spencer reminded me there was still good in the world. What the hell was I going to do without him?

Diego had gotten back from Columbia earlier that day. Even after three months with him away, I had still dreaded his return. He'd want sex for sure. Hell, he always wanted sex. No doubt, he'd had his pick of women while he was gone, but that still wouldn't stop him from demanding it from me. The mere thought of his hands on my body made me want to throw up, but that wouldn't matter, either.

It wasn't like I could tell Diego no. That's a lesson I had learned the hard way a long time ago. When Diego wanted it, he took it, no matter what *it* was. One backhand across the cheek was all it took for me to realize it was easier to just give in. Diego would never turn down an opportunity to prove just how much power he had over me.

Two goddamn weeks without the tender touch of a man who respected my body, a man who wanted only to please me.

Two fucking weeks, trapped inside a burning inferno with no way out, not even a hope for tomorrow. And not a snowball's chance in hell of keeping my word to Spencer once I was hanging there, arms tied high above my head, legs shackled spread eagle to the floor.

"There, that should hold you."

"Diego, please. You don't need to do this."

With a fistful of my hair, he yanked my head back. "Have I been gone so long that you've forgotten how merciless I am when you disobey?"

"I'll remember next time. I promise."

Diego released my hair and slowly began circling me, one foot over the other like a caged lion about to pounce on his prey. I knew all too well that was exactly what he was about to do.

Anticipating the strike, my body tensed when he leaned in, only the strike didn't come. "You should've remembered this time, mi amor," he whispered in my ear, followed by two quick jabs to the ribcage.

Sonofabitch! That fucking hurt. The second I relaxed my muscles, he attacked like the coward he really was.

A real man wouldn't treat a woman like that. Spencer taught me that.

"It's just a stupid plant!" I yelled when I finally caught my breath, those two weeks away from the club leaving me on the edge of my sanity and totally without discipline. I knew better than to talk back.

Diego stepped back and delivered a perfect round-house kick to the same spot he'd just hit. "You know the rules. There will be no flowers in this house unless I buy them." A punch to the stomach followed.

Keeping the plant was a stupid thing to do, but even knowing that hadn't stopped me from doing it. I'd desperately wanted to believe the tiny green plant would bring me peace and harmony like Spencer promised.

The lily was so small when Spencer first gave it to me. I figured it'd be months before the thing was mature enough to flower, so I brought it home. And Spencer had been right. It had brought me peace. Every time I looked at the dark green foliage, I was reminded of his tender touch. When the flower bud first appeared, I almost threw it out.

Almost.

I just couldn't bring myself to do it. I'd spent nearly three months caring for the plant, a living thing that depended on me to survive. I loved my lily. Maybe even as much as I would have loved a child, if I'd ever been granted that right. So I kept the flower, hiding her behind the drapes in the picture window of the library. I thought for sure she'd be safe there.

Only, I was wrong.

Lily wasn't safe.

And neither was I.

Chapter Three
Spencer

The rocking of the midflight turbulence had nothing on my nerves. All the stress of sneaking around and hiding who I really was had finally caught up to me. I couldn't decide if I wanted to scream or get drunk or vomit—maybe all three—and not necessarily in that order. Spending Christmas at Jack's ranch had been a slap in the face I deserved for what I'd done to my family. After that trip, one thing was certain. It was time to end the charade of my marriage once and for all, for everyone's sake.

If I hadn't been sure letting Izzy go was the right thing to do before the trip to Colorado, I was absolutely certain of it after. Intimacy had long since been a thing of the past for us. Two full weeks together in the middle of nowhere and the only time we even spent together was when I took her out to celebrate her birthday a little early.

Before I snapped the fuck out of it and realized I was actually cheating on my wife, I hadn't hesitated to initiate intimacy with Izzy. Since I figured it out, we hadn't once shared the same bed. There was no way I could bring myself to have sex with Izzy now that I'd accepted what I'd done was beyond wrong.

There was only one woman for me, and her name was Ashlan Rivers. She was the face I saw when I closed my eyes at night. It was her body I craved to touch. It was her heart mine ached for. Ashlan was meant for me. And she was mine. *Only mine*. It was time for me to stop all the lying and be the man Ash needed me to be.

And I planned to start with Valerie, the psycho bitch that had called non-stop the past week demanding to see me. I tried reminding her that what we had was over, but it hadn't helped. She wanted to see me, and she was refusing to take no for an answer.

"Meet me at Esoteric, tonight, or Izzy will get a birthday present she'll never forget," Val had said before she hung up on me. Her threat left me no choice but to go. I'd spent more than half my marriage sneaking around and having sex in clubs. I owed it to Izzy to spare her whatever pain Val had planned because of the choices I'd made.

Getting involved with Val wasn't something I planned to happen. We ran into each other at a conference in Miami. There was just something about being back in the city where the three of us shared that magical weekend several years before that made me want to go back to that moment. I'd never seen two women so free and uninhibited—or so aroused. Even Izzy had loosened up that night, courtesy of the ecstasy Val told her was aspirin. A fact I didn't know at the time, or I never would've allowed the three of us to end the night in a tangle of sweaty limbs.

Seven year-old twins and a growing business left me longing for a time when life had been simpler, before the complications of marriage and family and responsibilities all got in the way. After a few drinks at the hotel bar, Val convinced me to join her at a public BDSM club she frequented. That night Val opened my eyes to a whole new world, a world where I finally felt like I belonged.

Val had read me like a book and gave me exactly what I needed, begging me to tie her up and whip her. BDSM instantly became more powerful than any drug I'd ever tried. Our first scene had been so intense there was no doubt in my mind I had to have more.

In the world of BDSM, Val was what you'd call a switch. Just as masterful a Dominatrix as she was an obedient sub. She'd taught me everything I knew about being a Dom, and I'd always be grateful for that.

That past year things had gotten awkward between me and Val. When quarterly trips to the club were no longer enough to satisfy the hunger inside me, the two of us started meeting every month. That's when things began to get weird. Val mistook my selfish needs for want, only it wasn't Val I'd wanted at all. It was the power I felt when I brought her to the edge. There was just something about knowing I'd done that. That I'd read her body and delivered exactly what she needed at the precise moment she needed it. *Control*, that's what I really craved.

When I suggested we cool things off for a few months, Val seemed to be okay with my decision. Actually, until last week I hadn't heard from her at all since the night I'd told her I needed a break. I figured she'd moved on, but apparently she was just doing exactly what I told her to do: cooling things off for a few months. It'd been six months, and she was ready to heat back up. But once I found Ashlan, I wasn't interested in being with anyone else. Not inside the club or out.

Ending things with Val once and for all wasn't going to be an easy conversation, which was why I reserved us a private room at the club. Val didn't always play by the rules, but she took her role at Esoteric very seriously—

whichever role she was playing. Lately, she'd been back to Mistress Val, but tonight she'd dawn her sub hat. That was the best way to get her to move on: demand it. She'd never refuse her Dom a direct order.

"Too your knees, sub," I snapped when Val walked through the door, the distinct sweet smell of gardenias giving her away.

She dropped to her knees in front of me, her hands folded behind her back, her eyes cast toward the floor the way I liked. I rose to my feet, deliberately putting space between us. There'd be no playing around this time. No mincing words or beating around the bush. After tonight she'd finally understand it was time for her to move on. "We're not here to play."

• • • • •

Ashlan

Being away from Esoteric had proven harder than I'd imagined it would be. Or maybe it was being away from Spencer. By the end of the first week, I was finding myself thinking about him almost nonstop. My body ached for the kiss of Master Spence's whip and the gentleness of his touch that always followed. If I closed my eyes tight enough, I could feel the warmth of his breath against my skin.

Oh, God, his soft, wet lips tracing every inch of my naked body. "Mmmmm," I moaned out loud, the tiny bundle of nerves between my legs pulsing with need.

Diego's arm snaked around my waist. "Still thinking about last night, mi amor?" he asked.

Dammit! Busted again. Last night was the furthest thing from my mind, but I couldn't tell him that. If he even thought I was dreaming of another man, he'd beat me to a bloody pulp.

I was still pretty banged up from Diego's first night home when he found the peace lily. The safest thing for me to do was to seduce him. Swallowing the vomit that had risen to the back of my throat, I traced my finger along the arm he had wrapped around my waist. "Actually, I was thinking about today."

His hand traveled from my waist to my breast. "Today, huh," he said, his fingers already tugging at my nipples through the thin fabric of my shirt. "I can arrange that."

The sweet smell of Diego's cigar combined with the woodsy scent of his cologne churned the acid in my stomach. It took every ounce of strength I had not to throw up in his mouth as he kissed me. My mind wondered to that safe space inside my head as I accepted my fate. I had no one to blame this time but me. If I hadn't been caught in that lustful daydream, this filthy pig wouldn't be shoving his dick inside me.

"Is this what you wanted?" he grunted as he pumped in and out of me. "You love having me inside you, don't you?"

"Yes," I said, my answer as much a lie as his love. I hated having him inside me. The feel of his hairy body touching mine, the accent I once thought sexy as hell making my skin crawl.

He pumped harder, every thrust of his hips taking him one step closer to the edge. "Tell me you love it," he said between breaths.

The stiffening of his legs told me he was close. Luckily for me, I knew exactly what he needed to hear to find his release. "Oh yeah, baby, your dick is so hard." I ran my fingertips over his perfectly sculpted back. "I love the feel of you inside me." Diego wouldn't worry himself with concerns over my pleasure, so at least I didn't have to fake an orgasm, which was a good thing considering I was barely holding on to last night's dinner as it was.

Sliding my hands under the waistband of the briefs he hadn't bothered to remove, I cupped his firm ass in both my hands. His thrusts came faster and faster, his release a matter of seconds. "That's right, baby. You feel so good. Give it to me harder."

"Ahhhhh," he roared as his orgasm ripped through him.

An involuntary smile crossed my face. I'd used Diego's weakness against him. All it took was a couple strokes to his ego, and he blew his load like a goddamn teenager. I'd never been happier for the wham-bam-thank-you-ma'am kind of fuck Diego enjoyed in all my life. The victory may have been small, but it had been mine.

Nearing the end of the second week, my skin had begun to crawl with need. Every look Diego gave me, every touch, every move, every sound he made had my skin crawling. I was well beyond *want* at that point. I *needed* the pain my Dom delivered to quiet the storm that was building inside me.

Without that reminder Master Spence's whip brought, I'd found myself pushing back against Diego and his demands. That's how I ended up lying in yet another hospital bed.

The good news was when Diego realized I'd be out of commission for a while, he flew to Palo Alto. Secretly, I was hoping he had some piece of ass on the side and would end up staying, or better yet, someone would finally put a stop to his reign of terror. Controlling the distribution of illegal drugs was a dangerous business, after all.

Two days in the hospital was all I could take. It didn't take a genius to figure out my injuries hadn't come from a fall down the stairs. The staff hadn't even pretended to believe me that time. The last thing I needed was another lecture about being brave or smart or courageous. None of them knew jack shit about the courage it took to face that demon day after day. I didn't need counseling or the damn pain meds they were feeding me.

All I needed was Spencer.

Chapter Four
Spencer

Last night things hadn't gone as planned with Val. Six months away from her and I'd forgotten how to read her signals. I was so sure she'd accept any order I gave. Seeing her go ape shit when I told her about Ashlan proved just how wrong I was.

Val had become the ultimate dominatrix, knowing exactly what I needed then molding herself into her role as a sub to give it to me. Her reaction left no doubt she'd only been playing a part all along. That's why things were so different with Ashlan. Ash wasn't pretending. Her submission was so ingrained it could've been woven into her DNA.

After Val's blow-up, sticking around the club didn't seem like a smart thing to do. As soon as I had the chance to bolt, I took it. Esoteric wouldn't tolerate a domestic argument on site. They'd just as soon revoke both our memberships than disrupt the serenity of the other members. Not that I could blame them. People came here to escape the stresses in their lives, not play witness to a full on tantrum.

Nothing was going to keep me away tonight. It'd been seventeen long days since I last saw Ashlan, since I felt that connection only *my* sub could give me. The thought of waiting even one more minute was pure torture. That's not what had the hair on the back of my neck standing on end, though. Ash was late, and she was never late.

A stiff drink would've gone a long way toward calming my nerves as seconds became minutes. Too bad Esoteric didn't serve alcohol. They wanted to know the choices you made were your own. Safe, sane, and consensual were part of the oath.

My nerve endings were so raw with need for Ashlan, I knew I wouldn't be able to hold out much longer.

What the hell was taking her so long?

Fifteen more minutes. That's how much longer I'd wait before going to get the drink I desperately needed to calm my nerves.

Fourteen minutes thirty-seven seconds. *Dammit.* I couldn't even call Ash to check on her. We'd never exchanged personal information. No phone numbers or social media contacts and most certainly no addresses. Considering the club allowed members the use of aliases, Ashlan Rivers might not even be her real name.

If Ash didn't show up my only hope of finding her would be through the person who sponsored her membership. Unfortunately, that was Val. I sure as hell couldn't ask her for help after the conversation we had last night. Val said I was dead to her, and the stone cold look in her eyes said she meant it.

For what felt like the millionth time that night, my eyes scanned the room looking for Ash. Five more minutes was all I was going to wait.

Relief washed over me the instant I finally spotted her, those dark brown curls falling around her face as she made a beeline for the women's locker room. Watching

Ash move, that warm feeling that had washed over me when I finally spotted her quickly turned to ice.

With shoulders rolled forward and eyes fixed downward, that wasn't the confident, perky, defiant woman I'd left here safe and satisfied two weeks ago. Every time her right foot hit the ground, her face tensed up. A subtle wince most people wouldn't even notice. But I'm not most people. I'd spent the last six months studying every look on her face, every curve of her body, every sound she made. No one knew Ashlan's body as well as I did, not even her. Pain was one thing I'd never miss on her face.

I watched in anticipation, my patience wearing thin as I waited for Ash to emerge from the locker room. I couldn't stop wondering what the hell she was hiding. She'd said her body was only mine. Had she meant it? Or had she just been telling me what I wanted to hear to get the release she was craving?

Hell no!

That wasn't behavior I'd tolerate, especially not from Ashlan.

• • • • •

Ashlan

Surrounded by Spencer's energy, every nerve in my body came alive when I walked through the double doors at Esoteric. My skin ached for his gentle touch, the warmth of his naked body pressed up against mine as he took me to heights I could only reach with him. My soul ached to be caressed by his kindness, to be wrapped in his strong arms, knowing nothing in this world could possibly hurt me at that moment.

Too bad I still had at least another hour of prep work to do before I could get close to my Master. Latex was a given tonight. That way Spencer couldn't insist I take off my clothes. If he saw the bruises all over my body, I'd have a lot of explaining to do, and I didn't want to explain shit, least of all the hell Diego put me through the past two weeks. All I wanted was to forget, scream it all out, then savor the pain of a man who only wanted to please me, a man that knew my body better than I knew it myself.

That was what this lifestyle did for me. It meshed my two worlds together in a way I could live with. I needed the tears to rid the demons that haunted my soul. Every harsh word, every punch, every kick, every ounce of pain I endured at the hands of a man I'd once loved unconditionally, tightened the hold on me. The pain Spencer gave me set me free, if only for a little while. It was the slice of heaven inside my life of hell.

"Jesus, Ash," Carly, another submissive said when I walked into the ventilated painting booth inside the locker room. Her body glistened from what looked to be the last layer of her pink and gray school girl costume. "What happened to you?"

"What can I say?" I said, shrugging my shoulders, doing my best to play it off like it was nothing. "I like it rough."

"Rough? Is that what you call this?" she said, waving her hands over my body. "I can't believe Master Spence is taking you into a scene with bruises this deep."

Picking up the sprayer filled with black latex body paint, I held it out toward Carly. "He hasn't seen them," I said honestly. "Now, help me spray this shit on so it stays that way." When she hesitated, I moved the sprayer closer toward her. "*Please.*"

After what felt like an eternity, Carley took the sprayer from my hand. "We better get started," she said finally. "You're going to need at least three coats, probably four, if you plan on keeping your little secret." I didn't say a word, simply turned around so she could start. "You owe me big time for this, Ash. If Master Nate ever finds out I helped you hide this from Master Spence, he'll punish me for sure." I turned to face her when the sprayer stopped. "I'm not like you," she continued. "I prefer pink to black and blue."

Little did Carley know, but so did I. Black and blue was Diego's fetish.

When the first coat was finished, I stepped in front of the blower used to speed the drying of the paint. Even with the help of the dryer, each coat of latex would take at least fifteen minutes from start to finish. Master Spence was probably already pissed that I was late, and not the kind of mad I enjoyed. Making him wait over an hour while I concealed my secret wasn't the smartest move for me to make, but what choice did I have? Carley had been absolutely right. Spencer would never take me into a scene if he saw the bruises the paint was hiding.

After the hell I'd endured the past two weeks, I needed him to take me into a scene more than I'd ever needed anything.

"What do you think?" Carley asked after the third coat was dry.

While the body paint did a decent job of covering the worst of the bruises, I could still see a few. If I saw them, so would Spencer. "I think I need another coat."

"Well, I think you should just tell Master Spence the truth, but I'll spray on another coat if that's what you want."

I nodded my response, Carley's words putting a lump in my throat. Keeping secrets from Spencer wasn't something I wanted to do. It was something I had to do. Master Nate was just as protective as Spencer. Carley would understand why I had to keep this to myself if she knew the truth about my injuries.

Of course, she could never know. My survival depended on me keeping the details of my life outside the club to myself.

"Carley," a growly voice called out from inside the locker room. "Are you in there?"

"I'll be right out," Carley called back. She laid the paint sprayer back on the shelf. "I better get going before Nate's voice gets any angrier," she said with a smile. "I'd give it five more minutes under the dryer if I were you."

"I will. Thank you for your help."

"You're welcome. But if you get caught, you better forget I had anything to do with this."

"Carley!" Nate snapped from the doorway.

"Already forgotten. Now go have fun."

She was out the door before I could finish my sentence, which is where I should've been over an hour ago. Just because Spencer hadn't tracked me down inside the locker room didn't mean he was waiting patiently.

There was no doubt in my mind I'd be punished for being late. Spencer's punishments were never fun either. The last time I was late, he took me into one of the private wet rooms upstairs, cable tied my arms and legs to the iron rings mounted into the wall, blindfolded me, and then tickled me with a feather until I almost peed myself. Granted, the shower Spencer and I shared after he'd proven just how deep his level of control ran was amazing, but the punishment was downright humiliating.

When I was certain the latex body paint was totally dry, I said a silent prayer Spencer wouldn't notice the bruises and walked out of the locker room. Ready or not, it was time to face whatever punishment Spencer had in store. No matter what it was, one thing was certain. Tonight I'd finally get the release I needed.

Chapter Five
Spencer

When Ashlan walked out of the locker room covered in latex, my suspicions were confirmed. Not even the strobe lights penetrated the material she'd painted on her body. There wasn't a single inch of skin visible from her wrists to her ankles. She'd gone way beyond the standard application. If it weren't for the pain covering her face, I would've thought she was hoping for a photo op with the extra thick coating of latex she was wearing.

The closer Ash got to me, the clearer it became what she was hiding. Unless she just finished playing in some private scene in the women's locker room, the raised welts all over her legs and torso were from a pretty heavy scene.

My heart rate spiked as the rush of adrenaline coursed through my veins. In through my nose, out through my mouth, I breathed, repeating the simple command over and over again in an effort to maintain my calm.

Ashlan lied to me.

She fucking lied!

With eyes cast down, Ash spoke first. "Sorry I'm late, sir."

Sorry she's late? Her body was covered with the fucking evidence of her betrayal and she was sorry she was late?

I tossed a pillow on the ground. "To your knees, sub," I barked. My nerves were revved too high to deal with her at that moment. I needed to get a grip before I lost control.

Ashlan dropped to her knees without question.

Good, girl.

She would stay that way for a while. One minute on her knees for each of the seventy-one minutes she spent in the locker room hiding her body from me sounded fair.

Seeing her struggle was killing me, even though I knew it was for her own good. She'd spent countless hours preparing her body for that type of latex treatment before she even got to the club, which meant she'd been fully committed to keeping her injuries from me.

The question was why, and it was up to me to find the answers. And that I would, just as soon as her mind slipped into subspace, that quiet place inside her mind she went when we were in a scene. That's where I'd find the answers I was looking for.

• • • • •

Ashlan

What the hell was taking Spencer so long? He'd left me kneeling almost an hour ago. My knees ached from being stuck in that position for so long. Thank God he'd let me up twice to rest my joints. I don't know what I would've done if he hadn't.

I'd already apologized for being late. The question that remained was how long this punishment would last.

Was he really that mad I'd been late? Or maybe he sensed I hadn't held true to my word. I tried to tell him I couldn't give him what he wanted. It wasn't as simple as that. I'd desperately wanted to uphold my promise and save myself for him. Somehow, I doubted he'd take solitude in knowing I'd had sex with the abusive asshole I call my husband but saved all my pleasure for him.

I shook all thoughts of Diego out of my head. Sex with him was the last thing I wanted to think about at the club. He could've been the devil himself, disguised by his wavy dark hair, espresso eyes that accented that baby face, and the perfectly sculpted frame spending six days a week working with a mixed martial arts trainer provided him. Diego wasn't a worthy Dom. He had no business at Esoteric.

Enveloped by Spencer's calming energy, I slipped quietly into that special place inside my head where nothing could hurt me. That one place where I could let go of everything and allow myself to feel, trusting without reservation that Spencer was watching over me. A trust that was absolute.

"There you are," Spencer said softly.

I hadn't heard him approach, although it wasn't surprising considering how far I'd let my mind drift. "Yes, sir. Is it time to play?"

He ran his finger down my jaw before tucking it under my chin where he easily tilted my head back. When his eyes locked with mine, he said, "Not yet, sunshine. Come. Sit with me. We need to talk."

Without waiting for me to respond, Spencer helped me to my feet. Only, I didn't want to talk. I didn't want to sit and listen either, and I especially didn't want to wait any longer. What I wanted was for him to take me into a scene. It had been seventeen days since I felt that release only the crack of a whip in expert hands could bring.

"Please, sir, I'm sorry I was late. Take me into a scene. It's been too long. I need this."

Ignoring my pleas, Spencer led me to a quiet area in the far corner of the club. He sat on the leather sofa and pointed to the foot stool in front of him. "Sit," he said in a firm voice that left no room for discussion.

Resolved to my fate, I sunk down onto the cushy leather stool.

"Who decides what you need, sunshine?"

"You, sir."

"That's right. I do, so you can stop all this pouty shit, because right now what you need is to talk to me. Tell me, what's going on?"

With downcast eyes I said, "Nothing, sir."

"Eyes to me."

Without so much as a second thought, my eyes snapped to his. I said a silent prayer he wouldn't see the torment that rested there.

I never said a word, then again, I didn't have to. Spencer could read my body language better than anyone. Hopefully, he couldn't read my mind too. "I asked you a question, Ashlan. I expect you to answer me honestly."

"Please, sir," I whispered. "It's nothing. *Really.*"

Despite the hard set of Spencer's jaw, he held onto my face with a lover's care. His soft brown eyes looked upon me with a warmth I wasn't used to seeing, a warmth that would surely melt even the thick layers of ice around my soul, which is why I had to look away. I couldn't tell Spencer the truth about Diego, ever.

Spencer pressed his lips to mine, his left hand sliding down my neck, under my breast, over my ribcage. I couldn't help the subtle flinch when his fingers brushed across the worst of the bruises, the deep purple ones that hid three fractured ribs. "How do you explain this, then?" he asked.

I bowed my head, ashamed of what I'd let Diego do, that I hadn't been strong enough to push past the fear inside me and run when I'd had the chance. "It's not what you think, sir."

"Eyes to me," Spencer said in a much firmer voice. When I looked up again, his beautiful brown eyes had narrowed to tiny slits but I could still see the turbulence inside them.

Clenching the muscles in his jaw, he asked, "Then *what* is it?"

"Please, sir. Don't do this. It's nothing. Really. Please, let's just move on."

Spencer's eyes floated shut and had yet to reopen. He seemed to be taking deep, cleansing breaths, but what worried me was how many he seemed to need.

I'm sure he thought I was playing outside the club while he was away. The truth wouldn't be any easier for him to accept. And he could never find out about Diego. Spencer would lose his mind wanting to protect me—the only problem—Diego had reach in the darkest of the shady places. If Spencer started making waves, it wouldn't end well for either one of us.

When Spencer spoke again, his voice was surprisingly soft. "No, Ashlan. We can't move on. Your life is your business, but your safety is mine. If you aren't ready to tell me what the hell is going on, I won't make you." He released my hands as he stood up. "But I won't take you into a scene, either. Be on-time tomorrow."

Confusion crossed my face. "Sir?"

"It's clear you don't trust me. Go home and think about why that is, then decide what you want to do about it. We'll talk tomorrow."

Sonofabitch!

I wanted to scream and yell, to demand Spencer take me into a scene. Didn't he know how bad I needed a release? Couldn't *that* override his need to know about a few goddamn welts and bruises?

"It's clear you don't trust me."

Yeah, well, I had news for Spencer. Trust was a two-way street. Why couldn't he just trust me when I told him it was nothing? I'd meant it. There was *nothing* he could do. Diego was my problem. Spencer James needed to learn to keep his nose out of my business.

Without even caring about the attention I was drawing to myself, I stormed off to the locker room, beyond pissed. Maybe that kick to the head I took had been harder than I realized. Then again, what I'd done before Diego snapped was downright ridiculously stupid in a too-stupid-to-live kind of way. Still, throwing a tantrum in a room full of Doms had to be the dumbest thing I could have done.

But my libido was screaming so loud I didn't care. I just wanted a fucking release!

Not getting the release I spent the last two weeks waiting for only heightened the pain in my ribs. Washing the four layers of latex off was going to suck for sure. It would've been worth it if Spencer hadn't gotten his panties in a bunch about a stupid bruise. He shouldn't have fucking asked me to refrain. I could have called up one of the Doms I'd used outside the club before and taken the edge off. Maybe then I wouldn't have baited the asshole I call a husband and ended up covered with bruises so dark not even four layers of latex could hide them.

Rubbing my soapy hands over my body only made Spencer's rejection sting that much worse. I'd come to depend on his soothing touch to calm the pain I felt inside. I needed the kind of pleasure only Spencer could bring me. I'd paid my toll the last two weeks with Diego. It was time to collect my reward.

Ugh! Why the hell did he have to be so damn protective? "You asshole!" I screamed.

"You wouldn't be talking about me, would you?"

A deep, gruff voice was not what I'd expected to hear. This was the women's locker room, *wasn't it?* Reaching for a towel, I shook the water out of my ears then turned to see who the voice belonged to.

Shit. Spencer!

Yanking the towel away from my body, he tossed it on the wet floor. "What the fuck, Ashlan? You're beat to hell."

No! No! No! This couldn't be happening.

I reached toward the shelf for another towel only to find Spencer beat me to it.

Dammit! Think, Ashlan. Think!

Before I could come up with an explanation that wouldn't make things any worse, Spencer had my wrists pinned to the tiled wall behind me. "Is this the *nothing* you were telling me about?" he bit out.

That fight-or-flight instinct kicked in before I could stop it. "One in the same," I snapped, my natural instinct always to fight.

"I'm going to ask this one more time, Ashlan. Lie to me now, and we're through. Do you understand what I'm saying to you?"

Tears ran down my cheeks. I knew exactly what he was saying. The crazy, dysfunctional D/s relationship Spencer and I had was the best thing I had in my life. I needed him, but I needed to keep us both alive even more.

The look in Spencer's eyes said it all. He wanted to know the one thing I couldn't tell him. As soon as the question left his mouth, my world would come crashing down.

I had to get away from him before he asked me for the one thing I couldn't give him: the truth about Diego. "Please, sir. Don't do this."

"Ashlan," he said in his low, growly voice that spoke straight to the bundle of nerves between my legs.

Shit. Shit. Shit.

I had to shut him down before it was too late, so I said the only thing I could think of. "RED!"

Immediately, Spencer released my arms from his grip.

Without hesitation, I pushed past him, heading straight for my locker to dress. Without bothering to dry off, I wiggled my way into a pair of yoga pants and an oversized tee. The faster I got out of there the better.

When I turned around, Spencer was leaning against the locker beside mine, his arms folded across his chest. "I can't just pretend I didn't see that, Ash. As your Dom, you know I have a responsibility to keep you safe, and that protection doesn't end when we leave here."

Silent tears continued to fall. "I've already told you, Spencer. It has to. There are some things you just can't know."

Spencer dropped his head, a loud frustrated groan loosely camouflaged as a sigh passed over his lips. "Tell me one thing, Ashlan. Were you *playing* when that happened?"

Ignoring the question I'd been trying to avoid in the first place, I made a move toward the door. I couldn't tell him the truth. Not now, not ever. "I'm not doing this with you, Spencer. You shouldn't even be in here."

It took less than three steps for Spencer to close the gap I'd put between us. Wrapping his hand around my bicep, he turned me toward him, his reaction catching me off guard. "Cut the shit and answer the damn question, Ashlan! Were you fucking playing or not?"

"No."

Chapter Six
Spencer

Ash left me standing in the women's locker room, dazed and confused. Anger. Frustration. Guilt. Worry. I felt them all. When I'd followed Ashlan into the showers, I'd expected to find welts and a few bruises. Forget a few. Her body was covered in black and blue and purple and yellow.

Abused.

Fucking hell! From the looks of her, I'd say some asshole had been kicking the shit out of her since I'd left. She had bruises on top of bruises on top of bruises. One thing was for certain, I'd teach the son-of-a-bitch who put those marks on her gorgeous body how *not* to touch a lady, just as soon as I figured out who the prick was.

Whoever he was, one thing was crystal clear. She was scared shitless of him. All the color drained from her face when the realization of what she'd admitted sunk in. The widening of her eyes, the instant increase of her pulse, screamed sheer panic. I'd never seen a more frightened look covering her face.

Ashlan hadn't stuck around long enough for my mind to process all I'd seen, and now I didn't even know how to check on her. The club's privacy policy prevented them from giving me her address, but that wouldn't stop me from finding out if she was okay. Master Nate, another Esoteric member and one of the three club owners, was a private investigator. When I explained what was going on, he'd have no choice but to help me find her. His duty as a club master would demand it.

My eyes scanned the expansive space of the club's main room until I found him. Master Nate was monitoring a scene at the opposite end of the room. Dom Jay, Master Nate's newest Dom in training, was perfecting the Hishi pattern on the body harness he was tying. That was typical for Master Nate. Always scanning, making sure everyone was playing safely. Even if he wasn't a club Master he wouldn't be able to resist making sure Ash was okay. It was in his nature.

"Jay's coming along nicely," I said as I came up beside Nate.

Nate pushed himself off the support beam he'd been leaning against and nodded toward the juice bar, a slight smile crossing his face. "That boy's a natural with a rope," he said, having first-hand knowledge of the hard work and patience it took to master the art of rope bondage. "He could use a few lessons with a whip, though."

Yeah. Yeah. Yeah.

I knew what Nate was hinting at, but I wasn't in any condition to be giving lessons to anyone, not when my whole life had just been turned upside down. Couldn't he see I was barely keeping my own shit together? "Ash is in trouble," I blurted out, my nerves barely hanging on. I'd sent her home. Maybe even to the hands of the bastard who hurt her.

"What kind of trouble?"

"Someone did a real number on her, man. She's beat pretty bad."

Nate's jaw tightened, the natural dominant in him quickly rising to the surface. "Consensual?" It was the one question every Dom would want to know. Only, I didn't have the answer he wanted that time. When I shook my head, his fists tightened beside him. "Do you know who did it?"

I shook my head again. "That's why I need your help."

"Of course I'll help. You know we're family here, man. If Ash is in trouble, we all have a duty to protect her." Nate slowed his pace and looked over at me. "Just know I may not be able to disclose everything I find. As a club owner, I have a responsibility to protect the privacy of our members too."

"Look, I just need to know she's okay." I stopped walking, turning to face Nate full on. "Seriously, man, whatever you can do. I've seen MMA fighters come out of the cage looking better than she did tonight."

"*Tonight?*"

"Yes, tonight," I snapped. "I've been gone for two goddamn weeks. When else would I have seen her?" For someone so smart, Nate seemed to be playing catchup in our conversation, which was pissing me the hell off.

Nate's nostrils flared as he took off toward the bar, quickly closing the distance with long, determined strides. By the way his sub shifted on the stool, I already knew his sudden change of mood had something to do with her.

Carley knew it too.

"I told Ash to tell him," Carley said as soon as Nate approached with me one step behind him. "I told her it was a bad idea to keep this from Master Spence. She begged me to help her. I didn't know what else to do—"

"Enough," Nate snapped. "Save your excuses, sub. You knew what you were doing was wrong." He moved another step closer to her. "Tell me now, do you know who did that to her?"

"I swear I don't know, sir," she said, her voice already starting to crack. "All she told me was she liked it rough. It wasn't my place to challenge her."

Nate's voice dropped to a low, deep tone. "It wasn't your place to keep this from me, either." His chest rose and fell with every breath he took, his eyes narrowed to the thinnest of slits. "Now apologize to Master Spence for your behavior then go wait for me at the spanking bench."

Her whole body tensed as the words sunk in. Her fate tonight was set. "Yes, sir," she whispered.

Carley turned toward me and looked up. Unshed tears filled her otherwise sparkly green eyes. "I'm sorry, sir. I should've told Master Nate that another sub wasn't playing safe." She dropped her gaze back to the floor; "Or sane," she mumbled.

"Thank you," I said. "I'm glad to hear you accept responsibility for your mistake. Safe. Sane. Consensual. We all took that oath. Master Nate is right to punish you for forgetting. With any luck, you'll learn your lesson quickly."

"Thank you, sir," she said, unable to hold back the strain in her voice. "May I go now?"

"You may."

Nate and I watched Carley sulk across the floor to await her punishment. Most subs couldn't wait to be bent over for a good spanking. But Carley wasn't like most subs. She came to the club with no experience whatsoever. She'd never even been over her father's knee as a child. Nate sure seemed to be enjoying breaking her in. "If she's hiding something, I'll know about it soon," Nate said. "I've never met a sub with such a low pain tolerance. As soon as my belt comes off, she'll tell me everything she knows."

"Just call me when you know something. I don't care what time it is."

"You got it, brother."

Nate took off after Carley, who appeared to be chatting nervously to Master Dane, another club owner. What Carley lacked in experience, she sure did make up for in enthusiasm. Unfortunately for her, that wasn't going to help her case this time. She'd learn soon enough that whining to another club Master about her pending punishment wasn't a good idea.

There was no reason for me to stick around the club. Ash was long gone, and Nate would have his hands full in aftercare for hours after punishing his new sub. All I could do was wait and worry. Fortunately for me, I could do that at the hotel bar.

• • • • •

Ashlan

The second the word was out of my mouth, I knew it was a mistake. The tension in Spencer's body became palpable in the fraction of a second it took for those two letters to roll off my tongue.

Why did he have to ask me if I'd been playing? Playing required consent. And nothing I'd done with Diego the past two weeks had been consensual. Well, not in the truest meaning of the word, anyway. I learned long ago that fighting only made the sex last longer. Diego got off on seeing me struggle. It was better if I just laid there and let him have his wicked way with me.

Damn Spencer and his Dom look, that magic weapon that had me blurting out the truth without thinking. One more minute around him and I would have told him everything, every sordid detail of the hell I'd lived. I couldn't do that to him, which was why I had to get as far away from him as possible.

Tossing my bag over my shoulder, I'd bolted. There was no reason to look back. My time with Spencer had come to an end. I should've known it was only a matter of time. Talk about kicking a man while he's down. Or in this case, a five foot five, one hundred fifteen pound woman. Karma was not the fickle bitch I thought she was. No, sir, he was an evil bastard. Only the cruel hand of a man could break me, and losing Spencer was going to do it.

Last night I didn't have any other choice but to leave. I'd told an experienced Dom that I'd been abused. His duty to me wouldn't allow him to let it go until he had the answers he needed. Having Spencer poking his nose around would mean trouble. If Diego ever found out what I'd been doing, he'd kill us both. Ashlan Rivers could be no more. From that point forward, it would only be Ashlan Rivera, terrified wife of a drug lord.

Why did Doms have to be so fucking territorial? What Spencer and I had worked and he ruined it. Like Ashlan Rivers, our relationship was a thing of the past. It was the only way to keep Spencer safe.

Boarding the plane home was harder than I'd expected it would be. The thought of leaving Spencer sitting at Esoteric waiting for me was breaking my heart. Leaving like that after dropping the bombshell, after letting him see the bruises with his own eyes, without giving him the answers he was desperate for, was going to kill me inside. The not knowing would torture the Dom inside Spencer. And knowing I was responsible for that torment would torture me.

Running was a cowardly thing to do, but it was the only way. Spencer had proven last night he could evoke any truth he sought from me, even a truth that could get us both killed. If I'd gone back to Esoteric there was no doubt in my mind Spencer would've found out about Diego, and he'd be out for blood. Only, it'd be Spencer's blood that was shed. No one could touch Diego, not even the five foot eleven wall of muscles named Spencer James.

The thought of going home scared the hell out of me, even if Diego was still in Palo Alto. It wouldn't be long before he tired of his latest piece of ass, then he'd be home to finish the job he started. No one would stop him, either. Everyone feared El Loco, with good reason. He was a cold, heartless shell of a man who would torture and kill his own mother if the mood struck him. He sure as hell wouldn't hesitate to do the same to me, especially after I spoiled his plans earlier with my trip to the hospital.

I was so thankful when Val said she could help me get away from Diego that I hadn't objected when she insisted I had to go home for the plan to work. Not that objecting would have done any good, anyway. What Val wanted, Val got. Period.

At least I could take solace in the fact that I'd be staying in a hotel. All I had to do was survive one night.

Tomorrow I would die.

Chapter Seven
Spencer

Sleep eluded me most of the night. Every time I closed my eyes, Ash's battered body stared back at me. In the ten years I'd been living the BDSM lifestyle, I'd never seen bruises as bad as those. Then again, those bruises *weren't* like the ones I was used to. They hadn't been meant for anyone's pleasure but the bastard who'd put them there. Whoever the hell he was. Nate may have come up empty last night with Carley, but that didn't mean I wouldn't get the answers I was after, just as soon as Ash showed up.

"Where's that new sub of yours?" a snarky voice called out from behind me.

I didn't have to turn around to know who it came from. I'd recognize that low, husky tone anywhere. After Val's blow up the other night, talking to her about Ashlan couldn't possibly be a good idea, but ignoring her wasn't a good idea, either. That left me only one option: dealing with her. "What do you want, Val?" I asked through gritted teeth, my nerves already raw from waiting for Ash to arrive.

Val rounded the couch I was sitting on and took a seat on the table in front of me. One look at the deep plunge neckline of her strapless leather dress paired with those knee high spiked leather heels, and I knew the true Val had shown up. There was no more pretending. She was one hundred percent Dominatrix.

"So sweet of you to ask, Spence. If I didn't know any better, I'd say you were a gentleman." She sat up straighter and arched her back, purposefully exposing more of her scantily covered breasts. "But after what you've done to your wife, we both know that's a lie."

"Is there something you needed? Or did you just come here to tell me I'm an asshole?"

"Oh, Spence, babe, I'm hurt that you've forgotten. I much prefer the show." She leaned forward, her long blonde hair cascading over her breasts, momentarily capturing my attention. "Telling you you're a lying, cheating, bastard who broke my heart wouldn't have near the impact as showing you."

"Showing me? What the hell are you talking about?"

An ear to ear smile crossed Val's face. "The timing couldn't have been more perfect, really. I only wish I could be there to see the look on Izzy's face when she opens that package."

Package? What the hell was she talking about? I scooted forward to the edge of the couch. "What did you do?"

"Oh Spence, did you honestly think I was going to let you cheat on my *best* friend and not tell her about it?"

Sonofabitch! She didn't. She wouldn't. I jumped to my feet. "So help me, Val—"

"That's right, Spencer," she said, slowly rising to her feet in front of me, her breasts rubbing up against my chest. Pressing a gloved finger against my lips, she continued, "You'll be begging for my help before this is all over."

She leaned in and kissed me on the check, her hands planted firmly on my chest. "Tell me, Master Spence," Val said as she pulled her hands away. "How'd you like Ashlan's new body art? Purple may just be her color," she added, twisting the knife she just jammed into my gut.

Without even thinking, I reached out and grabbed ahold of her arms. "What the hell did you do?" I shouted. "I swear to God, Val, if you had anything to do—"

A tight grip on my flexed bicep effectively stopped me in my tracks. I spun my head to see who the asshole was who dared touch me when I was pissed off.

Sonofabitch. Master Dane, another one of the club owners.

It wasn't until I let go of Val that he finally spoke. "Is there a problem here?"

Brushing her hair off her shoulder with her newly freed hand, Val took a step back. "Just a disagreement on proper coloring," she said. "But I'm afraid we'll have to finish our debate at another time. I've got a newbie waiting."

A frown crossed Dane's face. "Take it easy with this one, will ya? He's practically a baby. If I hadn't seen his birth certificate with my own two eyes I'd swear he was still a teenager."

Val rolled her shoulders back, her bare breasts practically jumping out of the outfit she had on, a mischievous grin on her face. "Don't you worry, Master Dane," she said before licking her lips. "I'm going to take good care of Andy." With that, she spun on her spiked heel and quickly disappeared into the Saturday night crowd.

Dane turned his attention to me. "We need to talk."

Great.

That was just what I needed, another one of Dane's lectures. I was still skating on thin ice with the club owners for kicking the shit out of that Dom. I'd been lucky they didn't revoke my membership then.

As realization dawned, I sat back down on the couch, my head resting in my hands. Dane had reminded me that as a club Master I had a responsibility to set a good example for other club members. Losing my shit with a Domme wouldn't qualify, especially after I'd promised Dane I'd keep it together.

He moved to the chair across from me and plopped down. "Nate's been asking a lot of questions about Ashlan. Wanna tell me what's going on?"

My mood lifted just a bit. He wasn't there to reprimand me after all. He'd come to help. Only, there wasn't much to tell. I didn't know what was going on with Ash, but she was hurt, and it was up to me to keep her safe. "Ash is in trouble."

Dane scooted forward in the chair, resting his elbows on his knees. "What kind of trouble?"

"That's what I'm here to find out." My jaw tensed just thinking about the possibilities. "Only Ash is late."

"Don't get too worked up about that. She's probably still mad you sent her home last night. Being late is just her way of getting back at you."

While that sounded like something my sassy little sub would do, after seeing her battered body I wasn't totally convinced. "Let's hope you're right."

"I'm here if you need me, man. You do know that, don't you?"

I nodded. Of course Dane would help. He was a club Master. They'd all help if any one of the club's submissives were in trouble. If only I knew where the hell Ash was so we *could* help her.

Dane slapped me on the shoulder as he stood to leave. "She'll be here. Give her time."

Time.

That could easily be the one thing Ash didn't have.

When midnight rolled around, I finally gave up hope that Ash was coming to the club. She'd been late a few times, but never that late. *Dammit!* Why the hell hadn't I followed her last night when she stormed out of the locker room? She'd told me she'd been abused, and I just let her walk away. A Dom's job was to look after his sub. And right then, sitting there, I definitely wasn't doing my job.

• • • • •

Ashlan

Strung out on caffeine, sugar, and about an hour's worth of sleep, I was a nervous wreck by the time Val's plane landed. Even staying in the hotel last night hadn't made me feel safe. Diego had eyes all over Malibu. All it would take was one phone call and I'd be done for. Lying, sneaking around, hiding out. Yeah, Diego definitely wouldn't take that lying down. It was supposed to be the day I died. Torture hadn't been part of my plan.

"Are you sure this will work?" I asked nervously as we waited outside the airport for a taxi.

"Of course it'll work," Val snapped. "As long as you do exactly what I tell you to do." She pulled my hand away from my mouth. "Now, stop biting your nails and get in the car."

I'd been so mesmerized by her tone that I hadn't even noticed a taxi had pulled up in front of us. With trembling hands, I opened the door and climbed in. Val rounded the car and took the seat behind the driver.

"Where to, ladies?" he asked when we were both inside.

"La Villa Contenta," I said, almost choking on the words. There was nothing happy about that place anymore. Not when Diego was around, anyway.

I turned to Val. "Do we have to go to the house? Isn't there another way to do this? If Diego—"

"Look, Ash," she whispered through gritted teeth. "We've already been through this. You're going to die in a car accident. Don't you think it'll be easier to convince Diego that it was *you* who died in the car, if it's *your* car that runs off the cliff?"

She was right. The only way for me to truly escape Diego's reach was by convincing him and everyone else I was dead. That wouldn't be an easy task. There weren't many people Diego trusted, and none of them worked in law enforcement. He wouldn't just take the word of some highway patrol officer without proof.

"What if Diego wants to see the body? Won't he know it isn't me then?"

"Charles said the body will be charred beyond recognition."

"I know, but he's your ex-husband. I mean, what if —"

Quickly, Val turned to face me. "Enough!" she shouted, not seeming to care that the cab driver was staring at us through the rearview mirror. "Charles may have been a lousy lover, but he wouldn't dare lie to me. If he says the body will be unrecognizable, then that's exactly what it'll be!" Smoothing out her shirt, she added, "Remember, Ashlan, you came to me for help. You need to decide, right now. Do you want it or not?"

I didn't just want her help, I needed it. There was no Plan B.

"I'm sorry," I said finally. "If you trust Charles, then so do I."

"Good. Now sit back and shut up already. You're giving me a fucking headache."

I certainly didn't like it, but my choice was clear. If I ever wanted to be free, I'd have to go back to the house that had held me captive for the last five years one last time. Shackled by a fear only years of abuse could bring, haunted by the knowledge that if I ever left, Diego would serve up a punishment far worse than anything I could even imagine.

Killing Ashlan Rivera was the only way I'd ever be safe again. Still, knowing my life depended solely on the success of Val's plan had me more than worried. She may have gotten me a new identity for the club, but getting a fake ID was one thing. Framing someone for a murder that didn't really happen was a whole different story.

Val's plan did sound genius: wife fleas her abusive husband only to end up dead at the bottom of a ravine. The only part I didn't understand was how Val was going to get Diego's fingerprints on the brake line of my car. She'd said it was all part of her *Frame the Asshole* package and that's all I needed to know.

Trusting she knew what she was doing was the only choice I had.

Chapter Eight
Ashlan

The taxi driver sped off after dropping us near the back gate. Sneaking onto the property to get my car was the only part of the plan Val had left up to me. To say I was nervous would be the understatement of the century. Scared shitless was more like it.

The plan was for me to fake my death, not actually die. Unfortunately, I knew the risks all too well. If Diego was home, I'd never get out of there alive. About the only thing worse than me having flowers in the house was me having a visitor. Diego didn't allow me to have friends. That was part of *his* plan. The *You have no free will because I own you* plan.

My heart was beating so fast I thought I might pass out as Val worked to pick the lock on the back gate. She'd already managed to disarm the security cameras and alarm system, a feat I didn't think was possible. Even that was doing nothing for my nerves. All I could think about was what we would find on the other side of the gate.

Click. "Got it," Val said as she tucked her lock pick set back into her purse. "Let's go."

Time was up. Ready or not, I was about to find out.

Slowly, I pushed open the iron gate and peeked inside the yard. A wave of warmth washed over me. There was no one in sight. If Diego were home, the perimeter would be crawling with security.

I blew out the breath I didn't realize I was holding then motioned toward the main house on the far side of the property. "This way."

Using the palm trees and shrubs as cover, I took off running toward the house. Movement outside the staff quarters stopped me dead in my tracks.

Shit. Shit. Shit. Shit. Shit! Please don't let it be one of Diego's men.

They'd rat me out in a heartbeat to gain favor with their boss. I turned to Val, who was holding her finger over her lips signaling silence. Neither of us moved a muscle. I wasn't even sure I was breathing.

"Who's there? I have a gun."

"It's just me, Maria," I said quickly. "Don't shoot."

Val threw daggers at me with her eyes for breaking the silence but she didn't know Maria like I did. Her motto was shoot first, ask questions later. A lesson she undoubtedly learned after years of service to a drug lord.

"Mrs. Rivera?"

I poked my head through the ferns only to find her standing in front of me, a 9 mm trained right at my head. "Jesus, Maria. Put that thing away."

Maria immediately lowered the weapon. "So sorry, ma'am. I wasn't expecting you home. Mr. Rivera said you would be gone for a while."

"That's right. I just came to pick up a few things I forgot to pack, but I'm not staying."

"What do you need? Let me help you."

"That's okay," I said quickly, too quickly by the look on Maria's face. "Really, it's nothing I can't manage. Besides, it's Sunday. There's no need to bother you on your day off."

"Yes, ma'am," she said, reluctantly.

I was relieved when Maria turned to walk away—until she spun back around. "Mr. Rivera will be back soon," she said, her voice barely above a whisper. "Please, Mrs. Rivera, you need to hurry. It isn't safe for you here anymore." With that, she was gone. She knew the beating I would face if that narcissistic bastard caught me there. She also knew her own fate would be worse if he found out what she'd just told me.

"You heard her," Val said from behind me. "We need to hurry."

I wanted to hurry, to get out of there before Diego found me, only I couldn't move. I wasn't sure if it was fear or just sheer stupidity that kept my feet frozen in place. Hell, I wasn't even sure I was breathing until Val slapped me.

Val's hand connected with my cheek again. "Snap out of it!" she yelled. "We have to get out of here or we'll both be dead."

Val took off toward the garage, leaving me hovering in the ferns like a coward.

This was my mess. I couldn't let her go in alone. If anyone was going to get caught, it should be me. "Wait for me," I called after her, hurrying to catch up.

My short legs were no match for Val's long stride, even if she hadn't been five steps ahead of me. Val didn't slow down. Hell, she didn't even turn around to acknowledge I was chasing after her. She knew.

"That one's mine," I said, pointing to the sapphire black BMW Z4 on the far end of the garage. "I'll get the key."

"We're going to need something with Diego's fingerprints on it for my plan to work, preferably something with a smooth, flat surface that I can lift a print from."

As soon as I opened the key cabinet, I knew just the thing. The shiny silver ignition key for Diego's Bugatti lay neatly on the center shelf. He loved that damn car, so much that he never let anyone else drive it. His prints should be all over the fob. I lifted it, careful not to touch the button that opens the key. "Will this work?"

Val pulled a zip top bag from her purse and opened it up. "That should do," she said, motioning for me to put the key inside. "Now, let's get the hell out of here."

She didn't have to tell me twice. I hopped in the car, waited for the bay door to open, then took off, the turbo charged engine of my Z4 hitting sixty in less time than it took for my brain to catch up to what was happening. I was really going through with it. No more dreaming about being free or planning my escape only to chicken out like the coward I'd always been. For the first time in my life, I was finally going to be free.

As we sped along the Pacific Coast Highway, the gravity of what I'd done started to sink in.

No more begging for my life.

No more wishing I was dead.

No more Esoteric or Spencer or the release only he had ever been able to give me.

It was a high price for my freedom, but one I had no choice but to pay.

• • • • •

Val arranged for us to meet Charles at the Molera State Park near Big Sur so we could get to the business of planting the fingerprints, cutting the brake line, *and* transferring the dead body into my car. This was it. My life was almost over. Even though I had no idea who I would become or how I would survive, all that mattered was that I *would* survive. In less than an hour, I would be free of the man who took away my freedom along with any hopes I'd ever had for a family.

"Park next to that tow truck," Val instructed.

Suddenly, the pieces were starting to come together. I'd wondered how I would get the car safely over the Bixby Creek Bridge after the brake line was cut. Seeing the tow truck made a lot more sense.

I pulled into the empty space and turned off the ignition. As I reached for the door handle, Val grabbed my arm. "Get in the tow truck. Charles and I will take care of everything."

"Won't it be faster if I help?"

Val tightened her grip on my arm. "Have you forgotten who you're talking to, Ash? You don't question my commands. You follow them. Now get in the damn truck, or go back to your husband."

The tightening of Val's jaw told me she wasn't playing around. What choice did I have but to do things the way she wanted? I couldn't go back to Diego. Well, not if I wanted to live.

When I finally nodded, signaling my acceptance of her order, Val let go of my arm and hopped out of the car. I quickly followed suit. I wouldn't feel safe until my car was a raging inferno at the bottom of the ravine.

"Hey, baby," the man I could only assume was Charles Barnes said to Val.

Val wrapped her arms around his neck. "Charles, so good to see you."

"You must be Ashlan," he said when he saw me. "I'm Charlie."

I held out my hand to shake. "Thanks for your help. You have no idea how much I appreciate it."

"You sure are a sexy little thing. Maybe you can show me just how much you appreciate me later."

Val pushed her way between us; her eyes narrowed. "Get in the damn truck, Ash," she said through gritted teeth.

I crawled inside the cab of the truck without further argument. Pissing off the one person who could help me wasn't the smartest thing to do.

Seeing Charlie pull the dead body from the large, black bag he'd laid next to my car made me realize just how real the situation was. Charlie was risking his freedom—and his life—for me.

No one had ever risked so much for me before. No one had cared that much, not even my own family. Sure, mom was hurt when I told her she couldn't see me anymore, but I always wondered if it was me she was sad to lose or if it was her dream of riches. Charlie didn't even know me, yet he was willing to put his future on the line. Deep down, I knew there had to be a catch.

Val and Charlie made quick work of transferring the fingerprints and loading the body. All that was left was to cut the brake line. Val explained they would wait until the car was loaded onto the tow truck to do that so we didn't leave any evidence behind. That was the most important part of the plan, making sure Diego believed I was really dead. If he thought for even a second that I was still alive, he'd stop at nothing to find me. No one betrayed Diego and lived to talk about it.

"You okay?"

My head snapped toward the raspy sound of a man's voice. "Jesus, Charlie, you scared the hell out of me."

Charlie laughed. "Damn, girl. I just opened the door."

"Yeah, well, knock or something next time."

The smile that rested on Charlie's face quickly disappeared. "That husband of yours must be some piece of work for you to be this jumpy."

My eyes fluttered closed as I worked to slow my racing heart. "You have no idea," I whispered.

"Who is this husband, anyway? Maybe I'll pay him a visit after this is all done."

My mouth dropped open, my eyes widening. Val hadn't told him who I was running from. No wonder he was so willing to help. He had no idea he was risking his life by even talking to me, much less helping me escape. "Charlie, I, um…"

"He's none of your business, that's who he is," Val snapped from behind him. "Now, if you two are done flirting, maybe we should get the hell out of here." She pushed past Charlie and climbed into the cab of the truck next to me. "That is, unless you want Charlie to die today too," she whispered in my ear.

Chills ran down my spine as her words sunk in. Charlie was in real danger, and he didn't even know it.

"Val's right. He's not important. Let's get out of here."

Chapter Nine
Spencer

I knew Nate would come through, that he'd find out Ashlan's real name, so it hadn't surprised me when he called so soon. Truthfully, his call couldn't have come at a better time. To say things were tense would be an understatement. Things at home were hell. Pure and simple. Pretending to be happily married when all I could think about was finding Ash had my insides twisted. It wasn't fair to Izzy, but neither was having her struggle through the pain of what I'd done.

Hurting my wife was the last thing I wanted to do. I loved her, after all. What I did at the club wouldn't ever change that. I should have told her the truth about me a long time ago. Would she have understood if I told her about my sexual needs? Would she have joined me? Even if she'd left me, things would have been different. At least then I could've held my head up about my honesty. Now, I was just the lying, cheating, scumbag Val told me I was.

Being away from Ash hadn't helped. Every second that ticked by without me knowing if she was okay was torture. I couldn't eat. I couldn't sleep. Since Ash walked away from me, alcohol had served as both my only form of nourishment and my escape.

Nate warned me I wasn't going to like what he'd found. That was probably why my flight to Chicago seemed to take twice as long as it usually did. I needed to know Ash was okay.

The elevator stopped on the tenth floor of the Langham where I booked my usual river view suite. Nate insisted we meet in private, another fact that had my heart pounding.

I tossed my bag in the bedroom then headed straight to the parlor for a drink. My nerves were on edge. Not even the view of the magnificent mile below would soothe me until I knew Ash was safe. This was a definite job for Jack. Neat. Didn't need any damn ice cubes getting in the way of the numbing effects I was craving.

Knock. Knock. About damn time. I marched toward the door and yanked it open. "What'd you find?"

Nate stepped inside the spacious suite. "Are we alone?" he asked as he looked around the room.

"Yeah, we're alone. What's going on?"

"Who knows you're here?"

"Jesus, man. You sound paranoid. Just tell me what you found."

Nate sat down on the sofa and laid open the file he'd brought with him on the coffee table. "Have you ever heard the name *El Loco*?" El Loco. The words rolled around my mind. Where had I heard that name?

Before I had time to formulate an answer Nate continued. "Daniel Barreta. He's a Columbian drug lord who's currently in U.S. custody on money laundering and drug trafficking charges."

"Okay," I said, wondering what the hell that had to do with Ashlan. "What about him?"

"Well, El Loco is known to have several aliases. One of those aliases, Vicente Rivera, was listed as the father on the birth certificate of Diego Rivera. You know, El Mismo Diablo, as in *the* Columbian drug lord."

"The apple sure didn't fall far from that tree," I said as I slammed back the rest of my drink, my patience wearing dangerously thin. "Look, I appreciate the history lesson here, but what does this have to do with Ashlan?"

"Hold on. I'm getting there." Nate pulled a piece of paper out of the file. "Five years ago Diego Rivera got married to a twenty six year old American girl."

The hairs on the back of my neck stood on end. Nate couldn't be saying what I thought he was saying. Ash couldn't be married to that piece of shit, Diego Rivera. At least, I hoped she wasn't.

"And?" I said, hesitantly.

Nate turned over the paper he was holding. My knees buckled forcing me to sit down before I fell. It was worse than I'd imagined.

Ashlan.

My Ashlan.

In a wedding gown. Standing next to who I could only assume was Diego Rivera.

Her *husband.*

Nate warned me I wasn't going to like what he found.

He was wrong. I fucking hated it.

Mrs. Diego Rivera. Not just married—married to a motherfucking drug lord, the wife of the devil himself. No wonder she ran when I questioned her. If he was anything like the monster the news made him out to be, she had to be scared out of her mind.

Not only was Ashlan in trouble. She was in *serious* trouble. The kind of trouble that could get us both killed. "I need to find her, Nate. Can you help me?"

"I don't know, Spence. This is the kind of nosing around that could end my career, if you know what I mean."

Yeah. I knew what he meant. It could get me killed too, but I had to risk it. Ash needed me, and right then I needed her more than I needed to live. Izzy was divorcing me. The kids were going off to college. Soon all I'd have left was what Ash and I shared at the club. "Please, just tell me where to start."

"Have you considered that Ashlan might not *want* you to find her? She's an adult, man. You saw the pictures. Marrying Diego was her choice. Just as staying with him is also her choice."

"You didn't see her that night at the club, Nate. She'd been beat to hell, and from her own lips I heard her say it hadn't been consensual. She needs help."

Nate closed the file and pushed it closer to me. "Read this. If you still want my help afterward, I'll do what I can." He stood to leave. "Know this, though. Diego Rivera is dangerous. He's not the kind of man you go around accusing of beating his wife. And he's certainly not the man you want to cross by sleeping with his wife, either. This is the big leagues here, Spencer. Diego will kill you, and he'll enjoy doing it, too."

I swallowed the lump in my throat. "Thanks, man. I owe you one."

"Just take care of yourself, will ya? If I'm going to risk my life for your sub, you can bet your ass you're getting a bill."

I reached inside my wallet and pulled out the wad of bills inside. I didn't need to read the file to know I was going to help Ash. "Can you find out where she is?" I asked, handing over everything inside.

"Not until you read the file."

"Nate, I don't give a fuck what's inside that file. Ash is in trouble. That's all I need to know."

He thumbed through the bills in his hand. "Just an address?"

I nodded.

"Fine. I'll call you when I get it. Seriously, though, read the file."

• • • • •

One look at Ashlan's medical records told me everything I needed to know. Diego was worse than I'd imagined. How the hell could anyone treat a woman like that? Page after page with the words *unexplained fracture* scribbled across it. That sonofabitch had broken almost every bone in her fragile body over the past five years.

Why the hell had she stayed with him? Diego wasn't just abusive, he was an asshole too.

What surprised me even more was that a woman with a husband as abusive as Diego craved the lifestyle as much as she did. Of course, Ash and I had a contract, one that included a list of hard limits. Limits she knew I'd never violate. Maybe that was the draw for her, that deep level of trust. Knowing I'd only take her as far as she was willing to go.

Diego was the suspect in more than a dozen gruesome murders. Although, it was unlikely the police would ever get the evidence they needed against him. No, a guy like Diego wouldn't be stupid enough to get blood on his hands. He probably had a whole staff of people lined up who wouldn't mind ripping me from limb to limb.

After reading everything inside the file, I was more desperate to find Ashlan than I had been before. Any illusion I had about her being safe went right out the window. Ash would never be safe around Diego. Her x-rays were proof enough of that.

Until Nate got back to me, all I could do was wait and worry and wonder why the hell Ash went back to him.

Chapter Ten
Ashlan

Watching my car plummet over the edge of the Bixby Creek Bridge brought a level a relief I didn't know was possible. This was really happening. Ashlan Rivera died in a fiery crash, and Lily Walker rose from her ashes.

With my new identity, I would be safe. Free from the psychopath who never really loved me. All I could do was hope that being away from Diego would take away my need for the release Esoteric brought, because there was no way I could go back there. Not now. Not ever. That was part of the deal Val and I made in exchange for her help.

Staying away from Spencer was the other part, the part I wasn't so sure I could live up to.

"LILY!"

The sound of Val's voice bellowing in my ear nearly sent me over the edge after my car. I jumped back away from the railing. "Sorry, I was lost in thought. What did you say?"

Val's nostrils flared ever so slightly, kinda like the way Spencer's would when I hesitated in a scene. Mistress Val had indeed arrived. With any luck, she wouldn't stay. That's the last thing I needed in this situation.

She sauntered toward me. I didn't dare move. Instead, I repeated my new mantra over and over again in my mind.

Never challenge a Dom.
Never challenge a Dom.
Never challenge a Dom.

I wasn't always that weak. No, Ashlan Parks was born a fighter. It took years of training for me to learn how to be a good sub to make me that way. Don't get me wrong, I'd always had submissive tendencies. The lifestyle taught me it was okay to let go, to give in to my inner desires, and most importantly in my case, to follow orders without question.

Val squeezed my chin in her hand. Her long, red nails digging into my flesh. "I said, we should get out of here before someone sees us. Now, get in the damn truck!"

Arguing would be pointless, so I did as she said.

"Now what?" I asked when we were all back in the cab of the tow truck.

Val lunged toward me. "Stop your fucking whining!" she said, as she jabbed her finger into my chest. Turned out, Mistress Val had decided to stick around.

Never challenge a Dom.

"God, what did Spencer ever see in you? You're pathetic."

Never challenge a Dom.

"*I'm* flying the hell out of California just as soon as Charles can get us to the airport. *You'll* do whatever the hell you want." Val moved even closer, her lips inches from my ear. "But if you ever speak to Spencer James again, I'll hunt you down and make you both pay. You think you're helpless now, wait until you see the man you love writhing in pain, knowing you'll be next."

Love? Spencer? Was that what those feelings were?

"Do we understand each other?"

"Yes, ma'am," I answered quickly, not wanting to anger her any further.

"Good. Now sit still and don't you dare say another word until I tell you to speak."

I didn't answer, and she didn't want me to.

In silence, my feelings for Spencer became so clear. I didn't just love him. I trusted him. Something I'd never done before. More than that even. I needed him. Four months ago I wouldn't have had the courage to leave Diego. Spencer did that. He gave me strength and kindness and passion...

Oh, God, the passion.

My sex tingled just thinking about how my body came alive every time Spencer was near. He'd made me come—many times—with just a look or a command.

Damn, I had it bad. Why hadn't I seen it before?

What have I done?

I made a deal with the devil, that's what!

I'm such an idiot.

I not only accepted the poisoned apple, I gobbled it up without a second thought. Only, I wouldn't lie in waiting for my prince charming to rescue me. I was damned to a life without the man I loved.

I knew karma was a man. Evil Bastard! What would it matter that I lived if I could never see Spencer again?

• • • • •

Luckily, the ride to the airport hadn't been too long. The only break in silence the entire trip was when we pulled over to use the emergency call box. Val and Charles got out while I stayed put, a strict order issued by Mistress Val. I couldn't make out everything that was said, but I saw Charles reading the license plate number off the note I gave him.

When the police arrived at the crash site, they'd find the badly charred female cadaver inside. Everyone would assume it was me. At least, that's what I was banking on. With any luck they'd find the cut brake line too. As long as Diego was a free man, I'd always be looking over my shoulder.

Charles pulled next to the curb in the passenger unloading zone at the Monterey Regional airport. "My flight leaves in an hour. Take this piece of trash out of here, and don't come back until I'm gone," Val said to Charles.

"Don't worry about it, baby. You know I've got you covered."

"That's the only reason I keep you around, Charles. Don't forget that."

Val hopped out of the cab without so much as looking at me. She'd said it all. To her, I was just a piece of garbage, no longer necessary and easily discarded.

"Lily, huh?" Charles asked as we drove away from the airport.

"It's my favorite flower," I said honestly. When I was deciding on a new name, I immediately picked Lily, knowing it would always remind me of Spencer.

After that epiphany I had during the ride to the airport, I was realizing my mistake. Every time I heard my name, I would think back to that beautiful white flower that sprung up in the middle of those deep green leaves. The irony of it was not lost on me. I watched the flower sprout and grow. I nurtured her and grew to love her so much that I risked Diego's reaction by my having a forbidden object in the house, all the while oblivious that

I was disguising my feelings for Spencer inside my love of that flower.

"Well it's a nice name and a beautiful flower."

A small, sad smile crossed my lips. "Thanks."

"We have an hour before we can come back to the airport. How about we get some dinner?"

"Sure," I said, even though food was the furthest thing from my mind. It's not like I had anything better to do. Hell, I didn't even have a plan. I guess part of me never thought I'd make it that far.

"There's no need to be scared. All that nonsense before was just to throw Val off. But seriously, she would kill me if I laid a hand on you."

Yeah, Val wouldn't get the chance. I'd kill him myself if he tried to touch me. Never again would I let a man touch me without my permission.

Spencer James was the only one I'd ever trust enough to put his hand on me. Then again, I didn't want a confrontation with Chares either so I'd agreed to have dinner.

But nothing else.

"What's the deal with you and Val, anyway?" I asked, breaking the awkward silence.

Charles glanced over at me before returning his eyes to the road. "Didn't she tell you? I was her first husband."

"Exactly. You *were* her husband. Why would you go to all this trouble for her now? I mean, you probably risked your medical license or jail time or something today."

Charles began to chuckle, his chest moving as a deep pitch escaped. "I'm not going to lose my medical license or go to jail or even get a traffic ticket. When the rescue crew pulls that body out of the car, do you know who they're going to call?"

"Oh, I don't know, the medical examiner, maybe?"

"You're close," Charles said, a crooked grin on his face.

He must've thought I was a real idiot. I mean, I had watched television this century. Criminal minds, Law & Order, and Detective Joe Kundra were three of Diego's favorites, and he'd forced me to watch the gruesome tales with him.

I couldn't help but roll my eyes at the arrogance of Charlie's statement. "Enlighten me then."

Before he could answer, his phone began to ring. He pointed to me. "Not a sound," he said, all playfulness gone from his voice.

He pulled the phone to his ear. "Dr. Barnes." He sat patiently as he listened to what the caller was saying, responding with the occasional "yes" and "uh-uh" before ending the call with a sentence that made the hairs on the back of my neck stand. "Tell Mr. Rivera I will meet with him after I've conducted the autopsy and not a minute sooner."

I've conducted the autopsy.

He was the medical examiner?

"Val said you were a plastic surgeon."

"That's right, I *was* a plastic surgeon. Now, I'm the lead medical examiner for Monterey County."

No. No. No.

The situation was worse than I thought. "You have to pull over. Let me out. You need to get as far away from me as possible."

"I'm not going to abandon you on the side of the road, Lily, especially not with Diego Rivera in town." He glanced at me again, his sharp look all business. "Bet you thought I didn't know you were married to El Mismo Diablo."

The blood quickly drained from my face. "Diego's here?" I asked, the quiver in my voice impossible to miss.

"He was still at the crash site when the officer called. The body is being sent to Big Sur. I expect he'll follow. He was demanding to see the body. The police told him he had to wait until after a positive ID had been made. It's standard procedure in a case like this, really."

That wasn't the answer I was looking for. Charles thought he knew Diego but he had no idea what a real monster Diego was. "No, Charles, you don't understand. Diego will kill us both if he finds me with you. Now pull over!"

"I know a hell of a lot more than you think. I've patched up more than one of Diego's tantrums. Young women he left permanently disfigured for complaining when he hurt them or waking him up when she got up to pee or breathing too loud..."

My jaw dropped open. Charles had known all along the danger he was in. "If you knew what kind of man Diego was, why did you agree to help me?"

"It's because I knew him that I was moved to help. I wouldn't have been able to live with myself knowing I had an opportunity to help save a life and didn't take it." He looked at me again, his baby blue eyes softer than they just had been. "You didn't deserve any of that, Ashlan. I'm sorry for all you've been through."

A wave of conflicting emotions rushed over me.

Guilt. Relief. Anger. Embarrassment. Shame.

Fear.

It was the last emotion that drove me to action. Diego was too close. *I* needed to get the hell out of there. "Take me back to the airport. I have to get out of town. Diego could have eyes anywhere."

"Exactly," Charles said calmly. How could he be so calm? He'd seen what Diego was capable of. "That's why you're going to a safe-house in Carmel-by-the-sea. They have plenty of security personnel to keep you safe. Plus, no one on the outside will know where you are, including me."

Questions flooded my mind and began to spill out. "Where's this place at? Who all will be there? How long will I have to stay there? How do you know I'll be safe?"

Charles reached over and touched my hand. "Slow down," he whispered. "First of all, I'm sorry Val didn't tell you about the safe-house. But please tell me you didn't think I'd go to all the trouble of killing you if I wanted you dead?"

"I guess not," I said, laughing at how ridiculously true what he'd just said was.

"Good. Now that we've cleared that up, let's get to those questions."

"Do you really not know where I'll be?" I asked. It was absurd of me to be so clingy to Charles. It was just, well, the thought of no one knowing where I was scared me.

"Really," Charles said. "That's how a safe-house works. You'll lay low for a few days, weeks maybe and, when it's safe to move you, you'll be transferred anywhere you want to go."

"Do you know these people? The ones that are going to help me?"

Charles nodded. "A few of them," he answered, the haunting tone in his voice sending chills down my spine. "Unfortunately, Diego isn't the only son-of-a-bitch in California," he continued.

Val was right, I was pitiful. I'd gotten involved in an underground rescue without even knowing it. I'd let her use my desperation to accomplish her goal. Val had gone to great lengths to make sure I was untraceable. No one would even know I was still alive, let alone where to find me. The same measures taken to protect me would also ensure I never saw Spencer again.

Chapter Eleven
Spencer

Leaving Chicago was rough. I'd spent every waking hour at Esoteric, hoping against hope that Ashlan would show up. Considering it was Izzy's birthday, I had to go home. I'd been a shitty father and husband lately. My son's call this morning made that pretty clear. He hadn't wasted any time elaborating on the details, and that had the hairs on the back of my neck standing on end. Especially with Val's threat weighing heavy on my mind. The last thing any of us needed was for Izzy to find out about all the secrets I'd been keeping.

It was noon when I pulled into the driveway at my house looking like a man who hadn't slept in weeks. Bags under my eyes, unshaven, hair tousled, and not in that sexy made up kind of way, either. Plus, I was still wearing the same clothes I had on yesterday. At that point, all I could do was hope the enormous vase of roses I was carrying would keep Izzy from noticing how bad I looked.

When I found Izzy she was sitting in her office, her back to the door. Doing my best to straighten my messy hair, I quietly walked inside and said, "Happy birthday, Bella."

It was the box on her lap I noticed first, the signature pink and silver wrapping paper from my favorite toy store impossible to miss. When my eyes reached hers, I swear my heart stopped.

Izzy jumped to her feet. "You have a lot of nerve saying that to me!" Heaving the box toward me, she continued. "You lying, cheating bastard!" she shouted through her tears.

That's when I saw the pictures, dozens of photographs of me and Val. *That stupid bitch!* Fuck. Fuck. Fuuuuck! "Bella, no, it's not what you think."

"Seriously!" she screamed. "Are you trying to tell me those aren't a bunch of half-naked women, all tied up, ready for sex? I may be naïve when it comes to that shit, Spencer, but I'm not fucking blind!" Izzy closed the gap between us, her tiny finger jabbing at my chest, tears falling in a steady stream down her face. "Just tell me this, you sonofabitch! Did you sleep with all these women? Do I need to get a fucking AIDS test or something?"

What have I done?

I hated seeing Izzy hurt. Knowing I was the asshole who caused her pain made it that much worse. No matter what happened, I had to make this better for her. I owed her at least that much.

Placing my hands one her slender waist, I did my best to soothe her. "Baby, please," I said, my voice barely above a whisper. "I didn't sleep with any of those women. You know how much I love you. I've never even seen these pictures before." None of that was a total lie. Val and I hadn't *slept* together, not in the way Izzy thought, anyway. And I certainly hadn't ever seen those pictures before.

Pushing my hands away from her, Izzy stepped back. "Stop," she cried, her slender arms wrapping protectively around herself. "Just stop. I can't take any more of your lies."

I couldn't have Izzy crumbling because I was too goddamn weak to resist my own selfish needs. Anger. That was an emotion that wouldn't wound her spirit. "Damn it, Bella," I snapped, throwing my hands in the air. "You have to believe me. That isn't me."

"If it isn't you, then why were they hand delivered to me?" she shouted, already heading toward the door.

Good, girl.

"Why the hell would someone send me this trash, then?"

"To hurt us," I answered, because it was true. That's exactly why Val had done it. She wanted me to suffer, and what better way then by hurting Izzy? It wouldn't even matter to Val that she'd hurt her best friend to make that happen.

Izzy stormed out of her office, leaving me surround by the visual reminder of just how low I'd sunk. I didn't try to stop her. She needed to put some distance between us while the anger was still driving her. As hard as Izzy had tried to mask it, the emotion in her voice was clear. Heartbreak. Confusion. Disappointment. And I'd done that to her. Val may have sent the pictures, but *I* was the one who betrayed the sanctity of my marriage. Ultimately, it was *me* who hurt my wife. I was no better than that piece-of-shit, Diego Rivera.

When I heard Izzy's feet on the stairs, I started gathering up the pictures off the floor, taking extra care to assure I got them all. Izzy didn't need another look at my betrayal. With any luck, she'd forget she ever saw them.

After stowing the box in the trunk of my car to dispose of later, I headed upstairs to grab a change of clothes. Izzy needed space, and I'd let her have it, but it'd been two days since I'd showered.

When I stepped out of the closet, clean clothes in hand, Izzy was sitting on the chaise across the room. Without looking up, she said, "Drew and Anna graduate in less than six months. They can't know about this before then."

"As far as I'm concerned, Bella, they don't ever have to know about those pictures."

Izzy stood up, her hands fisted at her sides. "I'm not talking about those disgusting pictures," she said through clenched teeth. "I'm talking about the divorce."

Divorce.

Izzy's words stung more than I expected. Sure, I had been planning on asking for a divorce for months, but hearing the words come out of her mouth widened the crack in my heart even further. "We don't have to decide that tonight, baby."

"No, Spencer! You don't get to call me baby anymore." She blew out a heavy breath. "And stop calling me Bella too!" she added before storming away from me for the second time that day. I wanted to command her to stay, to make sure she understood why I had to hide that side of me from her. That's not what Izzy needed, though, so I had no choice but to let her go.

· · · · ·

At dinner I broke the news I was leaving for Chicago. Sticking around would only make things harder for Izzy. Right then, she needed me as far away from her as I could get. I'd do anything to make things easier for the woman I'd loved almost half my life, the mother of my children.

Anna, our 'I'm almost eighteen years old' daughter, was disappointed I wouldn't be staying home longer this time. That's my Anna. She's been a daddy's girl since day one.

Her twin brother Drew, however, couldn't have cared less. Since he got that soccer scholarship to Embry Riddle, his whole life had been nothing but soccer. Half the time I doubted Drew knew if I was in town or not. I had to give it to the kid. When he set his mind to something, there was no stopping him. He busted his ass on and off the field for years to ensure he got a spot on that team. No amount of skill would have mattered if he didn't have the grades to go along with it.

Being able to get back to the club sooner was the only good part in all this crap. Nate had to be close to finding Ashlan. I needed to be there when he did. Every second that passed was a second she was in danger. Besides, after the stunt Val pulled with those pictures, a trip to Esoteric was definitely in order. There was no way I was going to let her get away with that shit. Esoteric had strict rules against photography inside the club. Yeah, we'd see who was laughing when her membership got revoked.

• • • • •

Standing in the lobby outside Master Dane's office, I was sweating bullets. I'd never ratted out anyone before, let alone a respected Dominatrix like Val. What if my plan backfired? *Sonofabitch!* What if I got ousted too?

"Master Spence, sorry to keep you waiting." I tensed up at the deep sound of Dane's voice. "Come on in." Dane motioned me through the open door and into his spacious office.

I was relieved when he shut the door behind him. What I had to say definitely needed privacy.

I sat in the center of the brown leather sofa in Dane's office, placing the box of pictures on the cushion beside me. "Thanks for seeing me on short notice."

"Not a problem, man. What can I do for you?"

Nervously, I ran my hand over the top of the box. There was no easy way for me to say it, no matter how many times I ran it through my head.

"Wanna tell me what's in that box you can't stop fingering?" Dane snapped, clearly fed up with my stalling. "You called for this meeting, asshole, now get on with it. I've got shit to do." Dane folded his arms behind his head as he leaned back in the chair, propping his feet on the coffee table as he did.

"I'm married—"

Dane burst out laughing. "Seriously, man, if that's what all this beating around the bush was about, I'm about to kick your ass."

The fact that Dane thought I'd waste his time really pissed me the hell off. I tossed the box of pictures on the table in front of him. "Privacy, that's what this is about," I snapped. "Take a look at what was delivered to my wife today."

Dane lifted the lid and pulled out a few pictures. His eyes widened as recognition dawned. There was no mistaking the Esoteric insignia. "Where did you get these? We sweep for cameras every day before we open and again after we close. How the hell could this have happened?"

"I know exactly how it happened," I said, my voice returning to a more respectable tone. "Mistress Val."

Dane looked up from the picture he was holding. "You better have some proof of that before you go around accusing a club Mistress."

"Aren't these pictures proof enough? That's Val, in every fucking shot."

"Just because she's in the pictures doesn't prove she took them. Have you talked to her? Does she even know about these?"

No. No. No. This couldn't be happening.

How could he sit there and defend the vindictive bitch that sent those to my unsuspecting wife. I had to make Dane believe me. "Val is the *only* person here who knows who my wife is."

"How can you know that for sure? If you told Val, someone could have easily overheard you."

It was that moment that I knew I'd have to tell him the whole story.

Every.

Sordid.

Detail.

I dropped my head into my hands to shield myself from Dane's disapproving glare. "Val and my wife have been best friends their whole lives. She was Izzy's Maid of Honor. She's the Godmother to our children."

Dane shook his head. "Now I want to kick your ass for a whole different reason."

"I get it. I'm a scumbag. A piece of shit who doesn't deserve to live. I deserve this shit storm and more, but Izzy was innocent. She didn't deserve to have a box full of pictures from my time here hand delivered to our house!"

Dane sat back in his chair again, his earlier relaxed posture slowly returning. "I'll have to report this to the other two owners. We'll run a full a sweep of the security tapes. If anyone placed a camera inside this club in the last three months, I'll find it." At my nod, he continued. "I'll be completely honest with you, man. If we come up empty, it'll be your membership on the line. We take false reporting just as seriously as we take rule violations."

Fuck! I jumped to my feet, the overwhelming feeling of desperation making it impossible to sit still any longer. It'd been six months since I was with Val. And who knew how old those pictures were? How could I even tell? "Those pictures are at least six months old, Dane. Who knows when she took them? But you have to believe me. You can't ban me from the club. Ashlan is in real trouble, and this place is my only link to her. I have to be here when she comes back.

Dane stood then too. "I swear to God, Spencer. I'm about two seconds away from pounding your stupid skull into the floor. If Ash is in that kind of trouble, you better start talking. What the hell is going on?"

• • • • •

The next hour was spent filling Dane in on everything I knew. As it turned out, I wasn't the only one who had been keeping secrets. I mean, who knew Master Dane, or Lieutenant Colonel Ronnie Dane as he was known to the men he commanded, was a retired Army Ranger? Dane no longer intimidated me. He scared the living hell out of me.

Luckily for me, Dane was on my side. Well, about saving Ash, that is. He made his feelings about what I'd done to Izzy perfectly clear when his fist connected to my gut. It was a small price to pay for his help, really.

One phone call from Dane and twenty minutes later I had Ash's address in my hand. Figures El Mismo Diablo would own a sixty million dollar Malibu mansion. I'd never be able to give Ashlan the kind of luxury she was used to, but I'd sure as hell never hit her, either. Well, not the way Diego did. Hell, after seeing the pictures of her injuries, I might not ever be able to take her into another scene.

Safe.

Sane.

Consensual.

Those conditions were absolute and non-negotiable. Wanting me to take her into a scene after what she's been through certainly wasn't sane in my book.

Thanks to the amazing satellite images Dane's military contacts got us, it didn't take long to identify two potential weak spots in Diego's security. According to Dane, the larger cluster of trees that provided privacy from his neighbors was our best option for getting a recon team in and out undetected. At first I thought the recon team was a waste of time. Time Ashlan may not have. Dane hadn't left any room for discussion. He was in charge of her rescue. If I wanted to be involved at all my only option was to fall in line.

"Zeke, Cowboy, you'll fly out tonight and get eyes on the ground. Rock, you and Matt meet me at Edwards at zero five hundred. We'll hitch a ride on a Helo from there. We rendezvous at the Del Rey Yacht club at zero six thirty."

"Yes, sir," the three men said in near perfect unison, their military training quite evident.

"What time is our flight?" I asked just as soon as Dane was off the phone.

"The club closes at ten tonight. We leave then."

Chapter Twelve

Spencer

Time had never moved as slow as it moved that night. Twenty more minutes until Esoteric closed. Then we could finally get on with saving the woman I didn't want to live without. All I could do until then was sit and wait. Every tick of the second hand felt like an eternity.

Tick.

Is she safe?

Tock.

Why did I let her walk out that night?

Tick.

Why the hell hadn't I pushed harder for answers?

Tock.

What if she's hurt even worse?

The questions played over and over in an endless loop through my mind. I'd failed as a Dom. Even worse, I failed Ashlan when she needed me most.

Before I went completely out of my mind with worry and self-loathing, I pulled out my phone to do a little recon of my own. I wanted to put a face to all the anger burning inside me. Plus, at that point I'd do just about anything to keep from losing my shit. Twelve more minutes and we'd be on our way. All I had to do was hold it together until then.

I typed Diego Rivera in the search box of my phone's browser and hit enter. Less than a second later, I was staring into the cold, dark eyes of the only man I'd ever hated: El Mismo Diablo. And hell if I didn't hate how goddamn good looking the bastard was. Perfectly styled jet black hair framing the kind of baby face women drooled over. Little did they know, behind all that creamy caramel flesh was pure evil. The devil himself reincarnated. With looks like his, I couldn't blame anyone for falling for his spell. Hell, if I were I woman, I'd probably fuck him.

Not surprisingly, my generic search returned over four million results. While I didn't know exactly what I was looking for, I was smart enough to know the last thing I needed at the moment was to scroll through page after page of useless information about the piece of shit who hurt *my* Ash. My nerves were already raw.

I modified my search and tried again: Diego and Ashlan Rivera Malibu California.

Nothing could have prepared me for the headline I was reading: Ashlan Rivera, wife of suspected Columbian Drug Lord, El Mismo Diablo, dies in single car crash.

There had to be some sort of mistake. All the stress and worry about Ash had me seeing things. Ash *couldn't* be dead. I scrubbed my eyes with the heels of my hands, saying a silent prayer I was right.

When I finally opened my eyes again, the headline was still there. With lightning speed, I clicked on the link to the article, my mind refusing to believe what I'd just read.

Seeing Ash's gorgeous green eyes fill the screen on my phone sucked all the air right out of my lungs. Emotions ran through me faster than I could process them.

Shock. Disbelief. Despair.

Ash.

My Ash.

Dead.

"NOOOOOO!" I roared when the air returned to my lungs. I jumped to my feet, only to end up a listless heap on the floor, my legs too weak to hold me. I was too late. Ash was already gone. "No. No. No. No. NOOOOO!"

The door flew open. "What the hell's going on in here?" Dane demanded.

"Too late," was all I could manage to say. I was too fucking late.

Ashlan.

She's gone.

Dane started to say something but stopped when his phone began to ring. He held up a finger indicating he needed a minute. "Shit. I need to get this." He moved toward the door as he answered the phone.

"Dane," he barked out. His voice trailed off as he walked to the opposite end of the room. It didn't matter who he was talking to. I'd played things his way, and Ash was dead. Nothing else mattered.

I pulled myself to my feet and staggered out of Dane's office, headed for the closest bar I could find. There was only one thing that could ease the pain in my chest now.

• • • • •

It hadn't taken Dane long to track me down, yet I was already finishing up my fifth shot of Jack Daniels. Getting shit faced drunk was my only plan. Not even Master Dane was going to change that. Losing Izzy was bad enough, but losing Ashlan too was going to destroy me.

"I get it, man," Dane said as he filled the empty space beside me. "I'm not here to bust your balls or even to try and stop you." Dane rested his hand on my shoulder. "Tonight, I'm here for you. Whatever you need, I've got your back."

• • • • •

That's all I remembered before drinking myself into oblivion that night. True to his word, Dane never left my side. He not only made sure I got home in one piece, he hosed me off and tucked my sorry ass into bed after I threw up all over the bathroom. A process I'd pretty much repeated every night since.

Find a bar.

Get shit faced drunk.

Throw up all over myself.

Wake up clean.

The only deviance in my new routine came when Dane brought me to his house. After the third straight night sleeping on the pull-out sofa in my hotel suite, Dane insisted I stay at his place until I got my head on straight again.

At first, I refused to leave the hotel, much preferring to be alone to wallow in my own self-pity. When Dane threatened to chain me up in his basement if I didn't come willingly, I gave up the fight. Chicago wasn't the safest city even when you weren't falling down drunk. Dane made it pretty clear he wasn't about to stand by and let me get hurt. Not when he was feeling responsible for Ash's death too.

Every day that passed since had turned my world a litter darker. Ash was gone. And thanks to that stupid bitch, Val, my family was gone too. The more I drank, the more I needed to drink.

Stretched to the outer edges of sanity, I desperately needed some relief. So far, nothing I'd tried had worked. Not even the biweekly trips home to check on Izzy and the kids had been able to ease the pain in my chest.

That morning, however, sitting in the dark watching Izzy sleep, I was way beyond conflicted. Her breathy moans had me shoving my hand down my pants. Four months had passed since I last felt the warmth of a woman wrapped around my dick. Until that very moment, the thought hadn't even crossed my mind since the night I lost Ash.

"No," Izzy moaned.

Squinting my eyes just right, I would have sworn that was Ash lying before me. Her perfect olive skin kissed by my whip.

"Oh, God, yes," I whispered, my breath beginning to hitch. Without so much as a second thought, I thrust my hips into my fist, harder, faster. "Yes. Ash. Don't stop. Don't ever stop." A few more strokes and my orgasm dangled just outside my reach. One more delicious moan and I'd be soaring, free from all the searing pain the past few months had brought. My balls tightened, and I knew I was close. Just one more moan.

Come on, baby. One more. That's all I need.

"Spencer!" Izzy screamed.

Fuck. Fuck. *Fuck me!* I was right fucking there. So close to the release I craved I could practically taste it. Nothing like the shrieking sound of your 'soon to be ex-wife' to instantly soften your dick.

Sonofabitch! Izzy probably thinks I was some kind of freak after seeing those pictures. How in the hell was I going to explain this?

Quick, asshole. Say something.

Before I got the words out, Izzy spoke first. "It was just a bad dream," she said.

Wait. She hadn't seen me?

"Just a stupid dream."

No. She hadn't. *Fucking miracles do exist.*

When Izzy reached for the light on the bedside table, I high tailed it the hell out of there, thankful to have dodged *that* bullet. Even with the massive case of blue balls I was left to deal with.

By the time I made it downstairs to the study, I was in desperate need of a drink. Immediately cracking the seal on the unopened bottle of Jack, I brought the smooth elixir to my lips, chugging a good portion down, not even bothering to waste time tasting it. Getting caught with my hand down my pants killed the buzz I'd shown up there with. Staying one drink ahead of the pain in my heart was how I'd managed to survive the past four months without Ash. Every time the buzz wore off, all the pain came rushing back.

Every.

Goddamn.

Time.

And that's one pain I couldn't bear. Ash was gone, and no amount of suffering would bring her back to me.

Fuck one drink.

What I really needed was a whole goddamn bottle. And a cigarette.

The bottle to occupy one hand.

A cigarette for the other.

And a numbing sensation deep inside my heart.

Yeah. That's exactly what I fucking needed.

Chapter Thirteen
Spencer

The light illuminating through the kitchen window pulled my attention away from the serenity of the early morning waves.

Dammit. Someone was up.

A slender silhouette hovered in the window like an angel.

Ash? Could it be her?

Yes. It had to be her.

Leaving the near empty bottle of bourbon on the beach behind me, I scrambled to my feet. Only Ash was moving away from the window.

No! Not again.

I had to get to her before she disappeared. I could save her, but only if I could stop her from leaving.

With heavy legs and the deep sand slowing my pace, I'd never make it to her in time. "Ash," I cried out at the top of my lungs. "Don't go, sunshine. Please don't leave me again."

Yes. It's working.

She turned and was headed right toward me. The rapid thud of my heartbeat was all I could hear. Ash was so close I could almost touch her.

When she stepped out of the sliding glass door, I swear my heart stopped. In that fraction of a second, Ash disappeared.

No. No. NO!

"Daddy!" Anna squealed as she ran toward me. "I'm so happy you're home!" She threw herself in my arms, oblivious to my inebriated state. Thank God for that, at least. Couldn't have my little princess knowing her dad was a piece of shit drunk on top of everything else. I'd already lost Ash and Izzy. Losing Anna wasn't an option.

Forcing a smile on my face, I said, "Good morning, baby girl. You're up early."

"Yeah, mom was yelling in her sleep again," she laughed. "I don't think she likes it when you're away."

"Really?" I asked, sounding pathetically hopeful.

"Oh, Dad, stop being silly. You know how much she loves you." Anna tightened her arms around me again. "How much we all love you."

Izzy still loves me?

If that was true, it meant there was still hope. Ash was gone forever. Maybe I wouldn't lose Izzy after all. For the first time in months, my mood began to lift.

I scooped Anna into my arms. "You look hungry. How about some chocolate chip pancakes?"

"My favorite!" she squealed, tightening her grip around my neck.

Anna squirmed in my arms as I made my way back to the house. "Put me down," she protested. "I'm too big for you to carry."

Only, I didn't let her go. In that moment Anna was my connection to a life I thought for sure was gone forever.

"I'll make the coffee," Anna said when we made it back to the kitchen. "You start the pancakes."

"How about some orange juice for me, princess?"

"Orange juice, huh? So that's the magic cure for hangovers?"

So much for my plan of maintaining that façade of perfection... "More like the ultimate cure," I mumbled under my breath.

"Oh, Daddy! That's ridiculous. We both know prevention is the only cure for hangovers."

What the hell?

"Oh, yeah," I snapped, not even trying to mask the harsh look on my face, "and exactly what do you know about hangovers, Anna?"

"Um..." she said, nervously twisting her hands. "*Nothing.*"

Too bad her body told a different story. Lip trapped between her teeth. Eyes averted. Cheeks colored darker than her lips.

I stepped closer, nostrils flaring.

"It was only a couple times," she blurted out. "You know...um...at a couple parties, with um...my *friends.*"

Oh hell no. *She better not be drinking with that asshat she's been dating.*

"You know how I feel about you drinking, Anna." The effects of my all night bender still lingered. I sucked in a deep breath to keep from flying off the handle before addressing an even bigger concern. "Especially with Eddie."

That last statement brought her eyes back to mine.

Strong. Sassy. Fierce.

Just like her mother.

"Yes, *father.* You've told me that a million times."

Closing the final step between us, I told her again. "Boys at that age only want one thing, princess. Adding alcohol to the mix of hormones is a sure recipe for disaster. Trust me, Eddie's no different."

Anna tried to move away, but I held her in place with both hands on her shoulders. It wasn't her I didn't trust. It was every fucking teenage boy. Anna and I'd had that talk too many times to count. Shy of locking her inside the house until she was older, all I could do was hope she'd heard me and was making good choices.

I leaned closer to her, softening the look on my face. "I just want you safe, princess."

"I'm always careful, daddy." Anna reached up and kissed me on the cheek. "I swear."

Silence filled the air as each of us worked on our separate tasks making breakfast. Despite my intoxication, I managed to make quick work of the pancake batter, a recipe I knew by heart. I'd been making the same pancakes for Anna since she was old enough to eat them. Once upon a time I made breakfast for both my kids, until Drew became too cool to hang with his old man.

Anna's soft voice finally broke the silence. "Look who's home," she said.

When I looked up, I saw she wasn't talking to me.

My God, Izzy.

My dick twitched at the sight of Izzy's silky robe hanging open, her nightshirt hugging her bare breasts. She must've felt me eye-fucking her, because she couldn't fasten that sash any tighter. Like two layers of that thin silk fabric could hide the gorgeous body I knew was under there.

Anna was rambling on and on about something. I sure as hell hoped it wasn't important, because I hadn't heard a word she'd said since I noticed Izzy had walked into the room. My mind was way the hell over there in the gutter thinking all sorts of nasty thoughts about my wife.

My wife.

Fuck me. She *was* still my wife. And from what Anna said, she still loved me.

"When did you get home," Izzy asked, her whispered tone sending a jolt of electricity down my spine, straight into my balls.

I glanced around the room only to find Anna was gone. The only thing standing in the way between me and my wife were two flimsy pieces of fabric.

Fuck. Me.

A broad smile spread across my face. "I've been home for hours, Bella," I said, moving closer to where she was sitting.

Her body stiffened ever so slightly, awaking my inner Dom.

That's right, baby. I saw you writhing around the bed, your body begging to be touched.

I imagined how well Izzy's pale skin would color from my expert touch. My dick came alive with every thought.

As soon as I was close enough to touch her, I leaned in and whispered, "That was some dream you were having."

When Izzy sprung up off the stool, I was certain she was about to leap into my arms. That's not at all what happened. No. She sprinted out of the room like the kitchen was on fire.

Wait. Was it?

After a quick scan revealed the house was not about to burn to the ground, I went looking for Izzy. It didn't take me long to find her. I just followed the sound I knew all too well, the sound of vomit hitting the toilet.

"You okay, Bella?" I asked when the convulsing finally stopped.

"I'm fine," she snapped. "And stop calling me Bella!" she added as she pushed her way past me.

If Izzy was still in love with me, she sure had a funny way of showing it. Maybe Anna was wrong? Was that all part of Izzy's master plan? Faking her feelings for the benefit of our kids?

I had to find out. My heart had way too many damn cracks in it to play games.

The bathroom door was shut when I made it upstairs to the master bedroom. Izzy's muffled cries told me she was inside. Quietly, I pressed my ear to the door. "Why is this happening. Why didn't I believe him?"

Why *didn't* she? As in, past tense. That could only mean one thing: she believed me now. Anna was right. Izzy did still love me. She just needed more time.

Chapter Fourteen
Ashlan

Four months. Not a few days. Not a couple of weeks, but four long months. That's how long Tony kept me at the safe house.

News of my death spread quicker than any of us thought it would. Had my death been staged as an accident, chances were the news would have blown over as soon as it began. Unfortunately, evidence of foul play was leaked to the press, and suddenly my death became a national interest. From domestic abuse advocates to talk show hosts, everyone seemed to be taking advantage of the hell my life had been.

The first few weeks were the hardest. Knowing Spencer thought I was dead tore me up inside. He'd been honest with his feelings. He wanted *more* with *me*. But now he thought I was dead. The tortured look in his eyes the last time I saw him still haunted my dreams. If only there was a way to let him know it wasn't true without risking both our lives.

Every day I held out hope that love would find a way, but deep down I knew all hope was dead. Like Ashlan Rivera, eternally incinerated.

Hell, until today even going out in public had been considered far too risky an endeavor, which was why I'd been at the safe house for so long. The day had barely begun when the state prosecutor's office announced they'd taken Diego into custody on the charge of first degree murder, along with a slew of lesser charges. Honestly, I stopped listening after I heard the words "first degree murder." Charles' plan had worked. Diego was going to prison for my murder.

Finally, I was truly free.

Tony, the man who'd watched over me like a hawk since I arrived at the safe house, was escorting me to Florida. Charles hadn't been wrong when he said I'd be relocated anywhere I wanted to go. Tony never even flinched when I told him I wanted to live on the other side of the country.

Thankfully, he hadn't asked me why that's where I wanted to go. Tony had that whole clenched jaw, narrowed eye look down. He would've seen right through me if I'd tried to lie, and he never would have agreed to take me to Florida if he knew about Spencer.

Traveling commercially was still too risky. All it would take was a single camera to catch a glimpse of me for the defense to prove reasonable doubt. Sure, the long, red wig and dark glasses helped, as did my newly lightened complexion thanks to months of being stuck indoors, but this was my life we were talking about. No risk was worth it in my book.

Luckily, Tony agreed and made arrangements for us to hitch a ride on an army transport from Presidio to Laughlin AFB in Texas. It'd take longer to get to where we were going, but honestly, after four months of being trapped inside that house with Tony and his too-sweet-for-words wife Toni, I was more than ready to be surrounded by other people.

Lots and lots of people.

• • • • •

Zeke, Tony's army buddy who was escorting us on the first leg of our trip, seemed to take great pleasure in making sure I was securely fastened into the ridiculous harness I was expected to wear. "Gotta make sure you're strapped up, sweetheart. It's about to get rough in here."

"Knock it off, dickhead," Tony snapped.

Without another word, Zeke sat back in his own seat and fastened his harness. "Cowboy's meetin' us at Laughlin," he said to Tony. "He'll escort you the rest of the way." Zeke turned his attention back to me, tapping my foot with his. "Anything you need after that, pretty lady, Cowboy will see you get it."

Tony narrowed his focus on me when he spoke. "The only thing either one of us needs from Cowboy is a lift," he barked out before turning his death stare back on Zeke.

Tony's possessive tone wrapped around me like a warm blanket. He'd made it perfectly clear from day one that he'd never let anything happen to me. Funny enough, I believed him. Even so, I couldn't let Tony get away with that growly shit.

"I don't know, Tony," I said. "I'm going to need a friend...and Cowboy sounds kinda cute."

Tony's growl had Zeke flinching which made me laugh. Tony growled louder but it didn't make me stop.

Shaking his head Zeke said, "Sassy little thing, aren't ya. Cowboy's gonna fall in love."

That had me shutting my mouth. Love wasn't meant to work out for me. If six years of torture at my husband's hand hadn't proven that, losing Spencer certainly had. No, there'd be no more love for me.

Even thinking about Spencer made my heart ache with the kind of pain that would last a lifetime.

Haunting. All consuming. The searing kind of pain that made getting out of bed nearly impossible.

Every day I prayed Spencer wasn't hurting too. He deserved to move on from all this. He had a wife and kids, after all. The last thing he needed was the drama that came with even knowing me. Maybe thinking I was dead was the best thing for him.

"Don't mind him—"

Zeke's breath in my ear sent a cold chill up my spine. "What the hell!" I shouted, waving my arms around like a crazy person.

In a blink of an eye, the words Tony had spent months drilling into my head kicked in. I stilled my arms, positioned to take the perp down.

Disable or be disabled.

As if on autopilot, my arm flew out toward Zeke's throat. Too bad I'd forgotten I was trapped inside that stupid harness.

"Dammit!" I'd never been so pissed off at myself. I let my guard down for one damn minute, and look what happened. A mistake like that could get me killed. "Get this thing off me. Now! I mean it, let me go!"

Heat seeped through my jeans where Tony's hand closed around my thigh. The unexpected warmth drew me back to my senses. But not even his deep, rich tone could stop the adrenaline rushing through my veins. "Relax, princess. Everything's fine."

Princess? Did he seriously just call me that?

I. Don't. Think. So.

"Jesus, Zeke. What the hell did you do to her?"

"Oh, put your dick away! He just surprised me. That's all."

"Yeah, *Tony*, put your dick away," Zeke chimed in.

Turning my attention back to Zeke, I snapped. "Shut up, asshole! You're lucky I'm strapped down. I'd slap that stupid grin right off that pretty boy face of yours." I stopped to take a breath, preparing to go at him again, when Tony's grip on my leg tightened. Something about it felt so familiar, instantly draining the fight right out of me.

Before I even let out the breath I'd taken, I'd crumbled into Tony's side.

One helluva a stern look from Tony shut Zeke down too.

Thank God.

None of us said much after that. With me still tucked into his side, Tony's body relaxed in a way that no longer screamed certain death, but there was no way to know for sure. Turned out, Zeke and I were both smart enough not to poke *that* bear while trapped inside the back of a transport with no easy way of escape. Well, no easy way for me. I didn't care how many parachutes they strapped me into, someone would have to shove me out of that plane. No damn way would I jump willingly.

By the time we landed in Texas, where I was officially introduced to Cowboy, I was too tired to care about his annoying flirting. My lack of interest in his southern charms certainly hadn't kept him from trying. When Tony threatened to put a foot up his ass if he didn't back off, I didn't care how protective he was acting. For a moment there I wished I was still tucked away inside the safe house, completely buffered from the chaos of the outside world. What the hell had I been thinking leaving?

Living there wasn't all that bad. I could've stayed. Right?

Tony sat down beside me just in time to stop that worry train. "Take this," he growled, shoving a blanket in my lap. "You look tired. Get some sleep."

Arguing with Tony was pointless when he was perfectly calm. Doing it today would be downright stupid considering how tense he'd been.

Besides, I *was* exhausted.

Doing the only thing I could, I accepted the blanket and then curled up with my head on Tony's lap. There was no other way to lay down with all the equipment he insisted I had to wear. What I wanted was a hot shower, a comfortable bed, and some time alone, but I'd settle for the warm lap of a man I trusted.

Chapter Fifteen
Spencer

By the time I woke up, the house was empty. What I'd meant to do was give Izzy a little space to calm down while I got cleaned up in one of the spare bedrooms downstairs. When I was sure she'd had enough time to cool off, I was going to sit her ass down so we could talk about all the shit between us. That had been the plan, anyway. Too bad I decided to have another drink first. The fact that I woke up still wearing the same clothes I'd intended to change out of told me all I needed to know.

Passed out. Again. But hell if my body didn't need the rest.

Thank God I passed out before I ended up doing something stupid. Alcohol made me weak and, from what I do remember about last night, it also had me hoping for things that would never work out. How could I ever be with Izzy again when Ashlan was all I could think about whenever I was sober? I'd done enough damage to Izzy. It was time for her to move on, find that Prince Charming she deserved.

As if the throbbing in my head wasn't punishment enough for last night's bender, the incessant ringing of my cell phone sure as hell was.

What the hell could possibly be so important?

Fumbling the phone off the bed beside me, I answered. "What!"

Soft laughter filled the line first. "Good afternoon to you too, Mr. James," Natasha, my executive assistant said, completely unfazed by my grating tone. "You know, if you'd answer an email every once in a while, I wouldn't have to wake you up in the *middle of the afternoon*."

The lighthearted note in her voice always made me smile. *Jesus!* Why was I such an asshole to her? She shouldn't have to put up with my shit.

"I've sent you three emails in the past two days with an urgent message from Mr. Hart. And, since you haven't bothered to call him....he stopped by a little while ago, and let's just say he insisted *I* call *you*."

Maxwell Hart, the newly appointed president of James Industries, had only called me a handful of times since I hired him. An urgent message from him had to be important.

Sonofabitch.

The office was definitely not the place to show up drunk, which is why I'd been avoiding it for months. I didn't know the first thing about our current projects. Surely, Max knew that. *Right?*

But then, what could he possibly need from me? "Fine," I finally agreed. "Get him on the line."

"He's holding now, sir. I'll transfer the call."

Max's husky voice filled my ear before I'd fully processed what Natasha had said. I didn't want to talk to him right then, not with booze still oozing from my pours. "Spencer, hey, I know you're busy, so I'll be brief."

Jesus. I'd become such a dick, not even bothering to take the time to return a goddamn email from the man who was running the day-to-day operations of my entire fucking business. At least that was something I could fix.

Pasting on the fakest smile I'd ever seen, praying it reached my voice, I answered. "Max, hey....Sorry I haven't called. What can I do for you?"

"I got a call from the GM at Starwood in Atlantic City the other day wanting to know how much longer our inspector is gonna be onsite. That project..."

Starwood? Atlantic City? I sure as hell hoped Max wasn't expecting me to answer that question, because I had nothing.

Absolutely.

Fucking.

Nothing.

"The problem I'm having is I'm looking at a final inspection dated last year....you know, when the project was finished."

Great, I missed part of the conversation and now Max was talking to me like I was an idiot. Why the hell had I crawled out of bed?

When I didn't answer, Max added, "I spoke to Dr. Barnes this morning, she said she was working on a special project you authorized, and she didn't have an end date."

Dr. Barnes? Why did that name sound familiar?

Wait? Authorized a project?

What the hell?

"Get Sabastian on the line. Tell him I want security video of the Starwood in my inbox in five minutes, or he'll be looking for a new job!"

"Alright," Max said. "It'd be helpful if I knew what this is all about before I start threatening the head of our security division. Wanna clue me in here? If we're running projects off the book—"

"We don't run fucking projects off the books," I barked out. It pissed me the hell off that he'd even think

I'd let that shit happen. "And I haven't authorized any projects you don't know about. Now, if you're done questioning my integrity, maybe you can get me the damn video I asked for." I didn't wait for him to respond before I ended the call. The last I checked, James Industries still had my name on door.

After that call with Max, my body screamed for a drink. I couldn't get caught up in that trap again, though. At least not until after I'd showered and put on clean clothes. Three days in the same shirt was two days too many.

With Izzy gone, I was at least able to shower upstairs. I'd paid special attention to the master bathroom when I rebuilt the house. Izzy's office had been my wedding present to her. The shower in the master bathroom was my gift to me. Tiled floor to ceiling, dark polished marble filled the oversized shower stall. The bench seat and second shower head had turned out to be more fun than I'd ever dreamt they would be when I first designed it.

My dick hardened from the memory of the first time Izzy rode me on that bench. She'd been so shy and timid about showering together. Too bad she hadn't remembered our first shower together. The one we shared that night in Miami.

Fisting my cock, I leaned against the tiled wall. The two shower heads pelted me with warmth from the front and back giving me more than enough lubrication for what I needed to do. When I reached the tip of my dick, I squeezed, thrusting my hips forward. I had half a mind to draw this out, to take my time savoring every stroke, but I had shit that needed to be done.

It'd been so long since I found pleasure, a few more quick strokes was all it took to find it now. My balls tightened. Semen shot like a rocket onto the wall only to be washed away by the heavy stream of water. It took all my strength not to collapse in a heap on the wet floor which was why I sat down on the bench while my orgasm rocked through my body.

Stepping out of the steamy hot shower, the cold air slapped me out of my orgasmic stupor right back into reality. Wrapping one towel around my waist, running another one through my hair, I made my way to the closet.

Even in Florida, April could be cool, especially this far up the Gulf Coast. I pulled on a pair of jeans over my boxer briefs then rummaged through my closet until I found a warm enough shirt. Well, shirts, in this case. It was definitely a flannel and t-shirt kind of day.

• • • • •

Between the full night of sleep and the hot shower, not to mention what happened in the shower, I was feeling pretty relaxed. Even the cold air hadn't managed to grate on my nerves. You'd think seeing Sebastian's email would only enhance that euphoric feeling inside me. And it had—until I hit play.

Valerie fucking Russell!

She'd done gone and lost her damn mind. Getting her membership to Esoteric revoked apparently wasn't enough for that crazy bitch. She was looking for a trip to jail. Or maybe the looney bin would be a better place for her.

First she went and screwed with my marriage, now she was messing around with my company? Whatever game she was playing, hell fucking no was she getting away with that shit.

Before I could stop myself, Natasha's cell phone was ringing. "Tell the GM at Starwood that so far everything looks good with the inspection," I barked into the phone as soon as Natasha answered. "Tell him we'll be out of his hair by Saturday. Offer to pay the full rate for Dr. Barnes' stay. Apologize. Whatever it takes to make sure this is handled quietly." We sure as hell couldn't have our clients knowing James' Security had allowed a security breech inside their own company. Without giving Natasha a chance to formulate her typical laundry list of questions, I added, "And get me on the next flight to New Jersey."

"Wait..." I heard as I reached to disconnect the call. I hung up anyway. Natasha would just want answers, and I wasn't in the mood to give them. Nope. I was in the damn mood to *get* some answers.

Starting with Valerie!

Heading straight toward the airport, I tore down the highway like a bat out of hell. My plan was full of holes, but one thing I knew for sure was I'd make Val pay for messing with me. Stupid bitch thought she could screw up my life and get away with it.

Fuck that!

By the time I finished with her, she'd wish she never met me or my wife.

• • • • •

Atlantic City was a crisp fifty-five degrees when I arrived at the hotel. The guest services clerk was more than happy to get me an extra copy of the room key to the suite James' Industries had been occupying for over two months.

No wonder the GM had his panties in a bunch. Val had taken over one of the hotel's most expensive rooms. Sebastian would have some serious ass kissing to do if he planned on saving the account.

If I didn't find Val soon, she'd not only destroy the reputation I'd spent over twenty years building, she'd bankrupt my damn company.

A full sweep of the three room suite revealed more than I needed to know. Paddles, cuffs, canes, a whip—

What the hell?

My hands reached out toward the familiar implement, the custom designed leather handle calling to me on a level so deep I couldn't stop myself from touching it. Tracing the rough edge where Val carved my initials, there was no denying it. That wasn't just any whip. It was *my whip*. The one Val gave me to celebrate my membership at Esoteric. But how'd she get it?

Dragging my hand along the soft leather, images of Ash flashed through my mind.

As if the whip had burst into flames, I withdrew my hand with a swift motion. Fire pulsed through my fingertips where I'd made contact with the leather tail. Val must've coated it with capsaicin oil. She loved using that shit. Hot pepper soaked through my pours, creating one hell of a burning sensation. I don't know who she was playing with now but whoever was on the receiving end of that had to be a masochist, because that shit fucking hurt.

Snap out of it, fucktard. Dane's words rang loud and clear in my mind. It wasn't the time for a hard on. Besides, without Ash my days as a Dom were over. Shattered, like the rest of my dreams.

Plus, I'd come there to do a job: *make Val pay*. Too bad she wasn't in the suite so I could get on with it.

Two full loops around the casino floor, and I'd lost all patience. Every passing second I had to look for Val only fueled the raging fire that burned out of control inside me. No amount of the cheap bourbon I'd been drinking seemed to calm me down.

One drink here. Two drinks over there. As long as I kept dropping quarters in one of their slot machines, the wait staff kept my glass full. That night, however, was not the time to let go of appearances. Good thing there was plenty of space for me to get lost in.

Normally, I wouldn't drink at all while on a job. Nothing about this trip was *normal,* though. And as long as I didn't draw attention to myself, no one would ever find out what *business* I was really there for. Val screwed up everything. But, by the time I finished with her, she'd feel every ounce of pain I'd felt since my life fell apart. My inner Dom was dead. All that remained was a cold, heartless, shell of man. Not that any of that mattered, because tonight, I damn sure wouldn't be *playing.*

• • • • •

Sometime after midnight my body started to shut down. No doubt from the dozen or so drinks I'd had. It was a miracle I made it back to the room at all. The last thing I remembered was bellying up to the bar as I slipped deeper into the abyss, that dark spot that formed inside my soul the day Ash died. Thank God Val never showed up. With the direction my mind was taking me, neither of us would have made it out the same.

This morning was a new day. Time to find Val and put a stop to all the shit she was causing before it went any further.

I'd never been as angry as I was last night. If I would have found her and hadn't been able to convince her to back off, God only knows what I would have done.

I called down for breakfast—toast and a nice tall glass of orange juice to settle my stomach and calm my raging headache—before hopping in the shower. Last night I realized the fatal flaw in my plan: the sheer size of the property. If I was serious about finding Val, I'd need technology. Luckily for me, security systems were my specialty.

A quick trip to the local electronics store and I had everything I needed to hack into the hotel's security system. Facial recognition would take some time, but not nearly as much time as the one man search team plan I tried last night.

I hated to admit it, but Dane was right. I was a moron when I drank. If I'd slowed down long enough to think before I hopped a plane to Atlantic City, I could've already found Val. Not only did I pay full fare for my last minute plane ticket, but I was out another three grand for electronic equipment I could've brought with me if I'd slowed down long enough to use my damn brain.

Idiot.

Access to hotel blueprints were a definite benefit when running any security detail. That's what made the *industries* part of James' Industries so ingenious when I'd first added it. Remodeling upscale resorts gave us access to all sorts of information our security division needed. James' Securities had capitalized on that decision a million times over, making us number one in personal security on the entire East Coast. From the powerful, Wall Street types to uptight politicians and even the rich and famous. Our customers took their safety—and their privacy—

seriously. And they didn't mind paying top dollar for what we provided.

Attaching my newly acquired equipment to the hotel's security feed was a breeze. Of course, knowing the exact location of every fiber optic cable running through the entire resort was the reason for that. What was going to take forever was downloading and installing the facial recognition software on the new computer I had to buy.

Fucking moron!

Dinner time had come and gone hours earlier, but I'd been too busy to care. Once the computer was finally doing its thing, I made a call to room service. Going downstairs was far too risky since I'd switched to Plan B. If Val came back to the room and saw all the equipment I had set up, my entire plan would be ruined. Plus, that morning I promised myself I wouldn't drink until after the job was done. Tempting myself with a never ending flow of alcohol wasn't a good idea if I planned to keep that promise.

• • • • •

I set my empty plate down on the end table and kicked back on the couch. Nothing like a big, juicy burger to lull me into a near comatose state. Almost two hours after the scan started and nothing. Not even a *possible* match. Patience was proving harder than ever.

What I wouldn't give for a drink right now.

Just one more drink. Surely, it'd take the edge off, make waiting tolerable?

Like a bolt to a magnet, the mini bar pulled me in close. My hand whipped the door open before I could stop myself.

One drink won't hurt you.

117

The liquor inside called to me. Deep down I knew the devil was my temptress. Too bad that didn't stop me. My inner Dom was dead. It was a weak, pathetic excuse for a man who reached inside the stocked cooler.

I'd emptied two bourbon shooters before my mind caught up to the rest of my body, the warm amber liquor awakening all my senses for the first time that day. Two drinks hadn't hurt me. Just the opposite, I felt *alive*. Surely one more drink wouldn't hurt, either.

When the software alert sounded, I knew I'd been right. *Found you, bitch.*

Drinking didn't hurt me at all.

Chapter Sixteen
Spencer

Last night I'd been wrong. Drinking *had* hurt me. If I had been sober, I would've seen Val's evil plan unfolding before it reached out and stabbed me in the heart. I'd found her because she wanted me to find her. She took great pleasure in watching the pain overtake my features as I opened the text she'd sent.

"Oh look, Spence," she'd said. "I brought you a gift." After the *gift* she sent to Izzy, I should've known it was a trap. Too bad alcohol had clouded my mind. The second I opened her text and saw the picture of Izzy and that rich bastard, Alec Payne, all the fight in me drained. In my inebriated state I couldn't seem to remember that Izzy and I were days away from our divorce being finalized. All I could see was the look in Izzy's eyes.

Desire. Lust. Adoration.

Almost twenty years of marriage and Izzy had never once looked at me the way she was looking at that asshole.

When the initial shock wore off, I somehow managed to get my point across to Val. "Come near my family or one of my clients again, and I'll choke the life right out of you," I'd warned.

I just hoped like hell she got the message.

• • • • •

Ashlan

Knowing Spencer had a wife was one thing. Being close enough to touch her was a whole different story. Spencer never told me how beautiful Izzy was. She had that long, lean, body of a runner. Soft brown hair...smooth, porcelain skin...*probably not a single scar on her entire body.*

Izzy James wasn't just gorgeous. She was absolute perfection.

Not an ounce of fat jiggled as Izzy sprinted past me, seemingly oblivious to the fact I was hiding in the mangroves. That's when I saw it. Head held high, shoulders back. Isabella James wasn't perfect for Spencer at all. No wonder he'd come looking for me. His wife didn't have a submissive bone in her perfect little body. From her workout clothes to the way her ponytail swayed with her movements, everything about Izzy screamed control.

Izzy stopped then turned right toward me.

Shit. How am I supposed to explain this?

Heart pounding, I ducked down as low as I could get then held myself totally still, not even taking the breath my body desperately craved. Despite the cool weather, beads of sweat covered my forehead.

Izzy would think I was a psychopath.

Oh God, what if she calls the police?

I couldn't get arrested. My cover would be blown. Diego would be let out of jail.

Please, God. No!

Seconds away from a full blown panic attack, I caught the subtle movement on Izzy's face as her arm pressed protectively against her side. Tightly drawn eyes, the slight opening of her downturned lips... Pain was one look I knew well.

Strangely, I couldn't take my eyes off Izzy's face as she struggled through whatever pain she was having: acceptance, release, *pleasure*. Oh yeah, those flushed cheeks were quite telling.

Then it was gone. Just that like.

Shoulders back once again, Izzy took off, heading toward home. Maybe I'd misjudged her before. Maybe she was more submissive than I gave her credit for.

After Izzy rounded the block and I was no longer in danger of being seen, I stood up, legs burning from squatting for so long. Walking home was gonna suck. Good thing I didn't live far.

Tony would have my head in a vice if he found out I rented a house three blocks away from my past. He and Toni reminded me constantly how dangerous it would be for me if my real identity were ever discovered. Of course they were right. Only, Spencer wasn't the past I wanted to be hiding from.

As long as Diego stayed in jail, my past couldn't hurt me. At least that's what I prayed.

It wasn't like I planned to tell Spencer I was alive or anything. I just needed to see him. One quick glance so I'd know he was okay. But so far, I'd come up empty. The James' house got more visitors than that nightmare Malibu mansion I lived in ever did, yet, all I'd managed to see of Spencer were the taillights on his oversized Ford pickup truck.

Luckily, the torture of hiding out, begging, pleading, praying, not knowing—all that would end tonight— thanks to the do-it-yourself wireless security kit that finally arrived. With that delivery, I had the last piece I needed to override Spencer's security system and replace it with one of my own.

Spying on the James family was wrong, I knew that, but I *had* to see Spencer. Some days I needed it more than air. Every day I'd pray I would get the chance to see him and that he was okay, that the Dom in him hadn't been too damaged by what I'd done. What I had no choice but to do. Spencer's instinct to protect me at all cost was the exact reason I had to run.

If I hadn't faked my death Master Spence would have found me for sure. He'd told me not to run once. After begging to come for two straight days, my orgasm so close I could almost touch it, feel it tingling in every nerve, only to be denied time and time again, I promised him I wouldn't.

But I had.

"Running from me, are you?" Master Spence's voice surrounded me in the tiny space. Baiting a Dom was never a good idea, but I'd still done it. My skin was sticky from the hot summer night. The pool had been tempting me all day, crisp, cool water splashing against the tiled edge as the pump ran. All day I'd planned it. When the sky was finally dark and the threat of further sunburn gone, I was going for a swim. No matter what Master Spence said.

Unfortunately, I'd mistaken the closet door for the exit and found myself trapped. He'd called for me, but I didn't answer. How could I when my mind was unable to form actual words?

Master Spence stalked toward me, his eyes scorching holes in my overheated skin. Reaching out, he fisted my hair firmly, tugging until I had no choice but to look at him.

"Never. Fucking. Run."

Tingles ran down my spine, the bundle of nerves between my legs coming alive. *Oh, God. Master Spence...*

Focus! Tony's sharp reprimand rang loud in my ear, instantly shutting down the orgasm that begged to be let out. During my 'survival training' as Tony called it, *focus* had been his go-to phrase, telling me distractions could kill.

Just like always, I knew Tony was probably right. Now was not the time for distractions, but I would definitely be saving that delicious memory for later. What I needed to be doing was getting all the crap together that Cowboy insisted...*more like demanded*...I had to take with me on today's mission.

The military grade wireless jammer Cowboy loaned me took up most of the space in my backpack, making it almost impossible to get everything else in. It wasn't like I could leave the damn thing behind, though. According to Cowboy, this monstrous piece of equipment was *mission critical.* It just so happened, *that* blue eyed, sandy blonde, five foot ten wall of lean, cut, all-American cowboy, wasn't the type of guy you argued with.

Besides, considering this whole plan was Cowboy's idea, I would have been an idiot not to do exactly what he'd said *over* and *over* again.

Stepping into my neighbor's kayak, confident they would never know it was gone, I took off, one step closer to finally getting to see the man my body burned for.

Turned out, water access was a real advantage for criminals. The beach behind Spencer's house would make for the perfect access point. At least, that's what Cowboy said.

All I had to do was get into position and wait for everyone to leave. Thanks to Cowboy's buddy, Rock, who was apparently some sort of information gathering genius, I knew exactly when that should be.

Sheer determination propelled the kayak alongside Beachview Drive and around the bend to the backside of the James' property. Determination to smell him...feel him...*please him*. Every movement of my hand against the smooth, hard paddles spoke directly to the bundle of nerves between my legs. Every pull forward sparked the still sensitive nub—another foot closer, another wave of pleasure.

Oh, God, yes.

It'd been months since I'd felt the warm touch of a man. Skin against skin. Pleasure ripping through me as his strong hand landed sharply on my bare ass over and over again.

Yes.

I craved to be touched....to be spanked and whipped and fucked...pleasured to the point where I couldn't remember my name.

I craved Master Spence.

His house was so close.

Oh, God. Only a few feet stood in the way of me and the man my body craved.

Excitement ran through me with an urgency I hadn't felt in months. I was almost there. In minutes I'd be enveloped by Spencer James... Cocooned by the raw, spicy scent of his body wash....

My body shook with the force of the orgasm that was building.

Yes, Spencer. YES!

"Shit. WHOAAA!"

"Jesus, Ash, get it together!" I shouted to myself as I worked to stabilize the kayak.

Shouting *Ash* whenever I was pissed at myself was a bad habit I hadn't been able to break. Thank God there was no one around to hear me. Blowing my cover was not in the plans.

Neither is falling into the water with thousands of dollars' worth of borrowed equipment, in a stolen kayak.

By the time I had both the kayak and my screaming libido under control, I was gliding to a stop on the private beach access behind Spencer's house. The fact that Spencer had left the perimeter of their waterfront property unprotected gave me reason to pause. He was a security expert. Surely, he wouldn't go to all the trouble of erecting an iron gate across the front of his family home while leaving the most vulnerable access point unprotected. There had to be an alarm somewhere.

Knowing Spencer and his attention to detail, he'd probably have some heat sensing, motion activated pressure monitor or some crap like that. Too bad for him none of it mattered.

All those months spent wrapped in the safety of Spencer's arms during aftercare, I learned quite a bit about security, including how to get past it.

"No system is impenetrable," Spencer had said.

And I was about to find out if he was right.

Scanning the James' property as I dragged the kayak ashore, I veered toward the bed of sea oats. The tall natural grass on the berm was my best bet for hiding the brightly colored vessel that would serve as my ride home when I finished the job.

One step into the grass was where I found the trip wire. Wire so thin the narrow blades of grass had no trouble disguising it.

Very cleaver, Spencer James.

Too bad for him, I'd been trained to find the sneaky little suckers, just another part of Tony's Survival Package.

Avoiding the wire altogether was a much safer plan than me lifting a boat that weighed more than I did over a trip wire.

Praying no one would notice the neon green vessel, I ditched it on the sand and sprinted toward the patio chairs. I turned my head to the right, then the left, then behind me, in front of me, looking for any signs that someone was watching me. Breaking into Spencer's house meant risking exposure, but it was a risk I had to take.

My heart had to be beating a million times a minute. Every breath I sucked into my lungs was a struggle. I needed oxygen so I could think. I'd spent more time perfecting my *I'm lost* cover story than I spent studying the plan to get inside the house. What was I supposed to do next?

The weight of my backpack as I slouched to the ground was just the reminder I needed: Cowboy. It took him almost a week to get his hands on the military grade Wi-Fi jamming system, the one that was currently making it hard for me to get up off the ground. The one I forgot to turn on before I came ashore.

"Damn it, Ashlan!"

Jesus, I couldn't believe I called out my old name again. It was like I was begging to get caught or something.

Knowing Spencer, he'd have a wireless security system covering every inch of his property that the hard-wired system missed. Getting caught on camera would be suicide.

I wrestled the heavy bag off my back and flipped the switch. Unfortunately, activating the device now wouldn't erase the footage his system had already captured. Thank God Cowboy was on standby. I pulled out my phone and sent him an urgent text.

Forgot to turn on jammer. What do I do?

His response came almost immediately. **IS IT ON NOW?**

While I wanted to tell Cowboy off for assuming I was an idiot, time was a real issue. Besides, I *was* an idiot for not turning it on when I was supposed to. I typed, "Yes!" and hit send. Maybe he'd get the point I wasn't in the mood for his growly shit.

Cowboy's reply came a few seconds later. **Good. Rock can clean up your mistake. NOW FOCUS! FAILURE IS NOT AN OPTION!**

Little did Cowboy know I'd grown numb to the effects of shouting, conditioned since birth to block out the angry sounds and hurtful words. Besides, Cowboy would never hurt me. His eyes held a softness so unfamiliar to me, I couldn't help but trust him. Plus, he was right about one thing for sure. Failure was definitely not an option.

Gathering up my nerve with a few deep breaths, I sprinted toward the back of the house, taking cover under the closest window. The short run wasn't enough to wind me, yet I couldn't seem to get enough oxygen into my lungs. My recon suggested the house would be empty, but there was no way to know for sure. Plans change. Schedules change.

Oh, God. What if Spencer is in there?

I wanted to see him. *Oh, how I want to see him.*

But would seeing him be enough to satisfy that desire deep inside me? Would I be strong enough to walk away without touching him?

Breathe in.

Breathe out.

My mind was spinning so far out of control even essential life functions seemed to be shutting down.

Heat spread over my face, my chest, *oh God,* my arms.
Breathe in.
Breathe out.
In. Out.
In.
Out.

Chapter Seventeen
Ashlan

Once my breathing slowed and oxygen returned to my brain, I was able to reel in the building anxiety before I completely lost my shit. Spencer couldn't possibly be inside the house. Cowboy confirmed that Spencer had flown to New Jersey a couple of days ago. His return flight wasn't scheduled to arrive until later that afternoon. There was no way Spencer could have gotten on an earlier flight without Cowboy knowing about it, not with his Jedi Master, Tech Guru, he-who-can-find-anything-electronic friend, Rock. According to Cowboy, no piece of information was safe from this guy.

Failure is not an option.

With Cowboy's words in my ear, I took one final calming breath then peeked inside the kitchen window. Of course...the kitchen was empty.

Jesus, Ash. I'd almost given myself a heart attack for nothing.

Shaking my head, disgusted by the weakness I'd shown, I moved to the next window. A quick peek inside and that one also came up empty, as did every other window I looked through. There was no one home.

After pulling out the map Cowboy made for me, I quickly located the cable access point on the north end of the James' house.

Shrugging the backpack off my shoulders was a lot harder than it sounded. It took me a good thirty seconds to unwind the thick straps from my tiny arms, the weight of the bag making the job almost impossible. Inside the bag in a pocket labeled # 2, I found the electronic gadget I was supposed to use next. The radio wave jammer I was lugging around on my back being the first.

Small, white, square with rounded edges, this new device looked a lot like a shrunken version of an iPhone charger. Only *this* powerful piece of technology would serve a much bigger purpose than providing power to a phone. In the right hands, it could be used to hijack any security system. The second I plugged it in Spencer's entire security system belonged to me, well, technically it belonged to Rock, but that was kinda the same thing.

When I found the sliding glass door unlocked—I'm not going to lie—I was disappointed. For a security specialist, Spencer's home security fell way short of my expectations. Plus, I worked really hard learning how to use the lock pick set waiting for me in the pocket labeled # 3.

This was it. *The moment of truth.*

I was about to walk through the door of Spencer James' home.

Can I do it?

Or would I fall apart at the smell of him?

Failure is not an option. Cowboy's words gave me the strength I needed to keep it together. He was right. No matter how much this was going to hurt, I had to go inside. It was the only way to see Spencer, and I *needed* to see him.

With all the courage I could summon, I stepped inside. Spencer's house was not at all how I pictured it would be. Soft, earthy tones filled every space on the main floor, nothing like the Spencer James I knew. Then again, I wasn't the Ashlan Rivers he knew, either. Spencer never got to know the real me. Ashlan Parks. Not Ashlan Rivers, or Ashlan Rivera, but Ashlan Parks, the girl I was born to be.

Whoever that was.

Surely, Spencer knew who I was by now. On some off chance he hadn't managed to figure out my true identity soon after I dropped that *I'm being abused* bomb and split, it'd be impossible for him not to have put it together by that point. Not with my picture plastered all over the media.

"Notorious El Mismo Diablo Arrested in Connection to Wife's Death," one headline read. *"Diego Rivera Behind Bars Awaiting Trial,"* read another.

Too bad it had to come to that for Diego, locked up in jail for a crime he didn't commit. Toni helped me realize it wasn't my fault, so at least I stopped beating myself up over it. What's done was done. And besides, if he hadn't bought off the police, they would have locked him up for domestic abuse a long time ago. If Diego had been in jail, I wouldn't have had to die, and he wouldn't be facing life in prison.

A cold chill ran through me as I thought of Diego, the heartless bastard who stole both my innocence and my life. He could have avoided jail altogether if he'd treated me like a human being instead of his punching bag....

Dammit, Ashlan, stop it!

Shaking my head, I took a deep breath to slow the rising panic. It wasn't the time to go down that path.

"Get in. Get out." Those were Cowboy's instructions. Instructions that, just like all the others, he repeated over and over again.

He'd wanted to come with me. We argued about it for days. Only this time I hadn't backed down. Being at the safe house, surrounded by all that strength and power of both Tony and Toni, I learned to be strong, fierce, and unafraid to fight for what I wanted.

When Cowboy finally realized I wasn't about to give in, he made it clear that if he couldn't come with me, then I had no choice but to accept a twice a day training regimen. He went on and on about safety and responsibility to protect and a bunch of things so jumbled I couldn't make out his words.

Cowboy handled my refusal to accept his protection the way you might expect a toddler to handle someone taking away their favorite toy: red face, neck veins bulging, stomping around the room making all sorts of demands. Arguing with him would have been pointless, which was why I hadn't bothered. Besides, that constant drilling of commands had come in pretty handy so far.

After placing hidden cameras in every common area downstairs, I headed upstairs to do the same. The top of the stairs, the end of the hall, outside the master bedroom...

Oh God...the master bedroom.

The intoxicating smell that was Spencer James wafted through the open door of his private domain. Black leather and Jamaican rum swirled around the sweet smell of tobacco.

Rich. Intoxicating. Sensual. Wild with inhibition.

Oh, how I've missed that scent. Complex and dark, just like the rebel Spencer was.

I inhaled deeply, drawing his scent as far inside me as humanly possible, soaking in as much of that warm, comforting smell as I could. That magic mixture of spicy and sweet that enveloped every inch of me during our scenes.

Trust. Kindness.

Hope.

Love.

There was no stopping the tears that rolled down my cheeks. Tightness gripped my chest; heat filled my limbs, yet I felt numb, empty.

Every night at the Safe House, I'd dreamt of lying next to Spencer, wrapped in the security of his strength....softly stroking his face as he slept....his warmth healing the wound in my heart.

I threw myself onto the bed, burying my face deep in his pillow. "Oh, Spencer," I cried. "I'm sorry. Sorry I didn't tell you who I was. That I didn't come to you when I needed help. That I made a deal with the devil to save myself."

The tears came faster, harder. My whole body shook from the realization of what I'd lost forever.

Oh, God, what have I done?

• • • • •

One look at the clock on the bedside table in the master bedroom, where apparently I'd cried myself to sleep, had my heart racing all over again.

Sonofabitch!

I jumped out of bed. It was after three, and I hadn't even finished placing the cameras.

Stupid. Stupid. Stupid!

How the hell had I let that happen? If anyone had found me there I'd be dead—for real. It'd take the police all of five seconds to figure out who I was. Diego would be released. He'd hunt me down, and my life would be over.

O.V.E.R.

There was no time to place the final three cameras. School ended two hours ago. Spencer's kids could be home any minute...

Shit. What if they're already here?

All I could do was pray the camera's I'd already installed would get me what I hoped for, because right now I *needed* to get hell out of there. Fast!

I was seconds from the stairs when I heard him.

"IZZY!"

No. No. No. This couldn't be happening.

"IZZY! Where are you?"

Oh, God. It was really him.

What do I do? I couldn't let him find me there.

His footsteps were getting louder. My brain screamed run, but my legs wouldn't move.

Spencer.

He was so close. Close enough to feel the vibrations coming off his body. Close enough to smell the spiciness of his scent. Close enough to know I was about to get caught.

Before it was too late, I made a beeline for the bedroom closest to the stairs.

"Answer me, dammit! I know you're here. I can smell fear a mile away."

Doing my best to hide, I took off my oversized back pack and ducked behind the door, even though I knew it wasn't safe. Secretly part of me hoped Spencer would find me.

Oh, Spencer. It's me. I'm not dead. I'm here, for you.

For us.

For more...

"IZZY!"

Spencer's tortured scream tore a new hole in my heart. Even though he was close, his voice sounded so distant and cold.

Through the hinges of the open bedroom door, I watched as he staggered toward the master bedroom. My heart sank even more when I saw the haunted look resting on his face. Gone was the life that used to dance in his eyes. Nothing but emptiness lived there.

How long had it been since he'd slept? Or showered, for that matter? Seeing Spencer like that, so broken, was worse than a punch to the gut.

I had to get out of there before the acid churning in my stomach ended up on the floor.

As quickly and quietly as I could go, I ran out of the room, down the stairs, and out the sliding glass door.

Back to the kayak.

To my life of living hell.

Karma.

You evil Bastard.

Chapter Eighteen
Spencer

The sight of a petite, dark haired woman sprinting across the yard had me doing a double take: long brown hair that swayed frantically with her shorter steps, those too thin arms, narrow waist, that tiny frame moving with such familiarity. Muscles that, beneath those jeans, I knew were well-defined and firm. I'd spent hours touching her, memorizing every inch of that sexy body. I'd recognize it anywhere. But I had to be imagining things. I couldn't possibly be seeing what I thought I was seeing? Could I?

Ashlan?

"No," I snapped, my booming voice bouncing off the glass, blasting my ears with sound. It couldn't be Ash. Her charred body was found at the bottom of a ravine months ago.

Pressing the heel of my hands firmly against closed eyes, I rubbed, hoping to clear the mirage that would surely haunt me. Blinking rapidly, I reopened my eyes.

Fuck! Still her.

Quickly, I rubbed again, even harder that time. She couldn't be real. All the alcohol must've been messing with my mind. The coroner had made a positive ID from what was left of her DNA.

Hell, that bastard she was married to was awaiting trial for her murder. Yet still, when I opened my eyes for the second time, she was there.

Taking the stairs two at a time, I hurried outside. I didn't care what anyone said...the police...the doctors...none of them. There was no denying what I had seen. The woman running from my house was without a doubt, *my* Ash.

"Ashlan!" I called out as soon as I made it to the back yard. When she didn't stop I called again. "ASH, TO ME!" I yelled as loud as I could, not caring who heard me. If that really was Ash...*and it is*...stopping her was all that mattered.

Dammit! The retreating figure still didn't stop. She didn't even slow down or turn to look at me.

Maybe I was seeing things after all. There's no way *my* Ash would've denied her Dom a direct order. If that were her, she would've turned around and knelt at my feet before I had to tell her twice.

Only she didn't.

Maybe the ocean breeze was too strong for her to hear me.

Yeah, that has to be it. I'd have to get closer, shout louder.

Running as fast as my legs would take me, I called out again, "AAAASHLAN!"

Still, she kept moving.

"ASHLAN, STOP!"

Surely, she heard me that time, so why wasn't she stopping?

Because it isn't her, dumbass.

NO! *It is her!*

It had to be her.

The muscles in my legs were already burning when I hit the deep sand, every step a sheer force of will. Heart pounding, clothes clinging to my damp body, fire gripping my thighs and strangling my calves, nothing was going to stop me.

What the hell is she doing dragging that flimsy ass kayak toward the surf?

Hell no!

"Sunshine, no, don't go in the water."

As if working in fast forward, Ashlan moved the small vessel deeper into the ocean.

Fuck! Why isn't she stopping?

"Ashlan! Stop. Fucking. Running! Let me help you."

With one hand steadying the boat, she lifted her leg.

Sonofabitch! She's going to climb in.

"Don't climb in! You're gonna—"

Not flip...Thank God for that.

By the time I got to the water's edge, I'd lost sight of the neon colored kayak. Tiny shoeprints in the damp sand served as the only remaining proof I hadn't been hallucinating the whole damn thing. Someone had definitely been there.

Fuck that! Ash had been here.

Blood beginning to boil, I headed back toward the house. No sub had ever disobeyed me like that before. She wanted to run? Well, game on. It was time to put those high-priced security cameras I installed to good use. I'd prove Ashlan was there. Then I'd find her, and when I did, I wasn't about to let her go. I'd tie her up if I had to. Chain her to the bed until she finally got it through her thick skull that she wasn't to run from me.

But first, I needed a drink. It was going to take every ounce of strength I could manage to force myself to watch the security footage. What if I was wrong? What if it wasn't Ash I saw?

I couldn't get to the house fast enough. The need to know picked at my frayed nerves. Any minute they could snap. Losing my shit was the last thing I needed at that moment.

What I fucking need is a drink.

"Where the hell are you?" I grumbled as I searched the liquor cabinet, looking for a bottle of Jack Daniels. There had to be one in there somewhere. Hell, I'd been buying them by the case lately. Drinking was the only thing I'd managed to take seriously these past four months. I swear, if I screwed that up too...

Well, hello there, old friend. I knew there was a bottle in there.

I'd already failed as a father, as a Dom, and as a husband. I couldn't fail as a drunk too. Alcohol was all I had left. Just me and my buddy, Jack.

Crack. The sound of the seal breaking on the brand new bottle of bourbon had my mouth watering. That warm, soothing sensation called to me with the promise to numb my pain.

Screw the glass. My nerves were far too gone for that. I threw my head back and began to chug. "Ahhh," I moaned, when I came up for air. That involuntary sound of pleasure escaping without warning, a pure, unadulterated, only you can satisfy me, kind of pleasure.

I threw my head back again. A couple more drinks, then I'd watch the video.

"Fucking yellow walls," I muttered about half a bottle into my liquid courage. Izzy loved the sunshine yellow the walls of what was supposed to be *our* office were covered in. I hated that color, now more than ever.

Bright. Always cheerful.

Screw that!

Black, that was the color the walls should be.

Deep. Dark. Cold. Just like my soul.

Being in that yellow fucking room was a constant reminder of why I'd never be again: happy. Without Ash, all my dreams were shattered.

Too bad I hid the security system in there.

Cleverly disguised as a mirror, no one had ever noticed the false wall. A quick swipe of my finger over the pressure switch, hidden at the midway point on the top rail of the frame, and the mirror slid open. Inside the wall, the best security monitoring system money could buy.

From the white noise spread across the split screen, the screen that should've been rotating between the two dozen cameras protecting my property, it also appeared to be one that wasn't working.

Sonofabitch!

All twelve hard wired cameras: out. The thirteen wireless ones, also out. There wasn't a chance in hell something like that happened unless the entire system was down. *Jesus.* I couldn't even remember the last security check I'd done.

Fucking yellow walls! Now I'd never know for sure if that was Ash.

Mad as hell at my stupidity, I stormed out of Izzy's office with the half empty bottle of Jack. If there was ever a time when I *needed* a drink, it was now. The *not knowing* was going to drive me stark raving mad, and there was nothing I could do about it.

Lifting the bottle to my lips, I took a long drink, all but emptying the contents that time. There might not have been anything *I* could do, but Lieutenant Colonel Ronnie Dane, retired Army Ranger, *he* was a different story. And that bastard owed me. If it hadn't been for him, if he hadn't stopped me from going after Ashlan when I wanted to, she might still be alive.

Dane might not have been the asshole who cut the brake line on her car, but he sure as hell shared responsibility for her death.

With slowed, clumsy movements, I finally managed to pull my phone out of the front pocket of my jeans. I scrolled through my contacts, landing on Dane's number. "She was here," I said the second the phone stopped ringing, my voice coming out a lot more slurred than I'd hoped.

"What the hell, Spencer? It's the middle of the afternoon. Are you drunk, already?"

I didn't take offense to his sharp tone. I knew how much Dane hated it when people got drunk. There was no time to worry about that, though.

"Who cares if I'm drunk? Didn't you hear what I said? She was here, Dane. Ash was here."

"You're shit-faced, man," Dane snapped. "You're hallucinating."

I knew it. I knew if I didn't have proof no one would believe me.

Goddammit!

"Think what you want to think, Dane. I know what I saw. Ashlan is alive. You have to help me find her."

After a long moment of silence, Dane exhaled loudly into the receiver. "Look, Spencer, there's something I need to tell you..." He paused, the slow intake of breath the only indication he was still on the line. The hesitation ate at my recently soothed nerves. Was he going to tell me or not? What kind of mind games was he playing?

My top was ready to explode when he finally spoke. "Not like this. Not drunk. Sleep it off. We'll talk tomorrow." With that, the line went dead.

That sonofabitch hung up on me. He had to be fucking kidding me with this shit.

When Dane didn't pick up after the umpteenth ring, I finally realized he hadn't been kidding at all. That asshole was keeping something from me. No way was I waiting until tomorrow to find out what it was.

Fuck that.

If he wasn't going to answer his phone, I'd show up at his doorstep.

It didn't take long to fill my carry-on full of allowable items, mostly clean clothes. I was half a second from the bottom of the stairs when the front door opened.

"Dad?"

Dammit. Drew. I swear that kid could see right through me. The way his nostrils flared when he said my name, the tight set of his jaw, his defensive stance. Yeah, he knew I was drunk.

"You going somewhere?" he asked, pointing to my bag.

"Business trip," I said, keeping the answer short, hoping he wouldn't notice just how drunk I was.

"Bullshit! You're drunk! Then again, when aren't you drunk these days? When you're home that is. Why don't you stop all this lying and just try the truth for once?"

Drew fired questions and insults faster than I could process them in my inebriated state. It seemed he hated my drinking even more than Dane, something I didn't think was possible.

"Are you cheating on mom? Is that why you're never home? And why you're shit faced when you do bother to show up? Are you having an affair?"

That's when I felt it. The crack in my armor split wide open by the force of all my pent up emotions. Izzy. It was always about Izzy with him. Was it so inconceivable that *she* cheated on *me* and that's why we're getting divorced? Hell, she's the one who wanted the divorce.

A divorce Drew doesn't know about.

Izzy left *me*. Why should I be the bad guy in all this? "She left me, Drew," I blurted out. "Four months ago. Your mother filed for divorce."

"Very funny, Dad."

"No, Drew, it's not. It's not funny at all. She left me." I scrolled through my text message from last night and opened up the picture Val sent me, the picture of Izzy and Alec Payne. I turned the phone so Drew could see it. "How do you know your mother wasn't the one having the affair?"

"Is that the picture from the paper?" Drew asked, his eyes, widening with what—surprise, shock, or was it *recognition*?

What picture? What paper?

"Wait here," Drew snapped out before storming off toward the kitchen before I had to chance to ask. When he returned less than a minute later, he was carrying what appeared to be a crumpled up newspaper.

Fucking hell!

On the front page of the Gazette's business section was the same picture Val had texted me when I was in Atlantic City.

"Alec Payne, billionaire entrepreneur, reportedly in town to finalize the much anticipated purchase of the Bayfront Stadium, spotted having a romantic lunch at a local restaurant yesterday," the tag line read.

Perfect.

Now everyone who knew me would know Izzy had moved on.

Chapter Nineteen
Ashlan

What the hell was I thinking crawling into Spencer's bed? Just being in his house went against everything Tony taught me about protecting my new identity. Every scenario he drilled into my head for the past four months, forgotten the moment I inhaled Spencer's addictive scent.

Breaking into Spencer's house was bad enough, but crying into his pillow...that had to be the single most idiotic thing I'd ever done.

The kayak almost flipping had been a blaring warning to stay away. A warning I'd been too distracted to see. I let my guard down, a mistake I couldn't let happen again.

One thing was clear after that fiasco. My reckless behavior had to stop. My future survival depended on it. I'd come dangerously close to blowing my cover. If Spencer hadn't been drunk, he would've caught me for sure. Drunk Spencer had been hard enough to resist, but there was no way I could've resisted if my Dom had been the one calling for me.

Even if I had been brave enough to run, I would've been kneeling in front of him at his command, and *that* could get us both killed.

As it was, that haunted look I saw in Spencer's eyes would stay with me forever. Knowing I was the one who put it there made it hurt that much worse.

I should've known my plan to see Spencer was jinxed from the moment I almost flipped the kayak, dumping me and Cowboy's "you break it, you stole it" high tech jamming devi—"

Sonofabitch!

Cowboy's equipment!

No, no, no, no, no.

I didn't.

I couldn't....

Damn it! I did. I left my backpack in the bedroom where I'd hidden from Spencer.

"Dammit. Dammit. Dammit," I shouted at myself. How could I be that stupid? I didn't just leave behind some high-priced piece of technology, I left behind equipment traceable to the United States Army. If anyone found my bag, I was as good as dead. The Army would find out the jammer was stolen, and my fingerprints were all over the damn thing!

Shit! The plug.

Make that two pieces of traceable equipment I left behind. "Damn. It!" I'd been wrong when I thought climbing into Spencer's bed had been the dumbest thing I'd ever done, because *that* was the single most idiotic, ridiculous, your-too-stupid-to-live, kind of thing I could ever do.

"Get in. Get out. Nothing else." Those had been Cowboy's instructions. Instructions he'd repeated too many times to count. Now I had to tell him that not only did Spencer see me, but I left behind the equipment he made me promise not to let out of my sight. I could already hear the disappointment in Cowboy's voice.

As pissed as I was with myself, I couldn't help the grin that crossed my face as that last thought settled in. Cowboy would be *disappointed*.

Not angry or furious or *brutal*.

He wouldn't freak out and lose his mind, and he certainly wouldn't hurt me.

Four months ago a mistake like that could have gotten me killed. Or damn close to it, anyway. Disappointment was *not* an emotion the coked-out masochist tolerated, especially not from me.

A cold chill ran up my spine at the thought of Diego.

Stop it, Ash!

I couldn't let my mind go there. I wasn't Ashlan Rivera anymore, a beat down, shell of a woman full of pessimism and fear. I was the strong and fierce Lily Walker, and *she* had hope. God had given me a second chance at life, and I had no intentions of blowing it. Lily would get Cowboy's equipment back before it fell into the wrong hands. There was no way *she* was letting a moment of weakness—that one stupid decision to bury my face in Spencer's pillow—take away the freedom I'd had to give up my life to find.

· · · · ·

The midnight sky made my new hiding spot behind the line of trees on the north side of the James' property the perfect place to scope out the house unnoticed. As long as no one shut down the jammer I left behind, I wouldn't have to worry about being caught on video. If I hadn't been able to see the white charger thingy I'd plugged into the fiber optic cable box, I might've been more worried about the jammer being turned off. As long as that device was plugged in, Rock owned the entire security system, alarms included.

After attaching the telescope to the short tripod Cowboy loaned me for the recon phase of the operation, I situated myself into as comfortable of a viewing position as I could find: my front to the ground, left forearm folded in front of me helping to prop my upper body high enough to see through the telescope.

Who knew how long I'd have to lie there and wait? Going inside the house when the family was home was risky enough, so I'd lie there at least until I was certain everyone was asleep. Then I'd sneak in and grab my backpack.

The cameras I placed would have to stay behind. They were so small I doubted anyone would ever find them, but even if they did, the cameras were untraceable and way too small for a good print. They'd cost me most of the money I had left, but I hadn't cared. Blinded by my desire to see the man I didn't realize I loved until it was too late, the man I could never have, had stolen my ability to reason.

With my right hand guiding the telescope, I began to scan the second floor for signs of movement.

Stay out of Spencer's room.

Stay out of Spencer's room.

Stay out of Spencer's room.

I repeated the phrase over and over in my mind in hopes my body would get the message, every inch of which tingled with desire to be near him, to feel every glorious inch of his smooth, hard body on my tongue. Heat radiating—

Dammit, Ash! Focus!

My eyelids snapped shut, allowing me a chance to reign in my neglected libido. My inner voice was right.

Spencer's pull was far too strong for me to be off my game. If I had any hopes of finishing this job without getting caught, I'd need laser like focus.

After a few more deep breaths to settle my nerves, I grabbed the telescope.

Stay out of Spencer's room. I began to chant the command once again as I resumed the scan I'd barely started.

Light danced against the blinds in what I knew to be Anna's room. The way the beams flicked back and forth, going from dark to light then back again, had to be the wall mounted flat panel television I saw when I was inside the house. After a solid two minutes—that felt more like ten—of peering one-eyed through the eyepiece, I was convinced Anna was sleeping, or at least not up moving around.

Metal scraping against the rough surface of the brick pavers on the pool deck drew my attention away from the house. My heart sped up at the sight of a man I hadn't noticed before rising from the chair. My eyes scanned up and down his body. Short, sandy brown hair, broad shoulders, a muscular build that was all too familiar.

All the air left my lungs on one startled exhale.

Oh God, Spencer?

Before I could get a better look to confirm what I already knew, the sliding glass door opened. What caught my attention, however, was the silhouette of the woman I saw there. Long, thin legs, narrow waist, bleach blonde hair hanging in perfect curls over her scantily clad breasts, breasts at least twice the size of mine.

I blinked a few times, just to make sure I wasn't seeing things.

Spencer's cheating on his wife?

That didn't sound like something the Spencer I knew would do. Sure, what he did at the club was technically cheating, but Spencer hadn't seen it that way, at least that's what he'd said to me more than once. For years he'd hid a pretty big part of himself from his family, but that was exactly the point. He *hid* it. Spencer would never flaunt his love—

"Sub!" I barked out before I could stop it. Seeing that woman kneel before him snapped the last thread of sanity I had left. Spencer had taken another sub?

Sonofabitch! He wasn't just cheating on his wife. He was cheating on me!

Jealously was a green-eyed monster alright. It took every ounce of strength I had not to run after them, to claw his sub's eyes out then take her place before him. If anyone was going to kneel before Master Spence, it should be me.

He was *my* Dom.

At least he used to be.

When Spencer reached out and touched her face, my breathing hitched. I'd seen him with other subs before, but this felt very different. We weren't at Esoteric, and I wasn't watching a public scene at a sex club. No, what I was watching was a private moment between the man I loved and his new sub.

It was wrong of me to stay there. Neither of them had invited me to witness their scene, nor did they know I was peering in the dark through the lens of a telescope. But no matter how hard I tried to stop myself—like a train wreck—I just couldn't look away.

Seeing Spencer run his fingers over his new sub's shoulder—that feather light touch trailing around her neck, down her back—every sensual touch burned a painful memory so deep into my soul, I knew I'd never forget it. The blonde before him, the one he had pulled so close to his body no light could pass, *she* was his sub now.

And he was *her* Dom.

Spencer had moved on.

That's what I wanted, *right?* To know he was okay, that my decision to fake my death hadn't destroyed the Dom inside him. Clearly, I hadn't thought the plan through well enough. Seeing Spencer command someone else crushed even the hope in Lily Walker's phony life.

Tears streamed down my cheeks in a steady stream as I feverishly packed up the telescope. Screw the army's equipment. I should've just told Cowboy the truth from the beginning. Maybe then the wound in my heart wouldn't have ripped wide open all over again.

Chapter Twenty
Spencer

"Ashlan," I whispered, stirring as light pierced the peacefulness of my dream. It was a strangled plea to hold onto the tantalizing moment just a little while longer: Ash's body tucked close to mine, wrapped in the safety of my arms.

Pulling the covers over my head in a vain attempt to block out the sunlight flooding the room, I returned my face to the pillow I'd spent the night wrapped around. The same pillow that, if I didn't know better, I'd swear held the fruity scent of Ash's favorite shampoo. A smell so intoxicating it had my dick pulsing with need.

Another deep breath and I knew I'd never find the sleep my body desperately needed, not with my throbbing cock begging for attention.

Reluctantly, I sat up, immediately wishing I hadn't.

Sonofabitch. How much did I have to drink last night? If the pounding in my head was any indication, I'd say it was too damn much.

Slowing dragging my ass out of bed, I snagged four Advil off Izzy's bedside table and then made my way to the bathroom. Every step I took was another reminder of my stupidity.

Jesus Christ.

My life really had gone to hell. I couldn't even drink right anymore. Every fucking drunk knows to take the pain killers *before* you go to bed.

Thank God, the Advil finally took the edge off my headache. That, combined with a nice hot shower and a tall glass of orange juice, were just what I needed to clear the fog from my mind. Too bad that included the recall of some pretty disturbing details of what I did last night.

Anna's note confirmed at least part of my somewhat hazy version of events. Apparently, I had in fact told Drew and Anna about the divorce. Worse than that, I'm pretty sure I also told at least one of them that Izzy was having an affair.

"BTW, Mom's on a *business trip* with that guy from the paper." Anna's note read, with the word *business trip* underlined three times. Clearly, she thought there was more to the story. A story I undoubtedly told.

After seeing the picture of Izzy and Alec together, I'd completely lost my shit, along with all sense of reason or responsibility. I'd made a promise to Izzy that we'd wait to tell the kids about the divorce until after graduation, a promise I'd had every intention of keeping before last night.

I'm such a fuckup!

Without Ash, I'd lost that connection with my inner Dom and, along with it, the control and self-discipline I used to have. I'd let myself become that low-life bastard I'd spent my life despising, the one who made selfish choices, who put their own wants ahead of the needs of those who depended on them most, who broke apart families and hurt their kids.

Yeah. That was me.

Cheating on Izzy hadn't even been the worst it. I'd let Anna down, and Drew. Hell, lately, drinking had become my only priority. Nothing mattered more than getting lost in the freedom of my alcoholic stupor where I could forget about all the hurt that came with losing Ashlan.

I'd failed as a husband.

As a father.

As a Dom.

Even worse, I'd failed as a man.

It wasn't until I noticed the empty bottle of Jack sitting on Izzy's desk that the memory of the blank security video returned.

Ashlan. She'd been here.

I closed my eyes, the memory of that perfect body, her hair blowing wilding in the breeze as she ran across the yard, the tiny footprints she left behind in the sand for me to find. Could it have been her?

My eyes flew open as the details from last night started to fall into place. "Dane!" I shouted, suddenly remembering the call I'd made to him. That asshole was keeping something from me.

And I was going to find out what.

· · · · ·

Sitting in Dane's office, I had the awful feeling of déjà vu that had the hairs on the back of my neck standing on end. The longer I waited, the more anxious I became.

Memories from the last time I sat in his office still haunted me. It was in that very chair where I found out Ashlan had died. Being there grated on every painful memory. A drink would've settled the nervous feeling in the pit of my stomach, but Dane insisted I show up with a clear head. "We do this sober or we don't do it at all," he'd said when I called him yesterday. He'd been so pissed off about my drunken call the night before that I didn't dare risk showing up with liquor in my system.

Not when Dane had information I was desperate for.

Sitting on my ass wasn't helping my mood, either. I hopped to my feet and began nervously pacing the room. How long was he going to keep me waiting?

Doesn't he realize how important this is to me?

Is Ash alive? Or is she really dead?

Not knowing was the hardest to take. Whatever Dane told me, as hard as it was for me to believe, I knew I had no choice but to accept it as truth. He wouldn't lie to me. The club's motto, *Trust above all else*, wasn't an empty promise. It was a pledge every Esoteric member made and one we all took seriously.

What the hell was Dane keeping me waiting for? He had to know how hard it was for me to be there. Every sight, every smell, every sound echoing down the hall reminded me of Ash, and of a life I'd never have again.

Five more minutes, I convinced myself. That's how much longer I'd wait. Any longer and I wasn't sure I could take it. Being in the club had my skin crawling with need.

The need to touch her...to taste her...to protect her.

Three more minutes.

From the desk to the door then back again. I continued to pace the room. From the desk to the door, back again.

What the hell is taking him so long?

From the desk to the door.

"Take a seat," Dane barked out when he finally entered the room.

"Well, look who's suddenly in a hurry."

Dane plopped down into his desk chair, pointing to the empty seat across from him. "Do you want to hear this or not? 'Cause I have plenty of other shit to do tonight."

That was all the encouragement I needed to sit down and shut the hell up. I'd been waiting all day to hear what it was Dane had to say.

"Now," Dane continued as he kicked his feet up on the desk. "What I'm about to tell you is top-secret. You even think about repeating this to anyone and I'll rip your arms off and beat you to death with them." His eyebrows drew together, his focus narrowing on my eyes. "That clear?"

I inclined my head as if my life depended on it, because really, it did.

"And you can't go all ape-shit on me."

I nodded again, more than ready for him to get on with the story.

With lightning speed, Dane sat up, his feet hitting the floor a mere second before his fist connected with his dark cherry desk. "This isn't a game, Spencer. You need to take this shit serious. I can't have you running off all half-cocked like you have been these past four months. Hell, I've been wrestling with whether I should even tell you this for fear you'll lose your damn mind."

Dane's eyes floated shut, the tiny muscles in his jaw twitching as he worked to reign in the anger I heard in his voice. After a few deep breaths, his eyes opened. "I'm not sure you can handle this right now—"

He's not going to tell me?

Consumed by desperation, I lunged at him over the desk. Before I knew what was happening, we were both on our feet, my hands locked in a death grip with his lapel. "Please, Dane, I have to know the truth. Can't you see the hell I've been through? I can't take it anymore. I'm going out of my mind." Hell, maybe I'd already lost my damn mind, manhandling a guy Dane's size. That didn't matter anymore. Nothing else mattered but knowing what he was keeping from me. "Tell me! Was that Ashlan? Is she alive?"

"Yes," Dane snapped, right before he shoved me off him. His lips continued to move, but I couldn't hear a thing. It was as if those three letters had sucked all the air out of the room.

My legs went limp as I processed what Dane said.

Ashlan is alive.

I stumbled backward, landing awkwardly in the chair I'd vacated a few moments earlier. Heaviness settled in my chest, my heartbeat pounding frantically in my ears as everything around me went black.

Ash is alive.

•••••

"Stay with me, man," Dane was saying as he slapped me on the cheek. "You've gotta breathe."

Breathe?

Yes, I couldn't breathe. I must've passed out.

Pain racked the back of my head, a sharp, throbbing, screaming kind of pain that made it hard to open my eyes. "What happened to my head?"

Dane helped me sit up. "Fainted like a little girl, that's what," he laughed. "You hit your head pretty hard. Probably have a concussion. Let me see your eyes." He didn't wait for my approval before blinding me with his flashlight.

"Jesus, Dane," I barked, batting his hands away. "Wanna tell me what the hell's going on here before you start shining shit in my eyes?

Ignoring my question, Dane helped me to my feet then guided me to the sofa so I could sit. He sat down on the cushion beside me as he continued to tease. "You've gone soft, man. One minute I'm telling you about Ash and the next I'm picking your ass up off the floor."

Ash?

Oh God, Ash. She's alive!

I jumped to my feet, swaying on wobbly legs. "Where is she? When can I see her?"

With a firm shove on my shoulders, Dane had me sinking back down onto the couch cushions. "You're not going anywhere right now, Spencer, so sit the fuck still." Handing me a bottle of water, he continued, "Like I was saying before you fell out of your chair, a few weeks back I got a call from an old army buddy of mine who needed help with a high risk relocation of a domestic abuse victim he was helping out. Told me her name was Lily Walker, but not much else." He took a long pull from his own bottle of water before continuing. "It wasn't until two weeks ago, when she landed in Pensacola, that I knew it was her."

Two goddamn weeks.

He's known Ash was alive for two fucking weeks and he didn't tell me? Didn't he know I'd been living in Hell thinking Ash was dead?

Knowing she was alive breathed new life into my Dom. Nostrils flaring, I fisted my hands on my lap, fighting to control the fire that had begun to burn once more.

Dane leaned forward, removing the space he'd created earlier. "This is what I was talking about, Spencer," he said, pointing to my tightly fisted hands. "This isn't the time to go all overprotective Dom. Whatever her reason for running, whatever her reason for keeping this from you, you can't forget what she's been through. Hell, man, how desperate would you have to be to leave it all behind? Family. Friends. Her Dom?" Dane leaned back in his chair, his right hand reaching into the front pocket of his jeans for his ringing cell phone. "It's up to *her* to decide if she wants to see you." Looking down at the screen, Dane stood. He was halfway to the door by the second ring. "And you need to be prepared for the possibility that she doesn't want to go there."

"Are we a go?" Dane asked when he answered the call, quickly disappearing down the hall and out of ear shot.

My heart raced with excitement. Ashlan was alive. That really had been her yesterday. I wasn't losing my mind. Ash had come to me. She'd faked her own death so we could be together. But then she ran.

Of course she ran, dumbass. You were goddamn wasted.

"Fuck," I growled as I hopped back up to my feet. I was such an idiot. I'd scared her. She saw the real Spencer, the filthy drunk without an ounce of control, and she ran.

Chapter Twenty One
Ashlan

Somehow, I managed to avoid Cowboy all week. Unfortunately, today my luck had run out. Cowboy's last message said he would be by my house at eleven thirty to pick up the package. No more stalling. It was time to decide. Either disappoint Cowboy or risk seeing Spencer and his new sub.

Ugh. Even thinking about witnessing another scene between Spencer and his new sub had my stomach churning. It's not like I had a choice. Cowboy and Tony were the closest things I had to family, plus, they were all I had left now. My own parents hadn't cared enough to fight to stay in my life, and my Dom, the only man I ever *really* loved, had moved on.

I couldn't stand to disappoint either Tony or Cowboy, much less both of them. It was time to put my big girl panties on and get the job done.

"Get in. Get out," I whispered repeatedly on my walk to Spencer's, Cowboy's earlier training charging me forward. This was my last chance to get back Cowboy's jammer before I had to tell him I'd failed my mission.

"Of course you failed, mi esclavo. You're weak, and pathetic, and too stupid to fucking live." Diego's harsh words popped

into my mind, threatening to derail my plan, but I immediately shook it off.

"I'm not weak!" I screamed before I could stop myself. But I couldn't let my mind wander down that road. Toni taught me how strong I really was. I'd lived in hell my whole life, yet I was still alive.

I survived.

Years of abuse at my father's hand hadn't killed me.

Six years of beatings, courtesy of the man I married, hadn't managed to stop me.

Not even the crushed soul that seeing Spencer again was going to cause would be enough to kill me. No. Karma was an evil, evil bastard who took pleasure in seeing me suffer.

Once my borrowed telescope was in position, I wasted no time getting to work. Get in. Get out. That was Cowboy's plan from the beginning and, from here on out, I was going to do things his way.

Scanning from left to right, I searched every inch of the inside of Spencer's house. Well, every inch I could see, anyway. No sign of movement upstairs; things were looking good so far. Downstairs appeared empty too.

That's when I made my move.

Once again, the sliding glass door was unlocked. The high tech security system Spencer had installed apparently had lulled the James family into a false sense of security. Spencer had to know security systems weren't fail-safe. Hell, their system had been down for over a week, and they hadn't seemed to have noticed.

Opening the door just far enough for me to squeeze through, I stepped inside Spencer's house for the second time.

Wuh- psssh!

The undeniable sound of my master's whip echoed through the downstairs hall all the way to the kitchen.

Wuh- psssh!

A pull so strong, it drew me in without thought or reason, each step forward strengthening its hold, pulling me toward the closed bedroom door at the end of the long hall.

Wuh- psssh!

When I stopped outside the door, I told myself not to look inside. When the knob began to turn beneath my hand, I begged. Only I didn't stop. No matter how much I begged my hand not to turn the knob, my body had a mind of its own.

Wuh- psssh!

The train barreled down the tracks, and I was tied, unable to avoid the inevitable pain. Floating, I watched from afar, powerless to stop myself from watching the scene in front of me.

Nothing could have prepared me for what I saw when my eyes came into focus. The Dom wielding the whip before me wasn't *my* Dom. Same sandy blonde hair, same piercing blue eyes, but the blood dripping off the end of his whip told me he definitely wasn't *my* Dom.

No, the man I was looking at was a thinner, younger, less experienced version. There was no denying the resemblance, the Dom before me could only be Spencer's son, Drew.

Not Spencer, but Drew.

From the flick of his wrist to the gentle way he caressed the raised welts on his sub's skin, he was a natural. Inexperienced, yes, but the way he studied her, seemed to read her body, left me no doubt that in time he'd be every bit the Dom his father was.

Drew.

Not Spencer.

This whole past week I'd spent grieving the loss of my Dom when it wasn't even Spencer I saw that night.

Drew lifted the whip high over his head. Waves of fear filled my mind, the stinging from the scars on my back begging him not to strike with that much force.

His wrist pulled back, ripping an involuntary gasp from my lungs.

Drew's head snapped toward the offending sound.

Frozen, I couldn't move or look away or breathe, not even when he dropped the whip and started toward me.

Nostrils flaring. Eyes blazing. Drew's focus never wavered.

Not until the voice behind him started to protest. "Damn it, Drew, we weren't finished!"

Recognition wasn't immediate, but before his attention returned to me, I'd identified his sub.

Val.

Four months of survival training finally kicked in, and I sprinted down the hall, back the way I came. Getting back Cowboy's jammer on my own was nothing but a pipe dream now. If Drew caught me, he'd see right through any lie I tried to tell. One look into those familiar eyes, and I'd be putty in his hands.

And if Val saw me there....*oh God.* I couldn't go there. Even the thought of what she'd do to Spencer while forcing me to watch had my skin crawling.

• • • • •

For someone who hated running, I sure seemed to be doing a lot of it as of late. Luckily, Drew hadn't been wearing shoes and gave up the chase pretty quickly, because if he hadn't, there was no way I would've gotten away. He closed half the gap before he even made it off the grass.

It took the rest of the walk home to calm my racing heart. Of course, it didn't help that I was beating myself up for leaving without the equipment, *for the third damn time.* The only thing that lessened the sting of disappointing Cowboy was one simple truth.

Not Spencer, but Drew.

· · · · ·

Time seemed to moving at warp speed as I waited my inevitable fate.

Ding. Dong. The sound, even though expected, still startled the hell out of me, so when the stool fell over from me jumping to my feet, I wasn't surprised.

A quick glance at my phone only proved what I already knew: it was eleven thirty. The time to come clean had arrived. On the other side of the door, Cowboy was waiting for me to answer, expecting me to return the equipment he put his ass on the line to get for me.

Disappointed. Not furious.

I reminded myself of that as I looked out the peep hole, just to be sure it was really Cowboy. One look at that tattered straw hat he was wearing and I had all the proof I needed. Only Cowboy would put something that hideous on his head as if it were some priceless treasure.

Disappointed. Not angry.

I took one final deep breath as I worked up the courage I needed to open the door.

Ding. Dong.

"Just a minute," I called out through the door.

"Hurry up. I ain't got all night."

Disappointed. Not cruel.

I reminded myself of that one more time before I opened the door.

Doing my best to look casual, I said, "Cowboy, hey. Come on in." I didn't wait for him to answer before moving away from the door. "Can I get you something to drink?"

"Why don't you pour us both one, darlin'," he said as he followed me into the living room. "There's somethin' we need to talk about."

Damn it. I should've known he'd figure it out. Why hadn't I just come clean in the beginning? Then I could've avoided the hell the past week brought with it.

Pouring two shots, I handed one glass to Cowboy before throwing back my head, letting the clear liquid in the other glass slide down my throat.

Hoping the tequila would help me through the confession I knew I had to make, I quickly slammed back another then blurted out, "Cowboy, I'm sorry. It was an accident. I never meant to leave the jam—"

Cowboy jumped to his feet, slamming the empty shot glass down on the end table. Before I could even blink, the gap between us was dangerously closed.

Face red, veins on his neck bulging, rapid breathing... I'd never seen Cowboy mad before, and let me tell you, it was not something I wanted to see again any time soon.

Fight or flight?

I took one step back then another and another.

Fight or flight?

Another step back and I was out of running room, my internal struggle decided for me since I was pressed up against the wall behind me with nowhere to run.

Less than a second later, Cowboy was in front of me, his face only inches from mine.

With flared nostrils, he finally spoke. "Don't say it, Ash. Don't you dare say what I think you're fixin' to say."

Ash?

Did he just call me Ash?

The room began to spin, the walls around me closing in. If Cowboy had found out who I was, surely others could too.

Oh, God. What if someone else already knew my real identity?

What if Diego knew?

Oh, God, please don't let him find me!

Diego would kill me for sure. *"No, mi esclavo, death is too good for you. Instead, I will break you, first your body and then your spirit. You belong to me always. There is no escape for you."*

The hate in Diego's words held so much power that even then, months later, it still threatened to choke the life right out of me.

No! Not this time. You're stronger now!

When a firm hand pressed into my shoulder, I knew I had to fight. Swinging my arms, hands squeezed into tight fists, I started to scream, "NO! LEAVE ME ALONE! DON'T TOUCH ME!"

My small fists were no match for Cowboy's hard body. He hadn't backed away, yet he didn't try to stop me, either. He just stood there, letting me pound into him like a mad woman.

Over and over, my fists connected with his chest while I screamed incoherently. Hell, I'm not even sure they were words I was shouting, but that didn't matter. I was standing up for myself, fighting for *myself.*

Never in my life had I experienced such a cathartic release. Every jarring blow a tiny victory, every jolt of pain through my knuckles empowering me that much more.

I swung and screamed until I couldn't do either anymore.

Seeing his opening, Cowboy took me by the shoulders and pulled me into his chest. The strength of his grip left no room for argument, even if I'd had the strength.

"Shhh," he whispered, gently stroking my hair. "It's okay. I'm not going to hurt you. I'm sorry I scared you. I'd never hurt you, okay?"

That's when the dam broke. Huge tears rolled down my cheeks. All the emotions of the past week...the past four months...maybe even my life, came rushing out of me. I'd left his equipment behind, yelled at him, hit him repeatedly...and *he* was sorry?

I didn't realize I was trembling until Cowboy's grip tightened, pulling me even closer to his hard body. "Shhh," he whispered again. "You're okay. I've got you."

The words he used to comfort me only made me cry harder. Quietly, Cowboy rocked me side to side, patiently letting me cry it all out.

• • • • •

"Did you know it was me all along?" I asked when I finally calmed down.

Cowboy relaxed his grip, allowing me to put some much needed distance between us. I took a step back, relieved when he let me.

A simple "nope" was all he offered, but somehow that tiny bit of knowledge comforted me.

Cowboy let me go and reached for the box of tissues next to the lamp, giving me the space I needed to gather my thoughts. If he didn't already know who I was, how did he find out? And who else knew?

Before I could open my mouth to ask any of my questions, Cowboy shoved a handful of tissues in my hand and then said, "You think if I'd known, I would've let you anywhere near your past? What is it about *me*, exactly, that suggests to *you* I like risking the lives of women?"

While Cowboy's tone was low and even, the hard set of his jaw told me he was holding back. Nothing about him had suggested he'd knowingly risk my life and, clearly, it pissed him off that I thought he would.

Actually, everything Cowboy had done since we met was for my protection.

"I'm sorry, that's not what I thought at all. It's just...well...how did you find out who I was?"

The tension in his jaw eased before he said, "It seems we have a mutual friend."

Friend? He couldn't be talking about Tony. When Zeke introduced me and Tony to Cowboy, it certainly didn't seem like the two of them had ever met before.

Goosebumps covered my body as ice replaced the blood in my veins.

Oh, God. Diego always said he had reach—

A firm grip wrapped around my arm. "Ashlan, look at me." Cowboy barked out, pulling me off that panic train but not completely settling my nerves. "I've already told ya, darlin', you're safe with me."

Pulling out of his hold, I snapped, "You want me to believe I'm safe? That you aren't some psycho sent here to spy on me? To report back to that sonofabitch who tried to destroy me!"

I took a step forward, every word I snapped out increasing the power I felt inside. I wouldn't ever be that fool again, blindly accepting someone's word simply because they were charming or sexy. I'd already learned that lesson.

At Cowboy's nod, I continued. "Then prove it. Tell me what *friend* of mine told you who I was, because I have to tell you, *darlin',* there are only a handful of people who even know I'm alive, and I highly doubt you know even one of them!"

"Ronnie Dane," he said, smiling like he'd just gotten the canary, "That name good enough for ya?"

Ronnie Dane?

Who the hell is Ronnie Da...oh, God...Master Dane?

But that didn't make sense. Dane didn't know me outside of the club. How could he possible know I was alive? And more importantly, *why* would he care?

• • • • •

Twenty minutes later, after the shock of hearing Master Dane had tracked me down had finally worn off, Cowboy and I were in his lifted Ford pickup truck headed toward Spencer's house to retrieve the borrowed equipment.

"Their next door neighbors are never home," I said as we drove closer. "We can park there."

"We won't be parking," Cowboy said in that calm voice of his.

The truck rolled to a stop at the end of the road. Cowboy turned to look at me. "Let's get this straight right here. I'm going in alone." He didn't wait for me to respond before he continued. "You'll drive around the block until you get my signal. You'll pick me up right over there," he added, pointing to an empty house one street over.

"But it'll be faster if I come with you. I can show you exactly where the bag is at."

"Not a chance, Ash. Dane will have my hide if I let anything happen to you. Turns out, that dumb sonofabitch you've been spying on wants to see you. If you ask me, it'd be a helluva a lot easier on us all if you two worked your shit out."

Spencer knows I'm alive.

Worse, he wanted to see me. God knew I wanted to see him. But that could never happen.

"If you ever speak to Spencer James again, I'll hunt you down and make you both pay," Val had said. The heat in her eyes when she'd said it had left no room for doubt, either. She meant business.

Seeing Spencer was way too dangerous. "No," I snapped, sounding much more confident than I felt. I looked out the window so Cowboy couldn't see the lie on my face. I was anything but confident. "I can't talk to Spencer. Not now. Not ever! It's too risky. Val will kill him if I..."

No. No. No. No. No! Flashing red and blue lights were not what I expected to see.

Police. Fire rescue. Ambulances...

Shit. Val must've recognized me earlier.

Oh, God. Spencer.

Fighting back the tears burning my eyes, I pointed to the scene unfolding in front of us. "Do you see what I mean? This is all my fault. *I* did this."

When I blinked, the tears I'd been holding fell. All I could do was wipe them away.

I did this.

Faced with the truth of the rescue workers in front of me, those words hit me like a ton of bricks. Spencer was hurt, and it was *my* fault.

Swiping at my tears, I whispered, "Spencer's not safe around me. Nobody is."

This time, when the fight or flight instinct battled inside me, I ran.

Chapter Twenty Two
Spencer

Knowing Ashlan was alive while not being able to touch her, to hold her, to *love* her, tested the bounds of my sanity. Add that to Anna's frantic call about Izzy and I was about to lose my shit.

Apparently, Izzy tripped on that damn silk robe she insisted on wearing and fell down the stairs. Anna said she had blacked out and had a nasty cut on her head. "Oh, daddy, there was so much blood," she'd cried. Izzy was taken to the hospital, but it sounded like she'd be okay.

Me, however, I wasn't so sure about. If Cowboy didn't call back soon saying he'd found Ash, I'd need to be sedated, and I didn't mean a bottle of Jack. Oh no, I'm talking about the heavy duty shit doctors used.

"How the hell did he lose her?" I asked for the hundredth time since we got on the plane. He had her in his arms and let her get away. She was right there. Close enough for me to touch, and now she's gone, *again*.

"What could possibly be taking so long? She's on foot, for Christ's sake. How far could she have gotten?"

"Do I need to you give the same lecture you gave your daughter before we took off?" Dane snapped. "Because *this* sure as hell isn't the right time or place for a

172

meltdown. Cowboy is one of the best trackers there is. If anyone can find Ashlan, it'll be him. What you need to do is calm the fuck down and focus on what I'm telling you."

Reaching into the messenger bag beside him, Dane pulled out his iPad and handed it to me. "Look, Spencer," he continued, "I get it. You're torn up about Ash. I would be too. Right now, though, we've got a bigger problem." Nodding toward the screen, he said, "Cowboy's helmet cam captured this image inside your house tonight. Add that to what Ashlan said right before she jumped out of his truck, and we've got ourselves one fucked up situation."

Steeling my nerves, I looked at the screen. What could possibly be worse than—

Sonofabitch!

Valerie.

"What was she doing in my house?" I demanded, the acid in my stomach churning at that thought. "Hell, what was Cowboy doing in my house?"

Dane cleared his throat. "About that..."

He spent the rest of the flight filling me in on everything from Ash's stay at the safe house after she faked her death to the military grade security equipment she left behind when she broke into my house. Dane's details surrounding the staged accident were full of holes. His army buddy, Tony, hadn't been involved in that part of the plan, and Ashlan hadn't talked about it even once in the entire four months she'd stayed at the safe-house. But she'd talk about it with me, just as soon as I wrapped my arms around her, reminding her of the power I wielded over her body.

By the time we landed in Pensacola, I was torn between going after the woman I loved and keeping a promise to my daughter. In the end, Anna's needs won out. Lately, I'd been a horrible father: drunk, obsessed, absent. Nothing like the father she needed me to be, the father she deserved.

And besides, Dane was right, if anyone could find Ashlan, it'd be Cowboy. Right then, my little girl needed me.

I couldn't show up at the hospital like *this*, though, a nervous wreck wound so tight I could snap without warning. Not without a little liquid courage, anyway.

The lure of strength waited at the bottom of a glass of bourbon. A lure so strong I was bellied up to the bar at the Fantasy Lounge before I knew what was going on. It'd been two days since my last drink and, after everything I'd been through today, I'd say I earned a couple.

A couple drinks turned into about half a dozen, and by the time I got to the hospital Anna was out cold. According to the nurse's aide watching over her, Dr. Leonard, our family doctor, had given Anna a mild sedative to help calm her down.

Drew was nowhere in sight. Hopefully, he'd checked into one of the hotel rooms I'd booked after my call with Detective Rux. The detective had said the house was considered a crime scene until the police completed their investigation so was off limits for the time being. Even though the police thought the fall was most likely accidental, protocol required a full investigation.

The door to Izzy's room was closed. A tall, gray-haired nurse sat perched at a computer station outside the door. Her hospital badge identified her as Nina Kline, Registered Nurse.

"Can I help you?" she asked when I reached for the door handle.

"I'm Spencer James. I'm here to see my wife." I intentionally left out the part about our divorce. It was none of Nurse Nina's business, and I sure as hell wasn't going to let a little thing like a technicality keep me from checking on her. We were married for nineteen years. You don't just stop caring about someone when the divorce is finalized.

"Mrs. James is resting, sir. I'm going to have to ask you to come back later."

The tone of her voice grated across every last one of my nerves. I was here to check on Izzy, to see with my own eyes that she was okay, and I wasn't about to let Nurse Nina stand in my way.

"She's my wife!" I snapped. "You can't keep me from her." I stepped forward, willing to push my way through the door if I had to.

Beep. Beep. Beep.

The loud tone radiated from behind the large wooden door. Nina pushed her way past me as I opened the door to see what was going on. It made no difference to me which one of us got in there first as long as she stayed the hell out of my way.

Two other nurses rushed in behind me as the beeping continued, the three of them swarming Izzy's bed while I stood frozen in place to the ground below me.

Seeing Izzy, lying bloodied and broken in a hospital bed snapped the last thread of self-control I had left. She deserved better than the lies I'd been telling her, hell, the lies I was *still* telling her.

When the beeping finally stopped and two of the nurses left the room, I moved closer to the bed. Nurse Nina was saying something and, by the way she was looking at me, she probably expected me to answer. Only problem? I hadn't heard a damn word anybody had said since I walked in the room.

Ignoring the death stare from the nurse, my eyes swept up and down Izzy's body, taking note of every inch of her petite form, now covered in tubes and wires and *blood*.

So much blood. How could this have happened?

I took a step closer, finally finding my voice. "Izzy, we were so worried."

Izzy's eyes narrowed to tiny slits, and I couldn't tell if it was pain or anger, until she spoke. "Why are you here?" she snapped. No "hi" or "nice to see you" or "thanks for coming."

"How did you even know I was here?" Izzy's venomous tone was deserved. I certainly couldn't blame her for being mad at me. The things I'd done were unforgiveable. I'd broken my vows, lived a life she knew nothing about. Izzy had every right to be mad.

"Anna called me," I said softly. "Just because we're divorced doesn't mean I don't still care about you, that I don't still love you."

Izzy held up her hand. "Stop, Spencer, just stop."

The exasperation in her voice was the punch in the gut I needed to pull my head out of my ass. What was I doing? I'd already hurt Izzy enough. How could I come here, after all I'd done, and tell her I loved her? Even if I didn't mean it the way she seemed to think I did. Izzy would always hold a special place in my heart but I had no right to say that to her anymore.

"I'm so sorry, Izzy," I said, dropping my head into my hands while I sucked in a deep breath. Once I looked up again, I continued. "I'm sorry about the pictures." I really was. I should've told her about the club, about Val, about that weekend in Miami with the three of us. She had a right to know she'd been an unwitting participant in my introduction to BDSM, that Val had drugged her, tied her up, used her body for all our pleasure.

Now wasn't the time for that conversation, though. "I'm sorry for lying to you."

Seeing the pain in Izzy's eyes broke me. All the emotion and stress of the last two days left my body in tears that streamed down my face. Before I could stop myself, the truth came tumbling out of my mouth. "I do know the woman in those pictures, Izzy."

Tears fell down Izzy face, too. "Who are they?" she demanded.

"It's only one woman and who she is isn't important. It should've never happened. It was a mistake. I hurt you. I hurt us."

Shut up, idiot! What the hell was I thinking, telling Izzy all that shit now?

At least I'd been honest. Val didn't matter to me, not in the way Izzy would think.

Val introduced me to the BDSM lifestyle, taught me how to be a good Dom, and while I'd always be grateful to her for that, I'd never wanted anything more with her.

I sat on the edge of the bed. "I tried to end it, but then she sent you those pictures. I'm sorry, Izzy. I'm so sorry."

Izzy flinched at my words.

Beep. Beep. The machine started again.

"Why are you telling me this? Why now?"

Beep. Beep. Beep.

The high-pitched sound of the alarm sent Nina running back in.

What the fuck are you doing, asshole! She's in the goddamn hospital!

Sobered by the pain on Izzy's face, I took a step back.

"Your heart rate is dangerously high, Mrs. James." I heard Nina saying.

Oh, God, what have I done?

As if lying and cheating weren't bad enough, I'd laid the burden of my mistakes on her when she was vulnerable. Hell, maybe I'd chosen then to tell her *because* she was vulnerable.

Nina glared daggers at me when she turned around. I could see her mouth moving, but I couldn't hear what she was saying, still lost in my own self-recrimination.

When Nina motioned to the door, I got the point. It was time for me to go. I didn't stand around and argue, mostly because Nina was right. What the hell had I been thinking telling Izzy that shit right now? I'd come to the hospital to check on her, not fucking kill her. Now I had a whole new mess to clean up. I'd need a good night's rest and a clear head first.

Too bad it was the bottle who beckoned the loudest.

• • • • •

Ten o'clock?

Ten o'clock?

What the hell kind of hotel bar closed down at ten o'clock at night? Thank God Cash's stayed open late. Even better that it was close to the hotel.

The taxi dropped me off at the familiar storefront shortly before midnight. I'd already decided to walk back to the hotel but, not wanting to sober up any more than I already had, I gladly accepted the ride to the liquor store.

Seeing Izzy lying in that hospital bed had all sorts of fucked up thoughts racing through my mind. I wondered what Ash had looked like when she'd been in the hospital. Every passing second of sobriety shattered my soul even more.

By the time I cracked the seal on the bottle of Jack, I was consumed by a longing to hold Ash, to protect her, to love her, to make sure no one ever hurt her again.

But first, I had to find her.

Chapter Twenty Three
Ashlan

Jumping out of Cowboy's truck had been an impulsive decision. A decision I was already regretting. The night air cut through the lightweight jacket I'd worn, making my bones ache. Every fracture I'd ever had made its existence known in the cold, damp Florida air.

I was thankful I'd at least been smart enough to wear jeans and sneakers. Of course, I *hadn't* been smart enough to wait until we were closer to some sort of public transportation *or* grab my purse before I bolted. Thank God I had my phone, or I don't know what I would've done.

Calling Tony was the last thing I wanted to do. Unfortunately, I didn't have any other choice. No money. No ID. And no chance in hell I could go back to my house. Not with a military tracker dead set on finding me. Getting away from Cowboy and as far away from Spencer as humanly possible was my top priority. Getting my ass chewed out by Tony for all the idiotic things I'd done since the last time he saw me, well, that was just an unavoidable consequence.

With cops crawling all over the place, I figured the safest place to hide from Cowboy would be near the chaos. He'd expect me to run which was exactly why I hadn't. Well, that and the fact that we were *miles* from civilization at that time of night, *and* the only money I had was the five dollar bill in my pocket which meant calling a cab was out of the question.

I ducked behind a row of houses across the street before circling back along the water to Spencer's house. Unprotected from the bay breeze, the path along the seawall didn't do anything for the cold shiver threatening to overtake my body but make it worse. Too bad the mangroves provided the best cover from passing cars, so it was the safest way for me to get to where I was going unnoticed.

As hard as I tried to hurry, navigating my way along the narrow rock edge on legs unsteady with nerves and cold had proven tricky. By the time I made it back to Spencer's, the ambulance was already pulling away. I hadn't been able to see whether they'd loaded anyone into the back or not, but the fact that they were using the lights and sirens told me they had.

Don't be Spencer. Please, don't be Spencer, quickly became my silent mantra.

What if Val really had seen me? She said she'd make me suffer if I even talked to Spencer again. I'm sure seeing me at his house wouldn't sit well with her.

Oh, God, what did I do?

The need to know who had been rushed to the hospital consumed me, quickly taking over as my top priority. Moving as close to the house as I could get without being completely visible to the couple in the driveway, I hid behind one of the pygmy date palms lining the circular drive.

Drew and a younger woman, one I'd seen there a few times before while I was doing recon, stood in front of the open garage as the last of the police officers loaded up in their cars and left. The light from inside the empty bay illuminated Drew's features: sandy blonde hair, square jaw, broad shoulders, long, powerful legs. The resemblance between Spencer and his son was so strong it's no wonder I'd mistaken the two of them that first night.

Dressed in what appeared to be a custom tailored tuxedo, Drew stood out next to the woman who was dressed far more casually in a pair of yoga pants and a Ft. Walton Beach high school hoodie. Blonde hair piled high on her head in a messy bun, she appeared to be quite a bit younger than me. The confidence in the way she held her body left no doubt she was older than Drew, though. And by the way he leaned closer to her as her hand snaked under his shirt made it clear they were into each other.

After what I'd seen earlier between Drew and Val, I wasn't sure if I should be surprised by Drew's interaction with the new woman or not. So, I tried not to think about it, focusing on the worried looked on his face instead, bringing me back to why I was there.

When Drew's *friend*—because I wasn't sure what to call her—started talking, I risked the move one palm over so I could hear what she was saying, hoping against hope for any clue as to what happened there tonight.

"She's going to be okay, baby," the woman said. "She's strong. It was just a fall. She'll pull through."

Drew wrapped his arm around the woman's shoulders, tucking her into his side. A protective move I'd experienced many times from the older version of the young man I was watching. "I know she'll be alright. Still... I can't get that picture out of my head." Drew rubbed his hands over his eyes. "God, Sara, I've never seen so much blood."

Sara wrapped both arms around Drew's middle and squeezed. Looking up at him, her features soft, she said, "How 'bout I drive you to the hospital? I'm sure Anna needs you."

He leaned down and kissed the top of her head. 'Okay' was all I heard as they walked further into the garage, too far for me to make out anything else that was said.

While I didn't know much about what happened, I'd heard one vital piece of information: Spencer wasn't hurt. *She's going to be okay...She's strong...*I didn't know who *she* was, but *she* wasn't *he* and knowing that was good enough *for the moment.*

Closing my eyes, I said a silent thank you to God. *Spencer's okay.*

As soon as the metal gate closed behind Drew's Jeep, I took off toward the back yard. My plan was to hide out on the small sailboat I'd seen tied to the dock several times before.

The long wooden walkway jutted out to the deeper water in the bay. The dock wouldn't have been so bad if it'd had rails or didn't move as I walked on it. I'd seen floating docks before, I'd just never actually *walked* on one....dragged a few times, yes, but never walked.

Even though I'd lived near the water my whole life, boats weren't really my thing. Then again, neither was spending the night in the cold outdoors. The small cabin wasn't heated, but at least it provided shelter from the breeze. Plus, the bed was a nice bonus. After all the emotional drama of the last few days, I was beyond exhausted.

As appealing as curling up under the fluffy down comforter sounded, there was one final thing I had to do before I could sleep. Pulling up Tony's contact, I said a silent prayer that he'd understand everything I'd done, and why, then hit send.

• • • • •

There was something about the way Tony yelled at me that I found oddly comforting. Not an ounce of hate resonated in his tone or his words of reprimand. Oh, he was plenty pissed alright, but there was no question in my mind he'd forgive me.

"Stay out of sight until I can get there!" Tony barked out. "Do you think you can handle that, *Ashlan?*"

Hearing Tony say my name for the first time felt weird. Maybe it was the way he'd said it, as if he didn't believe that was really who I was. Or maybe it was something else altogether. All I knew for sure was that when I'd come clean about my past, well, the part of it I was willing to share with Tony, he hadn't questioned me the way I'd expected. Didn't dig further, ask any questions, or even sound the least bit surprised.

Of course, he could've been biting back what he really wanted to say, but I wouldn't have known it. The only acknowledgement that he hadn't hung up during my whole *come clean* speech was the occasional grunt or groan when I told him about Diego.

When I'd gotten to the part about my *relationship* with Spencer and my *friendship* with Dane, he'd stayed completely silent. So much so that I stopped twice to make sure he was still on the line. I'd yet to decide if Tony's silence was a sign of acceptance or if he was afraid of what he might say when he spoke to me again.

"Damn it, Ashlan! I asked you a question. Can you handle staying put until I can get there? Or is that too much to ask?"

Okay, there was the anger I'd expected from the beginning.

"No...I mean...that's not too much to ask. I'll stay out of sight. I promise."

Tony's exhale was long and loud. "I'll be there as soon as I can." With that, he disconnected the call.

It was just as well that he'd hung up. Holding it together while I told him about my past was a lot harder than I'd expected it to be. I'd spent four months trying to forget Ashlan Rivera ever existed, so forcing myself to talk about that part of my life sucked.

I tried my best to add distance between the foolish girl I'd been and the fierce survivor I'd become, but no amount of pretending Ashlan Rivera was someone else or wishing none of the hell I'd lived through was real had shielded me from the uneasy feeling in the pit of my stomach. If there had been anything in there, I would have lost it for sure.

Knowing the kind of information Rock had managed to gather on the James family in an impressively short amount of time, I powered off my cell phone for the night. The last thing I needed tonight was Cowboy tracking me because I was too stupid to turn off my phone.

With Tony all the way on the other side of the United States, even if he'd jumped on a plane the second we hung up, it'd be daylight before he could get to Ft. Walton Beach. That left me no excuse. I had to at least try to get some sleep.

Chapter Twenty Four
Spencer

Even with the bottle of Jack I polished off last night, sleep somehow managed to elude me. Every time I closed my eyes, I could see Ash's battered body staring up at me from her hospital bed.

Eyes glassy with unshed tears.

Bloodied and bruised.

Spirit broken by the sonofabitch who hurt her.

And it fueled my rage. Ashlan was *mine*, and I had a responsibility to protect her. I *would* protect her too. Just as soon I found out where she was.

Thinking about Ash being alone, or scared, or *worse* had my inner Dom on high alert. Add that to the two security guards who showed up at the hotel this morning with a protection order for my kids, courtesy of Alec Payne, and I'd reached Def Con one. So, when I swung open the door to Izzy's hospital room, it came as no surprise to me that it was Master Spence who walked through her door.

Flowers.

Fucking everywhere.

"Who sent you these?" I barked out, not even trying to mask the irritation I felt.

"Does it matter?" Izzy snapped with an icy tone *Master Spence* sure as hell wasn't used to hearing. Only Izzy wasn't talking to him, she was talking to the ex-husband who'd cheated on her.

After taking a deep breath to reign in the emotion simmering near the surface, I said, "Izzy, wait. I didn't come here to fight."

"Then why are you here, Spencer?"

Fuck. She's really pissed.

I moved to the edge of the bed, instinctively lifting her hand in mine as I'd done hundreds of times before when I'd offered her comfort. "I came to check on you, to make sure you're okay."

Izzy ripped her hand from my grip, her eyes glaring daggers into me.

Quickly, I jumped in with the speech I'd worked over in my mind earlier before she could spew the venom I saw building behind her eyes. "I know you're mad at me. And you may never forgive me, but I still love you. I'll always love you."

When she deliberately looked away from me, I had to bite my tongue to keep from ordering her eyes back to mine. At the coppery taste of blood, I released my hold and continued. "Izzy, please, look at me, talk to me."

Please, dammit. Before I lose my goddamn mind and Master Spence takes over.

Oh no, cooperating had never been Izzy's style. Not the bull-headed, Miss Independent, Isabella James. She'd much prefer the fight.

"Seriously, Spencer?" she snapped. "I was drugged and attacked. And to top that off, you decided the best time to tell me about your affair was while I was lying in a hospital bed," she screamed. "It was bad enough knowing you cheated on me. But you didn't just cheat, Spencer.

You had an ongoing, intimate relationship with another woman! And I don't want to talk about this with you right now."

Izzy's tone threatened what little control I had left.

How many fucking times am I going to have to apologize for that?

"Damn it, Bella. I said I was sorry!"

"Sorry!" she shouted at the top of her lungs. "Sorry doesn't begin to cut it, Spencer. I said I don't want to talk about this. Now please, just go."

No. No. No. I'd come there to check on her, to apologize for being a dick, for cheating on her. Izzy needed to forgive me so we could both move on. She deserved to be happy. Happy in a way I had never made her. "Izzy, please, I need you to forgive me."

A deep, male voice I didn't recognize sounded behind me. "She said not now, Mr. James."

I turned around to see who it belonged to, my nostrils flaring as I took in the familiar sight of the man standing in the doorway.

"Well, well, well...if it isn't Alec Payne." Seeing him there, the man who had looked at my wife with heat in his eyes, was a slap in the face that had my inner Dom seething. "Now it makes perfect sense: that picture, the *business* cruise, Drew and Anna's security detail." I turned back to Izzy, all sense of reason gone as I processed what Alec's being there meant, and snapped. "And you're mad at me? Isn't that the pot calling the kettle black? Bella!" I added the hated nickname because I knew it would piss her off.

And it had.

"Not even close," she screamed. "I NEVER cheated on you, Spencer!"

Alec stepped between us with a look in his eye I knew well. He was in full-on protective mode, prepared to protect what he was clearly claiming as his. "It's time for you to go, Mr. James."

There was no point in arguing with him. I'd given up the right to a place by Izzy's side with the choices I'd made. Even if I hadn't screwed up, Izzy asked me to leave, and Alec intended to make sure I did. It'd be a tough fight if I wasn't hung over. Considering I *was*, I made the only choice I could.

"Fine," I said, managing to sound a hell of a lot more civilized than I felt. Opening the door, I added, "But at least I'm honest about what I've done, Izzy."

Now *that* snarky comment better suited my mood.

It wasn't until I was halfway down the hall that Izzy's words fully sunk in.

Drugged.

Attacked.

And no damn security video!

Goddammit! I'd failed. *Again.*

• • • • •

Ashlan

The gentle rocking of the boat lulled me into a sleep so deep, so peaceful, so relaxing, I hadn't noticed when the sun rose that morning.

I powered on my phone to check the time, but it rang before my eyes could focus clear enough to read the display.

Tony's face filled the screen, bringing forth a smile. "Good morning," I said, yawning.

"You're kidding me, right?" Before I could ask about his pissy tone, he continued. "It's twelve fucking thirty,

Ashlan. As in *after* noon. I've been calling you for over three goddamn hours. Do you have any idea how worried I've been?"

"First of all," I snapped in a pissy tone of my own. "I'm sorry I slept so long." While I wouldn't stand for his harsh tone, I had to admit my part in why he was mad. "Second," I continued, "my phone was turned off, so I had no idea that you called. And third, cursing at me is...well, it's rude!"

"Rude?" he said, laughing, although I got the feeling he didn't find any of this funny. "What the hell do you call turning off your phone so I couldn't reach you?"

"Uh, how about smart? Seeing how I only have one bar left on my battery, no charger, and no electricity. Not to mention that with my phone switched on, someone could've easily tracked me."

Tony's heavy growl filled the line. "Where are you?"

I rattled off Spencer's address and agreed to stay put, with my phone on, until he arrived. Which was harder than it sounded, considering I had one hell of a cramp in my back and I really needed to pee.

Tony said he wasn't far. All I could do was hope his idea of 'not far' was actually close by, because I wasn't sure how much longer I'd be able to hold out.

I crawled off the bed and did my best to make it. So much for removing all evidence someone had slept there. Between my overfilled bladder and the desperate need to stretch my back, the end result looked more like the job a five-year-old might have done. Maybe even worse. After a few minutes of struggling to reposition the oversized comforter, I gave up on making the bed. And on hiding, too.

Poking my head through the opening of the cabin, I listened for any signs of movement. When there weren't any, I climbed out of the tiny space into the open cockpit.

Stretching had been a top priority, until I stood up to actually do it. Last night, lying on the surprisingly comfortable bed, I'd appreciated the soothing rhythm caused by the ocean. Trying to balance on two shaky legs was a whole different story. As I struggled to get out of the cockpit and onto the dock, I actually found the movement annoying, maybe because my bladder was going to explode if I didn't get relief, and soon.

Exposing my naked butt to potential boaters seemed a better plan than the alternative, so I hopped off the dock, hid in the mangroves the best I could, and took care of business.

Of course, Tony would have to choose that exact moment to call.

"Wait...shit..." I fumbled the phone as I wiggled my jeans over my hips. "Sorry, hey, are you here?"

"Are you wearing purple panties?"

Dammit.

"Please don't tell me you saw me pee." *Please* let it be a coincidence that Tony knew I was wearing purple panties. He'd never let me live that down if he really saw me.

Tony's deep laugh reached me long seconds before he said, "Okay. I won't tell you. Now zip up and let's get out of here."

"O...kay," I said, ignoring the uneasy feeling I had about Tony seeing me in such a vulnerable position.

Dammit. Dammit. Damn it!

Looking around, I couldn't see any signs of the large man who was picking me up. "Where are—?"

Before I finished my question, Tony stepped into view by the corner of the neighbor's house.

Too freaked out to make causal conversation, I whispered, "I'll be right there," then disconnected the call before starting the climb over the rock barrier separating Spencer's dock from his neighbor's.

I found Tony leaning up against his rented car, arms crossed in a defensive stance, but the grin on his face said he was enjoying himself.

Bastard. He hadn't even offered me a hand, not even when I struggled over that last rock. "Thanks for your help."

"Hey, I was going to suggest you come through the yard. You know, seeing how no one is home and all. But you hung up on me before I had a chance."

Dammit! I'd climbed over the cold, slippery rocks for nothing. *Argh!* "Yeah...well...you watched me pee!"

Tony grabbed both my arms and pulled me into a bear hug. My body relaxed instantly against his warm strength. All the fight drained out of my body the second his arms closed around me.

"Again, you're the one who decided to drop trou in public, so don't go blaming me for seeing it." He hugged me until the tension in his arms relaxed too. With one final squeeze and a kiss on top of my head, Tony let me go.

"You owe me fifty bucks, by the way."

"Ha, you're funny." Seeing how I only had five dollars to my name, he had about as good a chance of collecting as I had living happily-ever-after.

"I'm serious." Tony's deep voice stopped my runaway thoughts. "Toni bet me fifty bucks you wouldn't last a month before getting yourself into trouble. I bet it would take you at least two."

Great, so they both bet on me to screw up. I couldn't help but roll my eyes. Neither of them ever expected me to make it on my own.

"Geez, Tony, thanks for the vote of confidence."

"Oh, quit your bitchin' and get in the car. You're the one who..."

I shut the car door before he had a chance to finish the rest of that sentence. I didn't need to hear, again, how much I screwed up.

Because I already knew.

Chapter Twenty Five
Ashlan

Tony drove me to the Greyhound station in Gulfport, Mississippi where we traded in the rental car for bus tickets. He said he'd had enough driving, and since I'd left without any identification, he wouldn't let me behind the wheel. Of course, without ID, flying commercial was out of the question and neither one of us wanted to risk using Tony's military contacts again. That left only one viable option. And that's how I ended up crammed against a very growly man in the too small seats for his muscular, six foot three body, listening to him grunt and groan as the kid behind him kicked at his seat.

"He's just a kid," I whispered, which earned me the deadliest glare I'd ever seen. From the looks of it, Tony was seconds away from blowing his top.

The kid kicked the seat again, hard enough to make Tony's head jerk. He jumped up as fast as he could in the small space and then spun around to face his tormentor.

Oh shit.

One hard glare was all it took for the toddler to shrink into his sleeping mother's side. To my surprise and, from the look on the little boy's face, I'd say his too—Tony smiled. Then took the blanket he'd been using as a pillow and covered the child up.

"What?" Tony said when he saw the shocked look on my face. "The kid was cold." Immediately, he closed his eyes, his arms folded over his chest.

I didn't say a word, sinking down into my own seat instead, forcing myself to relax.

We arrived in Houston early the following morning. After Tony's stern look last night, there was no more kicking of the seat, which meant we were both able to get some rest.

Before we left the bus station, Tony handed me a bag with a pair of sunglasses, some shears, and two boxes of drugstore hair dye inside and told me to 'get it done'. The hard set of his jaw and his harsh tone left no room for argument.

He'd told me in the car that he thought I should dye my hair. I'd adamantly objected when he pulled into the parking lot of the salon.

But now, standing outside the ladies room, bag of supplies in hand, I was regretting that choice.

• • • • •

"I look ridiculous," I said, for the fourth or fifth time. "Why didn't you tell me when we were at the salon? If changing my hair wasn't an option, I had a right to know!"

At the red light, Tony turned to look at me. Eyebrows drawn, nostrils flaring, yeah, he'd had enough. "The fact that you didn't think you *needed* to change your appearance after having to be relocated, for the second damn time, really pisses me off. You know that?" The light changed, but Tony didn't move. He wasn't done with me yet. "Instead of complaining about your damn hair, which will grow back, by the way, why don't you try thanking me for dropping what I was doing to fly cross country to save you?" The veins in his neck pulsed with every beat of his heart. Cars behind us honked for us to move, but Tony's focus remained on me. "Now, I suggest you either change your damn attitude or sit back in your seat and shut the hell up."

The rest of the drive to Galveston was quiet, with the exception of my apology. Tony was right. I was whining and complaining instead of being thankful for his help. Selfishness wasn't something I was used to and, after being put in my place for behaving that way and the awful way it made me feel, I knew I hadn't been missing much.

The coastal town outside of Houston was smaller than I'd expected. Getting lost in a crowd became easier the bigger the crowd grew. How was I supposed to blend in here?

To add to my surprise, when we pulled into the parking lot at the Wharf, a local restaurant and bar, Tony handed me an envelope and ordered me out of the car.

"What do you mean? *Get out?*"

"Look, Ash, I can't know where you are. It's the safest way. You have to trust me on this."

"But...I don't have any money, or a place to stay, or a job." I could feel the panic setting in. He couldn't leave me there. Alone. "And I don't know anybody here. I can't do this by myself. Please, Tony. You can't leave me here."

Tony gathered both my hands in his. "Look at me," he demanded. Instinctively, my eyes snapped to his. "You're stronger than you think, okay. And I wouldn't leave you here if I didn't think you'd be safe." It was then I noticed the tension around his eyes, too. Leaving me there wasn't any easier for him than it was for me.

"There's some money and a new identity inside the envelope, one that *no one* knows, okay. Not even me." His eyes closed and, when they reopened, nothing but seriousness remained. "Talk to Rod, he's the head bartender here and a good friend of mine. He doesn't know you're coming or that you know me. But tell him you need a job, and he'll hook you up." He let go of my hands then said, "Toni and I care deeply for you, Ashlan. We'll always be there for you. No matter what idiotic things you do."

Tony looked away from me. "Now go."

As much as I didn't want to get out of the car, to leave the safety of Tony's company behind, I knew I had to. He needed me to be strong.

With a quick 'bye' I was gone.

• • • • •

Spencer

Best damn tracker, my ass. It'd been two damn days and Cowboy still wasn't any closer to finding Ashlan. He'd tracked her as far as Houston, but the trail went cold at the Greyhound station. The good news was he'd been able to install facial recognition software on the city's traffic cam system at the bus terminal, train station, airport, and even the port authority. The bad news, there hadn't been a single sighting.

Dane's whole *let the experts handle it* approach was grating on every nerve I had left. Cowboy could be spinning his wheels for all I knew. Who was to say Ash hadn't already skipped town.

Coming home to find my house alarm turned off, again, did nothing to improve my mood. How the hell did I think I could keep Ash safe when I couldn't even get my own damn family to keep the goddamn alarm set! At least I would have video this time. I'd find out who turned it off and get that shit taken care of today.

I stormed off toward Izzy's office and the hidden control panel of my security system. Finding the door standing wide open was not what I expected.

"What the hell," I shouted as I walked further into the room to take in the scene in front of me. Broken glass littered the floor, couch cushions ripped to shreds, paint covered the walls: large, red letters that read *what's mine is mine*. Entire bookshelves had been emptied, drawers turned upside down. The artwork Izzy spent years collecting, slashed.

Not one surface in the entire room had escaped the wrath that had been unleased here. When I spotted the words *DIE BELLA* etched into the glass of the bay window, I didn't need the security video to tell me who was responsible for all the carnage. There was only one other person besides me who dared call Izzy by that nickname.

Valerie.

The mirror hiding the security control panel was shattered, but luckily the false wall behind it had held. After clearing the larger pieces of the broken mirror, I was able to lower the access panel and queue up the video. Two dozen cameras meant two dozen videos to comb through. First, though, I'd take a look at the one room I knew for sure the bitch had been in and trace her steps from there.

One look at those long legs ending in the perfect round ass, and my suspicions were confirmed: Valerie *fucking* Russell. The only question I could think of was why? She'd already won. Izzy and I were divorced. Ash was in hiding. I was fucking miserable. That's what she'd wanted, right? To ruin my life? Newsflash, she'd already succeeded. What the hell was she planning now?

Watching the video in reverse, I was able to track Val's entry point into the house. She hadn't broken in at all. She pulled right into the goddamn garage.

And deactivated the alarm?

I replayed *that* five seconds of video three times before I finally accepted it. She had the damn alarm code! The one I changed after Izzy was drugged and attacked.

How the hell did she get the goddamn code?

Hell, Izzy didn't even have it. Not that she needed it. Alec hadn't let Izzy out of his sight since that awful night when she was found lying in a pool of her own blood.

So how the hell had Val gotten it?

"Ohmygosh, Dad!" Anna's high-pitched squeal pulled me back to the present. "Are you hurt? Did you call the police?"

Sonofabitch. There'd be no getting out of calling the police now that Anna had seen the destruction. And I couldn't let the police see the video I'd just watched. How would I explain Valerie to Detective Rux? He already thought I was somehow involved in Izzy's attack. Knowing that the crazy person who tore Izzy's office to shreds had both access to the garage and the alarm code, and I'd be upgraded to suspect number one.

Fucking hell!

"Not yet, princess," I said, feverishly working to delete the video footage. "I wanted to check the security cameras first to make sure the perp wasn't still in the house."

"Oh, good idea," Anna said. "You see if he's still here, and I'll call the police."

Shit. It wasn't like I could object to her calling the cops. We'd all been on high alert since Izzy's attack.

Detective Rux grilled us about the importance of reporting anything out of the ordinary. Izzy's office being destroyed definitely qualified, but goddammit, there were too many videos. I'd never get them all deleted in time.

My only choice was to activate the emergency procedure. Both hard drives would be wiped of all footage just as soon as the restore function completed its cycle. I wouldn't be able to see everywhere Val had been but, by the time the crime scene unit arrived, the evidence I wanted to hide would be gone. It'd look like someone hacked in and wiped the data, just like last time.

Fucking great. That wasn't at all suspicious for a security expert.

Chapter Twenty Six
Spencer

"Dad! Wake the fuck up," Drew shouted as he shook me by my shoulders. "You drunk motherfucker. Couldn't even make it upstairs last night, passed out on the couch like the asshole you are."

What the hell? I had to be dreaming. My son wouldn't dare talk to me like that.

Slowly, I sat up, the throbbing in my head an unwelcome side effect of my still half-drunk state. And hell if that didn't tell me this fucking nightmare was real.

Looking up at the red faced boy in front of me, I barked out, "Who the hell do you think you're talking to, *son?*"

"Oh, I don't know, *Dad*, the liar, the cheater, the drunken asshole, or maybe it's the sadist I'm talking to. Who the hell knows with you?"

Sadist.

Hearing that word come out of my son's mouth was a slap in the face. My worst fears were materializing right in front of me, my two worlds colliding in a way I wasn't prepared to handle.

I couldn't let Drew know the truth about me. Not with everything else that was going wrong with my life as of late. Evade, that was the best plan. "Look, Drew, I don't know what you're talking about—"

"Really," Drew interrupted.

Turning around, he picked something up off the table: a box with pink and silver paper.

My heart raced as adrenaline rushed through my veins. He had *the box*. Those goddamn pictures Valerie sent. But how had he gotten them? I'd given them to Dane weeks ago.

"Because I've seen the pictures," Drew snarled as he tossed the box on the couch next to me.

Pictures spilled out onto the cushions as the box tumbled to its side. Only, the pictures that flew out weren't the same ones Izzy showed me. In these, my face was clearly visible. And that wasn't Val I had in leather suspension cuffs.

Sonofabitch!

"Where did you get these?" I demanded.

"Who gives a fuck where I got them?" Drew shouted, the veins in his neck starting to protrude. "You cheated. Then you lied. Then you blamed your divorce on mom." Nodding toward the pile of pictures beside me, he continued, "What happened, Dad, mom wouldn't let you tie her up and do those things to her, so you thought you'd get back at her by flaunting your little hobby?"

Realization hit like a tornado. The room spun around me, my whole world dismantling in the storm. There was nowhere to hide. Drew had seen the pictures. That part of me I'd spent years hiding had been exposed.

"What do you want me to say?" I finally asked. "That I'm sorry I hurt your mom? Sorry that I lied to all of you? Because I am." I buried my head in my hands for a moment to gather my thoughts. Drew deserved more than I'd given him. He deserved to know the truth.

"Hurting your mom was never my intention," I said when I looked up again. "That's actually the reason I started going to clubs, so I *wouldn't* hurt her. No matter how hard I tried, Drew, I couldn't hide who I was anymore. I was miserable. Your mom was miserable."

Tears welled in my eyes at the painful memories of the time when Izzy and I had separated. That was before I found the lifestyle, before I understood who I was and what I needed. "When I found the club, I found peace. And that peace is what finally let me be the husband your mother needed me to be."

"That's it?" Drew snapped. "Cheating saved your marriage, so that makes it okay?"

It was a fair question, not one I ever wanted to have to answer for my eighteen-year-old son, but what choice did I have? Pandora's Box was open, and it was time for me to deal with the wreckage. "Honestly, Drew, I convinced myself it wasn't cheating. It was a way to satisfy that need deep inside me *and* keep your mother safe."

Folding his arms, Drew said, "How do you keep anyone safe when you're drunk all the time? Hell, Mom was attacked, her office destroyed, and where were you? Drunk? Off *playing* with another one of your subs?"

Raw emotions had me snapping out, "No. I've been looking for her."

Drew's jaw twitched. "Looking for who?"

"Ashlan, the girl in the pictures. She's in trouble, and I can't find her." I ran my hands through my hair, the reality of what I'd just said twisting the knife in my heart. "How am I supposed to help her if I can't find her?"

"Maybe she doesn't want you to find her. Maybe she found out you were married and took off. Or maybe she just got tired of playing, Dad. Have you stopped drinking long enough to think about any of that?"

Drew's unrestrained cynicism reminded me of me—granted, a younger, less experienced me—the man I'd been when I was struggling to find peace. "You're right," I said, because it was true. "My drinking has gotten out of control. All this lying and sneaking around and hiding who I am, it sent me over the edge. I'm not making excuses. What I did to you and Anna, to your mother, it was wrong."

"Damn right, it was wrong," he interrupted. "And if Mom wasn't so happy living without you, I'd kick your ass for what you've done to her."

"And I'd deserve everything you had to give, too. But I can't change the past. I can't go back and undo what I've done. Hopefully you can take solace in the fact your mom is happier without me, that my life has gone to hell."

He nodded toward the pictures again. "Yeah...really looks like you're suffering to me."

"Believe me, Drew. I am. Ash is in trouble, and knowing there's nothing I can do to help her is a much worse fate than hell."

As much as I didn't want to look, to see Ash's hooded eyes staring back at me, Drew had seen more than enough. With tears falling in steady streams down my face, I gathered the pictures of a much happier time back into the box, every picture ripping me apart even more. "God, Drew, I just need to find her."

Drew's arms fell to his sides. "What good is finding her unless you get your drinking under control? Seriously, Dad, I mean, do you even remember the fight you had with Alec last night? You almost got yourself arrested. What good will you do anyone from a jail cell?"

Fight with Alec? Jesus, I really did need to stop drinking, and soon.

When I didn't respond, Drew closed the distance he had put between us, plopping down on the couch beside me. "I get it," he said after a long silence. "That need to protect someone you love, I mean," he added quickly. "Not about the other stuff. You know the whole Dom/sub thing. I'm still trying to understand all of that..."

Drew leaned his head against the back of the couch, his feet coming to a rest on the table in front of us. Looking up at the ceiling he asked, "Is it always like that? The BDSM lifestyle, I mean. Is love just part of the package?"

Drew's question had my senses tingling. I'd expected anger, not curiosity. Still, some things were just better left unsaid. "Let's not do this, okay? Talking about my life at the club isn't going to help anything."

Ignoring what I'd said, Drew continued. "When I saw those pictures, do you know what I felt?"

I thanked God I wasn't naked in the pictures Drew had seen. That would only make the whole situation that much worse. While I didn't know for sure what he'd felt when he opened that box, I had a pretty good idea— shock, surprise, disbelief, anger. "Drew—"

"Excitement, Dad," he spit out, stress thick in his strained tone. "That's what I felt when I saw that woman cuffed and bound."

That wasn't something I'd expected to hear.

Turning his head until he was facing me, Drew went on. "Do you have any idea how fucked up that is? I mean, she's *your* sub, tied up and waiting for *you*, and there I was with a fucking hard-on."

At whatever thought that went through Drew's mind, all color drained from his face. When he sat up, he looked like he'd seen a ghost.

I opened my mouth to tell him his reaction to seeing a beautiful woman was natural, that there was nothing for him to be ashamed of—when a horrifying thought came to mind. There was only one person who could've taken those pictures. Suddenly, finding out where Drew got them was a top priority.

Lifting the closed box, I asked, "Where did you get these, Drew?"

Only, Drew wasn't listening, lost in the torment of his own confession. "When she saw my reaction, she said it was in my blood. When she offered to teach me, I couldn't say no....and now everything is so messed up."

Teach him?

He's playing with a switch?

No. No. No. No. No! My blood began to boil. There was only one switch I knew who would take a newbie as her Dom.

Fucking Val. That bitch!

I'll fucking kill her.

As soon as I got my hands on Val, I planned to wrap my fingers around her damn neck and squeeze every last drop of breath from her, not letting up until her body hung lifeless in my grip. She was playing with my goddamn son!

"I want you to stop seeing her, Drew," I said when air returned to my lungs. "Val is bad news. She's the one who sent those pictures to your mother. She's only doing this to hurt me. She doesn't care about you. When she gets her revenge, she'll toss you aside and move on to her next victim."

Drew's hands fisted in his lap. "No, Dad, she won't. That's the problem. I tried to tell her what we'd done was a mistake. That it was just too weird because she's mom's friend, but she won't stay away. I even told her I'd found someone new, but that didn't work, either. Now, I don't know what to do."

My head was still spinning from what Drew just told me. How dare Val seduce my son? Eighteen or not, he was still a kid. He called her Aunt Val, for Christ's sake. "Ignore her calls, and if she shows up again, call me. I don't care what time it is. I'll deal with Valerie."

Oh, I'll deal with her, alright.

Chapter Twenty Seven
Spencer

True to my word, I'd stayed away from alcohol since my talk with Drew, which was a hell of a lot harder than I'd thought it was going to be. If not for the support of my new friends down at the Dry Dock, a local alcoholics anonymous meeting place, I never would have made it past the first day, much less the first month. Although I was still using the one-day-at-a-time approach, every day that passed without me taking a drink made me feel that much stronger.

Getting that thirty day chip really opened my eyes to a lot of things, or maybe it was just thirty days of sobriety, but either way, I realized how fucked up I'd let my life become. Drew was right. Drinking had started to control my emotions and, in turn, had been controlling my life.

The problem was, Doms weren't supposed to be controlled by their emotions and especially not by mind altering drugs. Too bad I'd had to hit rock bottom before I remembered that.

Giving up the bottle helped me see clearly for the first time in...hell, I couldn't even remember the last time I'd seen things without the fog of bourbon.

Things had been tense with Drew the first couple weeks of my sobriety. He'd completely avoided me at first, but after the initial shock of knowing my secret wore off, he came around more and the awkward tension between us started to fade. We'd even made great strides in repairing our relationship. In a strange way, my being exposed was a blessing.

After hearing more about Drew's time with Valerie, I was even more anxious to wring her damn neck. So far, all attempts to get ahold of her had failed. Even my unannounced visits to her apartment had been unsuccessful. Dane hadn't had any luck, either. Damn bitch was smart. She hadn't made a single credit card transaction or ATM withdrawal in over a month. Don't ask me how she managed to survive so long without money, but she'd found a way to do it.

Last night, Dane dropped a bomb on me. He'd come across some information that suggested Val might've been involved in Ashlan's disappearance. I knew the name Charlie Barnes had sounded familiar when I first heard it. He'd been Valerie's first husband, and the lead medical examiner that performed her supposed autopsy.

Even worse, Dane tracked the source of Ashlan's new identity, Lily Walker. Turns out, it was Val's connection that'd gotten her that. I was willing to bet Val planned the whole damn thing: Ash's death, framing Diego. If she had anything do with why Ash was hiding from me....

Fuck! I didn't know what the hell I'd do.

If there was one place I was certain Val would show up at, it was the twin's graduation. Hell, her new boy toy was graduating. No way would she miss that.

I'm sure she can't wait to celebrate with him.

The mere thought of her hands on my kid sent shivers down my spine.

"Bogey at nine o'clock," Dane said, the earpiece he'd fitted me with working loud and clear.

A glance to the left and there she was.

Valerie.

I knew she wouldn't be able to stay away. "Copy that," I said into the tiny mic inside my cuff link. I was doing my best to sound cool and calm, but on the inside fire raged through my veins.

The tension in my voice hadn't gone unnoticed with Colonel Dane. "Keep your cool, brother. This isn't the time to lose your shit. Try to remember why you're here. Okay?"

There was no time to respond, not that I even wanted to. Dane had no idea what I was going through. Let's see how he'd handle things if Val was messing around with his son. We'd see who lost their shit then.

Before I could even breathe, Val was standing in front of me. "Hey, Spence," she said, her hands running greedily over my shoulders down to my biceps. "I was hoping to get to see you today. There's so much for us to talk about."

"Cut the shit, Val." Shrugging her hands off me, I continued. "We both know you've been avoiding my calls for weeks. Where's Ashlan? What the hell did you do to her?"

Val ran her long, red nail from my temple to the corner of my mouth, the soft pad of her finger coming to rest against my bottom lip. She pressed firmly, urging me to open.

I resisted, at first. The mere thought of tasting her skin had my stomach ready to revolt. The punch to my gut got her what she wanted, though.

My mouth dropped open as I took a breath from Val's unexpected heavy hit, and she slipped her finger inside my mouth, quickly finding my tongue. I bit down, temporarily trapping the digit in place before yanking it out of my mouth.

"Enough!" I growled. "Your games aren't going to work this time, Val. Just tell me where the hell Ashlan is, and then get the fuck out of here."

Val smiled, a slow, devious grin covering her face. "Oh, Spence," she said, "haven't you figured it out by now? This isn't a game to me. It's revenge."

"Revenge for what? For my being married? For ending things? Because you—"

Val's spiked heel connected with my shin shutting me down instantly. "How many times did you tell me you were leaving Izzy?" she snapped. "How many times did you say you were tired of living a lie? I waited for you, Spencer."

The volume of her voice seemed to be rising with every word she spewed out. People were starting to stare, but Val didn't care. She made that perfectly clear when she continued. "I became a *sub,* for *you!* All because I knew, that one day, you'd finally be mine. And how do you repay me for all I've done for you? For introducing you to the lifestyle that set you free, for putting you in touch with the Dom you were born to be? For waiting patiently while you fucked my best friend?"

Val paused to suck in a breath before continuing. "By fucking lying to me! By leading me on. By toying with my emotions! And you think this is a *game?*"

My head spun from Val's verbal lashing. Before I could formulate a response, Dane's voice sounded in my ear. "Get out of there, Spencer. You two are making a scene. Place the tracker and go."

Dane was right. That's exactly what I needed to do. Unfortunately, my mouth had other plans. "I never lied to you, Val," I said, ignoring the grunt in my ear. "I meant all those things. I tried to leave Izzy, I really did. But even if I had, we wouldn't be together in the way you wanted. Our relationship would always only be in the club, and I never pretended otherwise. You knew the score and made the choice to play with me anyway. That's on you. It's Ash I love. Now tell me where she is!"

Val's nostrils flared as she took deep, deliberate breaths. Her eyes had narrowed so far I wondered how she could even see. After a few long seconds, she opened them again. I wasn't surprised to see her composure had returned. Her eyes even managed a smile. "Drew really enjoyed his graduation gift backstage. Ask him about it later. And make sure he doesn't leave anything out." She leaned close and whispered in my ear, the one with the fucking earpiece. "Not one flick of my tongue, not one thrust of his hips... Mmmm. Not one drop of..."

As soon as the air returned to my lungs, all control slipped. "Goddamn you, Val! He's a fucking kid."

"She's baiting you, Spencer. You need to place the damn tracker and get out of there. Now keep your shit together and get the job done!"

Dane's words came just in time. I'd been milliseconds away from blowing my top. Val was never going to help me find Ashlan. I sure as hell didn't want to hear another word about what happened backstage. Not from her, and sure as hell not as the graduates were being led to their seats. I leaned in and whispered in Val's ear, my hand brushing ever so lightly against her favorite diamond studded earrings, just enough to plant the microscopic device without her noticing. "You're playing with fire, Val. Stay away from my son."

It was a command and a warning all rolled into one.

She understood.

"Not until it's gone, Spencer. All of it. You played me. Now it's my turn. You know...that whole eye for an eye shit. You stole my innocence that weekend in Miami, and I stole Drew's. You broke my heart. Now I'm going to crush yours. Mark my words, Spencer James, by the time I'm done with you, you'll feel every ounce of pain you've put me through."

"Get out of there!" Dane shouted in my ear. "She's baiting you. She *wants* to make a scene, Spencer. Val loves the show, the attention. Trust me, nothing good will come of this. You have to leave. NOW."

As much as I hated to admit it, Dane was right. I couldn't let Val cause an even bigger scene in the middle of the auditorium as the ceremony was starting. Without another word, I walked away.

"You'll regret this, Spencer." Val called after me, but I didn't turn around. There was nothing else to say to her.

The GPS was planted. All there was to do now was hope Val would lead me to Ashlan.

Chapter Twenty Eight
Ashlan

Staying away from Spencer was a lot harder the second time around. Maybe it was because that tortured look I'd seen on his face haunted me every time I closed my eyes. Or maybe it was because I'd had to give up Tony and Cowboy too. I mean, sure, either man would still offer help if they knew I needed it, but that wasn't the same as having them around, and it certainly didn't make me any less lonely. Really, any of those things could have made it harder to accept my new life, but they hadn't. Deep down, I knew my heart ached because I'd never see Spencer again.

Working helped. Some. It gave me a reason to get out of bed, anyway, and a place I was expected to be. It wasn't much, but at least it was something.

Rod had quickly become my new best friend. Tony told me I could trust him, and I had. Instantly. He'd given me a job, just like Tony said he would. And when he found out I'd spent the night in one of the shipping containers down at the pier, he gave me a place to stay—after he chewed me out for being a 'dumb-ass'. And when I insisted on getting an apartment of my own, it was Rod who drove me all over town looking for one I could afford in a section of town that wasn't too dangerous.

Rod also introduced me to Dawn, the volunteer coordinator at the local teen crisis center where I now volunteered three days a week. Hearing the stories of what the teens there had faced seemed to give my past purpose. God had put this opportunity in my path, let me use my experiences to give others strength and knowledge, so hopefully they could escape at least some of the evil they were up against.

Hearing their stories also helped me see what Tony had said all along.

I was strong.

I was worthy of the kind of love that included respect, in all things. That hurtful words and constant control and physical abuse weren't acceptable.

More importantly, in a few short weeks, I'd come to understand that none of the abuse I'd ever endured was my fault. I didn't cause it, and I sure as hell hadn't deserved any of it.

Like a true friend, Rod had never pushed me for information about my past, but I suspected he knew more than I was ready to admit. Ironically, it was the fact that he hadn't pushed me for answers that proved he knew more than he let on. He was afraid to scare me.

Of course, it was *me* who ended up scaring *him*...with an embarrassing scene that included me getting drunk, stripping down to my bra and panties, and then throwing myself at him.

Literally.

Thank God Rod had been strong enough to catch me without either of us getting hurt. That would've made the sting of hearing he was gay hurt more than it had.

I'd been disappointed when he first told me he wasn't interested in women...mostly because I was drunk...and horny didn't even begin to describe the constant tingling between my legs the past few days.

Luckily, Rod had the good manners not to make a big deal about me throwing myself at him, and then he let me cry on his shoulder afterwards...because, damn, he was smokin' hot. All six foot something with muscles to spare...shaved head, smooth, chocolate skin...

Oh, God.

"Are you even listening to me?"

Busted. "Sorry, I was ogling your ass. What'd you say?"

Rod gave me a hard stare, followed by his signature charming smile. He liked the attention, even if I didn't have the right equipment to get him off. "Why do you torture yourself like that, baby girl? You're just ruining it for all the other men out there. You know, men who are..." He waved his hands over me... "Into all that."

I couldn't help the laugh that escaped. Rod had such a way with words. "Can't blame me for looking," I said when I finally stopped laughing. "Now, what was it you wanted me to hear?"

He grabbed my slender wrist in his much larger hand and pulled me closer to him. "Stand here. I'll just show you."

At my nod, Rod fitted the protective earmuffs over my ears. When his were in place, he picked up the Glock Tony had insisted I keep and demonstrated how to position my hands, then my feet. Rod reached for the loaded magazine, waving it in front of me as if what he was about to show me was important, then shoved the clip into the pistol.

One final look at me, then Rod turned toward the target, lifted his arms, took aim, and fired. Shot after shot left the end of the gun, each one louder than the next. Even with the protective covering, the shots rang so loud in my ears I thought they might bleed. It was the vibration running through my body that made it all worthwhile.

When the clip was empty, Rod returned the weapon to the gun bench in the shooting stall and turned to me. I'd already taken the earmuffs off, so I had no trouble hearing him when he said, "Okay, your turn."

I didn't hesitate. Tony had made sure I knew how to use the weapon before we ever left California, so I wasn't worried. "Okay." I pushed my way in front of Rod and covered my eyes and ears with protective gear. In a move Tony would be proud of—I inserted a new clip, took stance, chambered a round, and then emptied the clip in three tight groupings on the target's head, chest, and groin.

"*Okay...,*" Rod said, slowly. "That was..."

"Awesome," I supplied. "Amazing. Cool as shit."

"Well, I was going to say unexpected, but yeah, what you said, too." He held the button that would return the target to the firing line where we stood. "How'd you learn how to shoot like that?"

"Tony," I said, before I could stop myself. "My...um...brother."

"You've been holding out on me, baby girl. I didn't know you had a brother." He gave me a hard stare. "What else don't I know about you?"

Dammit, me and my big mouth.

Before Rod could demand an answer, I moved the target back in place, picked up the Glock, and proceeded to empty two more clips.

• • • • •

Spencer

Why the hell did I let Anna talk me into such a big party? I should've known when she asked that she was down-playing the whole thing to get me to say yes. I couldn't even blame alcohol for the decision that time, either.

Thank God.

But still, I was such an idiot for actually believing Anna was capable of planning a 'small, intimate gathering with a few friends.' Small party my ass. In the end, the guest list had over a hundred names on it.

After the fight I had with Val at the graduation ceremony, I wasn't in the mood to entertain anything but a tall glass of Jack. Unfortunately, there wasn't a drop of the soothing elixir in the house. I'd thrown it all out the day I found out my uncontrolled drinking had ultimately led a sexual predator right into my son's bed.

I wasn't exactly happy with Drew right now, either. He was supposed to call me if that bitch tried to contact him. From what Val told me at the ceremony, it sure as hell sounded like she'd had more than *contact* with him.

Alec's security detail surrounded the perimeter in their all-too-obvious black suits, thin black ties, and earpieces. If you asked me, it was over the top, even for a control freak like Alec Payne. Not to mention, having them around was really starting to piss me off.

Wouldn't you fucking know it? Thinking about the bastard sleeping with my ex-wife had conjured him up like some damn magic trick.

Seeing Izzy and Alec together shredded the last bit of my self-control. This time when then waiter walked by carrying the full tray of champagne I didn't hesitate, lifting two glasses from the shiny silver surface.

To hell with sobriety.

From the tight bubbles forming in the champagne flute, I knew Anna had spared no expense when planning the party. Then again, I hadn't told her to. After Alec bought her a brand new car, I would have done anything to make my princess happy, including letting her paint the foyer crimson red and my new pool room jet black.

Grabbing a third glass of champagne, I headed inside, hoping someone had thought to bring something a little stronger.

And wouldn't you know it...

Hello, old friend.

Once that familiar buzz caught hold, there was no turning back. Jack and I were like thunder and lightning.

We belonged together.

Four shots in and I still wasn't ready to entertain. I poured myself a double and took a seat at the bar Anna had installed. How ironic that a guy who was supposed to be on the wagon had a brand new bar installed in his house? A bar that was surprisingly damn near fully stocked for the party.

Once again, the devil had tempted me.

And this time he won.

A familiar voice outside the door caught my attention. *Izzy.* Fucking great. I'd hoped, prayed even, that she wouldn't come. Sure, it was ridiculous of me to think she wouldn't, but that hadn't stopped me from doing it anyway.

Izzy stepped through the door, Alec's arm draped protectively over her shoulder, no doubt, from what happened the last time they were both here. Fuck, I couldn't even remember that fight.

"Do you like what I've done in here?" I asked, trying to sound casual. By the way Izzy jumped, I'd say my attempt had failed.

"My office," she gasped, the shock of what I'd done in the room written all over her face. "What have you done to my office?"

I couldn't help but laugh, the alcohol disabling my brain-to-mouth filter. "It's not your office anymore, Bella."

"Spencer, how could you? This is still half my house, and you know how much I love this room."

The bourbon that filled my veins acted as a truth serum. I no longer cared where I was or who was around to hear me speaking the cold, hard truth. "I couldn't stand the constant reminder of you, Bella." I slammed back another shot. "I changed it all, every room, every memory."

Izzy ran out of the room, tears streaming down her face, no doubt from the shock of seeing the changes I made to *her* office, or maybe it was my grating tone. Either way, I didn't give a damn. She'd made her choice to give up the space when she decided to play house with her new client.

Alec, who'd stayed behind when Izzy fled the newly decorated space, turned his attention to me. "Sober up, asshole. That's the mother of your children you're talking to, and this is their graduation party. The last thing they need is for you to get drunk and show your ass."

I slammed back another shot.

Fuck you, Alec Payne.

Chapter Twenty Nine
Spencer

Alec was right to put me in my place. I'd done exactly what I swore I'd never do again. I'd let my emotions control me then proceeded to get shit faced drunk. By the time the party ended, at least, I'd managed to sober up enough to make an appearance. Which was good, considering my parents were staying over.

Gladys James wouldn't much care for the drunken idiot I'd become. Mom never could accept that I wasn't perfect, no matter how many times my dad told her I wasn't.

Good ol' Steve James was one hard motherfucker. Third generation Marine veteran, he'd lived a focused life. From the time he was born, he knew he'd be a Marine. When I opted for college over the Corps, I thought Colonel James may never forgive me. He might not have, if it hadn't been for Izzy and the twins.

My cousin, Cathy, had decided to stay at the house too. Cathy and I were more like twins than cousins. Only a month separated us in birth, plus, we'd grown up next door to each other. Practically inseparable for most of our lives, Cathy knew me better than anyone, which is how she knew I was full of shit about why Izzy left me. All night she'd been asking questions, picking apart mom's story piece by piece.

"Drop the act, Spencer," Cathy said as soon as we settled into the patio chairs, alone. "What really happened between you and Izzy?"

Resting my elbows on my knees, I dropped my head into my hands. I was done hiding the truth, even from my family. "I'm an asshole."

"No shit, Spence, but why'd she leave?"

"I've been lying to Izzy for years, Cat. Hiding who I really was while sneaking around behind her back, having sex with other women." I sat up and looked Cathy in the eyes. "I'm not like other men. I've got this dark side. This side that craves things Izzy would never understand."

"You don't know what Izzy would understand, Spencer. She's a tough girl."

"Actually, I *do* know. She filed for divorce the second she found out the truth. She didn't even give me a chance to explain."

"Explain what? That you lied? That you've been cheating on her for years? I meant, you should have told her sooner, you dumbass. Of course she filed for divorce now. You *cheated* on her. You hid things from her, only proving you knew it was wrong, yet you continued to do it. Hell, if you ask me, I say you're lucky divorcing you is all she did. If a man ever pulls that shit on me, I'll cut off his dick and feed it to the dog."

A smile crossed Cathy's face, her attempt to lighten the mood working. "Seriously, though, if this life you're talking about was so important to you, you should have been honest with your wife about it. She may have still divorced your sorry ass, but at least you could've felt good about being honest instead of drinking yourself silly as the guilt eats you up inside."

Cathy didn't know the half of it. The guilt that was eating me up right now had nothing to do with Izzy. What I'd done was shitty, but she'd moved on. Izzy was a fighter. Not even my betrayal had kept her down.

Ashlan was who I was worried sick about. I'd let her go. Let her walk right out of Esoteric after she told me she'd been abused. That's the guilt that ripped me apart inside.

• • • • •

"What!" I snapped into the receiver, the constant ringing of my phone waking me from a deep, alcohol induced sleep.

"Get your ass out of bed, man. Nate's been arrested."

"Arrested?" I asked, my mind still playing catch-up at three in the morning.

"I'm tracking a lead with Cowboy, so I need you to go bail his dumb ass out of jail."

A lead? That was the first piece of good news I'd heard in days. "What's the lead? How can I help?"

Dane exhaled into the phone. "You can start by following orders. Get your ass to New York. Nate knows how to find Ash."

That was all I needed to hear. If it could help find Ashlan, I'd do anything Dane wanted.

I hopped out of bed and made a beeline for the dresser. Three minutes later I'd dressed, drug a toothbrush through my mouth, and was heading down the stairs. Thank God Cathy stayed over last night. She'd be able to smooth things over with my parents when they woke and found me gone. I tapped out a quick text to her as I waited for the gate to open.

Fucking gate! I squeezed through the narrow opening too soon, scraping the side of my truck all the way down the bed. I didn't care. Finding Ash was all that mattered.

Dane hadn't bothered to fill me in on the details of Nate's arrest, so while I waited for my flight to board I went online to find the arrest record. Another benefit of James' Security was the ability to run a nationwide background check at a moment's notice. All I had to do was login to my desktop remotely, and I'd have what I was after.

It took less than a minute to queue up Nate's arrest record. Less than one goddamn minute to tell me Nate was a bigger bastard than I could've even imagined. Charged with a class B felony, *Criminal possession of a dangerous weapon,* that sonofabitch was arrested while placing an explosive device at Alec's apartment. Not to mention, he was the lead suspect in a string of break-ins at Payne Enterprises, one of which ended in an explosion that injured several people. Master Nate, my ass, the stupid motherfucker. What if Izzy had been there, or worse, one of my kids?

"Sonofabitch," I barked out, which elicited more than one gasp from nearby passengers. Normally, I would have cared, probably even apologized, but not now. Not after reading Nate was wanted for questioning in Florida for Izzy's attack.

The rage inside me built to dangerous levels. At that moment, I swore if Nate had anything to do with what happened to Izzy, I'd fucking kill him, just as soon as he told me where the hell Ashlan was.

• • • • •

Waiting had never been my strong suit. Add in my desperate need to find out what Nate knew and my half-drunk state with the fact that the damn flight attendant had already cut me off, and the fucking plane couldn't fly fast enough. I wanted answers, dammit! And I wanted them now.

By the time I was in a cab headed for central booking, I'd decided I wanted answers before I bailed Nate out of jail. If he had anything to do with what happened to Izzy or with Ash's disappearance, I'd not only leave him in jail, I'd nail his ass to the wall. Nate and I shared a bond, a brotherhood only another Dom could understand. A betrayal like either of those would be unforgivable.

"How much farther?" I snapped.

Poor cabbie, it wasn't his fault. No, my foul mood at the moment had everything to do with Nate.

"Three more blocks, sir."

Three more blocks. Three more blocks to get my shit together. I couldn't go charging into the police station like a raging bull. I'd wind up in a cell of my own.

Two more blocks.

Breathe.

"This isn't the time to lose your shit." Dane's words came as a welcome reminder.

One more block.

Breathe.

There had to be a logical explanation for Nate's involvement in all of this, *right?*

One final deep breath and we were pulling up outside the police station.

"That'll be $65.41," the taxi driver said. I handed him a hundred dollar bill and climbed out of his cab. He'd earned every penny of that tip.

The inside of the station was bigger than I'd pictured it, but no less busy. I took my place in line and fucking waited.

And waited.

And then waited some more.

"Can I help you?" the officer at the empty window asked me, indicating it was finally my turn.

About damn time.

Trying to look more confident than I felt, I stepped up to the window. "My friend was arrested. I came to bail him out."

"Inmate's name?"

"Tyler Philips," I said, giving the man the alias Nate had used. "But I'd like to talk to him before I post his bail."

"Absolutely, sir. Inmates are allowed visitors on Wednesdays and Thursdays. You come back then and see your friend."

Sonofabitch. I couldn't wait four more days, not when Nate had information about Ash. I had to talk to him, and it couldn't wait. "Never mind. I'll go ahead and bail him out now."

• • • • •

Three hours and two cab rides later, after going to the bail bondsman's office and back, Nate and I were in yet another taxi headed back to the airport, me with a two thousand dollar hole in my bank account and Nate with a story to tell.

"You wanna tell me what the hell this is all about?" I said before we'd gotten fifty feet from the police station. "Are you working with Val?"

"Don't start with me, Spencer," Nate snapped. "Do you have any idea what I've been through since yesterday?" He turned toward me, deep wrinkles covering his forehead. "I was arrested for trying to blow up a damn apartment building. And did I mention I'm the prime suspect in a whole bunch of other shit I knew nothing about before today?"

Nate's nostrils flared, the anger inside him ready to explode. "She played me, man. That package I delivered today, I thought it contained divorce papers! Val told me that guy, Alec whoever the fuck he is, was her husband. Said he'd been dodging the process server for months so he could hide his millions before she divorced him. I had no fucking clue there were explosives in that box. Someone could have been killed! Hell, *I* could have been killed."

Nate's reaction told me what I need to know. I'd never seen him loose his cool like that before. He couldn't fake that kind of emotion if he tried. Still, there were a couple of things I had to know before I could put this behind us. "Did you break into my house? Attack my ex-wife?"

"Are you kidding me right now, Spencer? Of course I didn't. I'd never hurt a woman like that. You should know that."

Ignoring his irate tone, I continued my questioning. "What about Ash? Did you have anything to do with her disappearance?"

Slowly, Nate shook his head. "No. But I know where she is."

The space inside the cab began closing in around me. Nate knew? All this time I'd been searching for her and he fucking knew!

"This isn't the time to lose your shit." Dane's familiar words filled my head once more, tightening the grip on my rage. There'd be time to hear his lame ass excuse for keeping me from Ashlan later. Right now, he held the key to my whole fucking life: finding her.

"Spencer, are you still with me?"

I shook the fuzz out of my head then nodded. "Just tell me where she is."

"What do you think I just did, if you'd pay attention," he barked. "She's living in Galveston. Goes by the name Stephanie Reynolds. Works nights as a bartender at the Fisherman's Wharf. Volunteers with a local crisis center during the day. How much clearer do I need to be?"

Chapter Thirty
Spencer

Dane set me up with a flight into the Coast Guard station in Galveston where he and Cowboy planned to meet me later. As a condition of his release, Nate had to fly straight back to Chicago while the police sorted things out.

Before Nate left New York, he sent a private investigator he knew in Galveston to stake out the restaurant where Ashlan worked with orders not to let her out of his sight. Given that Ash had faked her own death to get away from her ex-husband, we all agreed approaching her at work would be too risky.

When I agreed to the plan, I hadn't expected Ash to still be working after midnight. I'd spent practically the whole damn day waiting. And it was fucking killing me. I was so close to Ash I could almost taste her, every last inch of her.

Not now, asshole.

Fuck. Now was not the time for a hard-on. I had to stay focused for when the PI called, which had to be soon.

Not knowing how Ash planned to get home had my inner Dom on high alert. I already knew there were no busses this late. I'd checked the schedule as soon as I found out she didn't have a car registered under any of her aliases.

Surely, she wasn't planning on walking this time of night.

When the pacing I'd been doing no longer calmed me, I began firing questions at Dane. "Is he sure she's still there? I mean, absolutely certain? What if she left without him seeing?"

Dane put his hands on my shoulders, stopping me in my tracks. "I get it, man. Really. But you need to calm the fuck down. You've been pacing around like a caged animal for over an hour, and it hasn't done a damn bit of good." Dane pulled his hands back. "This isn't the time to lose your shit, Spencer. Nate wouldn't have sent this guy if he didn't know what he was doing." He pointed at the chair he'd vacated moments ago. "Now sit down and let the man do his job."

I sat without another word. It was Lieutenant Colonel Ronnie Dane who'd shown up tonight. Retired or not, he took his job seriously. I wasn't about to cross him knowing he was fully loaded and ready for battle.

Besides, he was right, this wasn't the time to lose my shit. I needed to keep my cool for Ash. The last thing I wanted to do was scare her off like I'd done before.

An hour later Dane got the call. Nate's PI had gotten a look at Ash's address on the paycheck inside her purse. He hadn't said how he managed that, but I didn't care how he got the address. The only thing that mattered right now was getting to Ash before someone else did, especially since she was walking home.

Alone!

Dane, Cowboy, and I wasted no time getting to Ash's apartment, a run-down complex near the pier. The only plus about the place was its close proximity to the Coast

Guard Station. It had taken us less than fifteen minutes to get to the dilapidated building she called home.

Until now, that is.

There was no way I was letting the woman I loved live in a shithole. All it'd take was one strong wind and the buildings in her complex would fall like dominoes.

"Cowboy, you'll knock on the door," Dane said, interrupting my errant thoughts. "Spencer and I will wait over there for the all clear." He pointed to an overgrown bush a few buildings away. Cowboy nodded in acknowledgement then headed for Ash's apartment while Dane and I took cover so we could *wait* some more.

Every second that passed as we waited for Ash to get home felt like an eternity. Where was she? What was taking her so long? Had anyone followed her? The only thing that kept me from losing my shit was the knowledge that Nate's PI was tailing her. Any sign of danger and he'd step in. That was all the comfort I was going to get.

• • • • •

Ashlan

"See ya tomorrow, Steph," Rod called after me as I was leaving, that southern twang of his still making me smile even after a night as long as we'd both had.

"Night," I called back, giving him a big wave.

Working with Rod had been a blessing in disguise these past few months. Turns out, running from Spencer was a lot harder than I'd imagined. If it hadn't been for Rod, I don't know if I would have survived.

Walking home late on Saturday nights, alone, was the only part of my job I didn't like. It drove Rod crazy, too. He finally stopped badgering me about it last weekend after our trip to the range. One look at my paper target and he'd finally agreed I was perfectly safe on my own.

The only problem: I didn't feel safe at all. If Diego ever found me, I'd be dead before I could get the Glock out of my purse.

I'd resisted the idea of carrying a gun when Tony first suggested it but after he taught me to shoot, I came around. There's something to be said about a woman being able to protect herself. Diego was living proof of that need. If I'd known how to handle a weapon back then, my life could've been much different.

Lately, shooting had become my substitute for sex, those vibrations flowing through my body, making me tingle in all the right places.

Damn. I *needed* sex, not that vanilla, boring shit men offered me every night at work, but the kinky kind I craved. For that, though, I needed the safety of a club. Unfortunately, that was out of the question right now. Working at the Wharf paid the bills and that was about it. Until I found a better job, I'd just have to keep going to the range.

Thank God my apartment was close to work. After volunteering all morning then working a double shift at the restaurant, I was too beat to walk very far.

It was nights like these that made me forget my apartment was smaller than any place I'd ever lived, even as a kid. One bedroom, one bath with a kitchen barely big enough to turn around in, the closet sized living room the only thing differentiating the place from an efficiency unit. It was better than sleeping in the shipping container I'd used on my first night in town, though. And the independence that came with having my own place made me love the tiny space.

A dark figure caught my attention as I rounded the final corner to my building. Instinctively, I pressed myself up against the wall, sliding my hand inside my purse. Whoever that was lurking around my door, I wasn't about to face him alone.

Holding onto the gun like my life depended on it, I chambered a round, just like Tony taught me.

Leaving the safety of the building, I made a move toward my door, the weight of the weapon in my hand a reminder of how strong I'd become. It was that confidence that carried me those last few steps in the dark toward the unknown.

"Move and I'll shoot," I said in my best southern drawl.

"Jesus, Ash. It's me, Cowboy. There's no call for all of that."

No. No. No. No. No. How the hell did he find me? I'd followed all of Tony's rules this time, every damn one of them. I'd even cut my hair and dyed it this ridiculous shade of black. Yet still, Cowboy had managed to find me. And if he could track me down, so could one of Diego's men.

Evade. That's what Tony would do.

I dialed up the accent a notch. "Wrong answer, buddy. Name's not Ash."

"Oh yeah," he snorted. "Then what is it?"

"Stephanie," I snapped. "Not that it's any of your damn business."

Cowboy took a step closer. "Are you sure? You don't look much like a Stephanie to me."

Shut him down, Ash.

The longer I kept talking, the better the odds he'd figure out my accent wasn't real. I couldn't let Cowboy know who I really was, not unless I wanted to run—again.

And I didn't.

My life had been tossed and turned enough. I was happy living here, happy to be volunteering at the crisis center. Hell, I was even happy to be working at the Wharf. I didn't want to run. Not anymore!

Waving the pistol slightly to the left, I said, "You don't get outta here in the next five seconds and it won't matter what the hell you think anymore. Now beat it!"

His energy surrounded me before his deep vibrato. "Ashlan, lower your weapon."

Without even a thought, I did as my Dom commanded, my mind warring against my body, causing my limbs to shake. All the work I'd done to keep us both safe, ruined by one single command.

Quickly, Spencer moved in from behind me and took the gun from my hands. I hadn't tried to stop him. How could I? Master Spence spoke to my body on a level I didn't understand. He held the power to command my every move.

The world around me faded away as Spencer's arms tightened around my waist, my back pressed firmly against his chest. Neither of us said a word. But we didn't need to.

Standing on the porch, wrapped in the safety of Master Spence's arms, I collapsed, my whole body going limp at once. All the stress of hiding, of pretending to be someone I wasn't, of trying not to think about Spencer, released in the arms of the man I loved.

I love him.

Oh, God. I did love him. No matter how much I'd tried not to. I hadn't been able to stop myself from loving Spencer.

"I've got you," Master Spence whispered as he scooped me into his arms—strong, powerful arms—that held me ever so tenderly.

Silent tears ran down my face.

Spencer.

He's really here.

My Dom found me.

Chapter Thirty One
Ashlan

Light from the neon sign across the street peered through the thin curtains in my bedroom.

My bedroom? What the hell?

I jolted upright in bed, eyes darting from left to right and back again as I scanned the room. How did I get in bed? Screw that, how did I get home? Or in to my pajamas?

I squeezed my eyes closed, looking for answers I couldn't find.

"Welcome back, sunshine."

One sound of Spencer's voice and all the memories of what happened last night came rushing in with a vengeance: the shadow, the gun, Cowboy, Master Spence.

Oh, God. No. No. No. He can't be here.

It couldn't be Spencer. My mind had to be playing tricks on me. After everything I'd done to hide my identity, there was no way he could have found me.

My eyes flew open.

Spencer.

Three steps and he was standing beside the bed, so close I could feel the heat radiating from his body.

No. No. No. Didn't he know how dangerous his being here was—for both of us?

Spencer pulled my hand into his, and I lost it. He had to go. Now! One more minute and I wouldn't be able to stand letting him leave.

And he *had* to go.

My body declared war with my mind. The wild sensual scent of black leather and Jamaican run filled the space. Every breath I pulled through my nostrils had my sex pulsing.

Pulling my hand away quickly, I said, "You have to go—"

Spencer dropped down onto the bed beside me. "Not a chance, Ash. I'm not going anywhere." He pulled my hand into his once again, holding it tighter that time so I couldn't easily pull away. "I spent months thinking I'd never see you again. But then I did, and you fucking ran."

Spencer's eyes closed, a shiver rocking his body. Seven long, silent seconds passed before he opened them again. With control in his voice, he continued. "Now that I've found you, now that I've held you in my arms again, sunshine, I'm never going to let you go."

Cupping my face in his hands, he angled my head then leaned in and kissed my lips. A soft, tender kiss that spoke of passion and love and forever, the kind of kiss that shot electric sparks to all the right places, that gripped my heart with a strength strong enough to protect us both. It was the kiss I'd always dreamt of, and the kiss I knew I'd never get.

But there it was.

Oh, God. How will I ever let him go now?

"Ash," Spencer whispered when he pulled away, trailing slow, sensual kisses down my neck.

Goosebumps covered every inch of my exposed skin, and the tingling in my sex already had me ready to beg.

Every kiss, every feather light touch of his hands along my sensitized skin increased the throb.

God how I'd missed his touch.

When he reached my collarbone I couldn't stand it any longer. The ache in my sex was too strong to ignore. "Spencer," I gasped.

His only response came in the form of more sensual torture. His tongue circled my hardened nipple, not seeming to care that my pajama top stood in the way. His teeth closed ever so gently, eliciting an involuntary moan from deep inside me. A raw, primal sound I didn't even recognize. It'd been too long since I felt the touch of my Dom. Strong, experienced hands ready to send me over the edge.

Only it wasn't my Dom touching me.

It was Spencer, sweet, sensual, taking-way-to-long-to-savor-the-moment, Spencer.

One touch was all I needed. Just one touch to the swollen nub between my legs and I'd be flying higher than I'd ever flown before.

As if sensing my need, he bit harder.

"Ahhhhhhh," I screamed, not caring how desperate my voice sounded or that the neighbors most definitely could hear me through the too thin walls. Right now I needed Spencer more than I needed privacy or dignity or maybe even air.

I'm going to explode. "Please, Spencer," I moaned. "I need you inside me. Hard. Fast. Now!"

He looked up, heat dripping from his eyes. Not out of anger or frustration that I hadn't called him sir. We weren't in a scene, and the way he touched me—with the hands of a lover—told me he wasn't looking for my submission.

Without saying a word, Spencer ripped his shirt off, unbuckled his belt, and opened his jeans. The sight of his toned chest did nothing for the ache I was feeling down south.

"Naked. Now," he ordered, his deep vibrato causing my insides to quiver. Before I could even blink, he was standing, pants around his ankles, with his erection pointing straight at me.

I hurried to pull my chemise top over my head as Spencer stalked closer to me. He'd become the tiger, and *I* was his prey.

One knee on the bed between my legs, the other foot on the floor, he leaned closer. I couldn't get my panties off fast enough, which Spencer made clear when he tore them off me with a firm yank, his thick finger seeking my soaking wet heat.

"Nice and ready for me, sunshine," he said, that devilish grin on his face. "Good thing, because I'm about to fuck you." Spencer rubbed his heavy cock over my swollen clit, making me ache that much more. Circling his hips, he positioned himself at my opening. "Hard and fast, just like you *demanded*."

On that last word he thrust inside me. One, swift move and he'd lodged himself deep in my canal, my body fighting to accept his girth. Spencer didn't slow, and he didn't stop until he'd buried himself so deep I knew I'd feel it for days. Moving his hips, he slowly pulled out—all the way to the tip—before thrusting hard and fast.

"Ahhhhhh," I screamed again. Loud, unrestrained, full of raw emotion for all we'd lost.

It'd been almost seven months since I had a man inside me, felt the warm pulsing of an erection pushing past those sensitive nerves at my opening.

Stretching me.

Filling me.

Satisfying me.

Another deep thrust had me shouting his name.

Hanging by a thread, every thrust came with a promise to send me over the edge. My legs trembled as the quivering in my sex grew stronger. "Ahhh," I moaned again, pleasure taking over the pain of his swift intrusion.

Spencer pulled out.

No! I was so close to my release, I could almost taste it. Every nerve in my body was ready to explode and had me begging for release. "Please, Spencer. I need to come."

His smile widened. "Turn over" was all he said, but it was enough to get me moving. But struggling to turn with shaky limbs, I wasn't making much progress.

Spencer slid off the bed.

No. No. No. Please don't go. Don't leave me so close to the release I desperately need.

With a firm grip, Spencer's hands closed around my ankles. One second I was lying on my back, trying but failing to turn over, the next I was on my knees, face buried in the bed, my ass pulled high in the air.

Ohmygod!" I shouted when Spencer pushed inside me again, the new angle allowing him to slip even deeper.

Hard, fast, he fucked me just like I wanted him to, like I'd dreamt of too many times to count recently.

A quick snap of his hips sent his cock slamming into my cervix. "This hard enough for you, sunshine?" he asked in that deep tone I loved so much.

"Ohhhhh, ahhhh, ohmygod, yes!"

Spencer reached between my legs and gathered up some of the wetness from my arousal onto his finger before finding my clit. Pressing down on the sensitive bundle of nerves, he slowly moved in circles, increasing my need for release even more when I was certain that wasn't possible.

He increased the pressure, causing my breath to hitch. *Oh, God.* I was so close.

One command, that's all I needed. Three little words to send me flying.

Only, Spencer had other plans. "Who's body is this, Ash?"

"Yours," I blurted out without question, without thinking, and not just because I was hanging by a thread. I meant it. My body had never come alive for anyone like it did for Spencer.

He pressed harder on my throbbing clit.

"Oh, God. Only yours."

"That's right, sunshine. This body is mine. All mine." He thrust harder, his finger swirling faster. "Come for me," he commanded.

That's all I needed to hear. "YEEEEEES!" I screamed, all inhibitions lost as pleasure ripped through me. My body took over, sending contractions to my sex, squeezing the rock hard cock still buried deep inside me.

Hips bucking.

Legs shaking.

Screaming and moaning.

There was a moment when I may have even stopped breathing.

My back arched off the bed as every nerve in my body fired simultaneously, but Spencer didn't stop his assault on my clit. Circling, nibbling, biting, prolonging my orgasm until I collapsed in a pile of limp, sweaty limbs on the bed below him.

When the haze finally cleared, all I could see was Spencer lying beside me, an ear to ear smile covering his face, one arm tucked under his head, the other running barely there circles over my skin. I wasn't sure how I got to my side or the moment when Spencer pulled my body against his, but I didn't care. Right then, at that very moment, nothing else mattered but the man staring at me with eyes that would've melted ice.

Spencer pushed my shoulder until I was laying on my back, his still hard cock resting at the junction between my thighs. "Now that you've been thoroughly fucked, sunshine, I'm going to make love to you," he whispered softly before placing a gentle kiss on my lips.

Make love.

The words felt foreign to my ears. I'd never made love before. Not with Spencer or any of the Dom's I'd played with, and sure as hell not that bastard I married. What he and I did in the bedroom had absolutely nothing to do with love.

In, out, ever so slowly Spencer moved inside me again, his eyes firmly fixed on mine, drawing me in until everything around me faded and all I could do was feel.

Chapter Thirty Two

Spencer

This is where I belong. Buried so deep inside Ash she couldn't help but scream my name. Another thrust of my hips, another delicious sound.

"Oh, God, Spencer, please," she cried out that time, making my dick harden even more.

Not yet, sunshine. I had other plans tonight. Plans to send her higher than she'd ever gone before, so high she'd forget she wanted to run.

Another thrust, another moan.

"Please."

Ash didn't say what she wanted, and she wouldn't have to. I knew what her body needed. Increasing the pressure on her swollen clit, I slammed into her again, her inner walls already beginning to squeeze my cock, bringing me that much closer to my own release. A few more thrusts and I'd be done for.

Snapping my hips, I commanded, "Come for me."

"Ohmygod, yes! Yes! Yeeeeees!" she shouted as her walls clamped so hard around my cock, it sucked every drop of come I had right out of me.

When Ash's body finally began to relax, I rolled over to my back, taking her with me.

Feeling Ash's heartbeat against my chest soothed me in a way I didn't know was possible. As long as I could feel it beating, I knew she was safe. All I had to do was convince her that wrapped in my arms was where she belonged.

As much as I hated to break the peaceful silence that had settled between us, I didn't have much time to get Ash to trust me enough for what I had planned. "A bartender, huh?" I said.

"Yep," she answered, without lifting her head.

That one word answer had my chest moving with laughter.

"What's so funny?" she asked, a hint of defensiveness in her tone.

I tightened my grip around her back, holding her securely to my chest—just in case she had any ideas of moving away from me. "You are," I said, simply.

Her body stiffened and I knew I was losing the moment. I pulled her tighter then kissed her forehead, the tip of her nose, chin, everywhere but the place I knew she wanted it most.

"And why is that?" She snapped. "What do you find so funny about me?"

Her feisty tone sent my tongue involuntarily darting out to lick her lips. What I really wanted to do was devour them, only this wasn't the time for that. I put her at ease instead.

"Your one word answer, the casual way you responded, like nothing in the world was more natural than you tending bar, when nothing I know about you suggests that's what you did for a living." When I leaned in this time, I captured her lips in mine for that kiss we were both craving. Breathless, I pulled away. "What else don't I know about you, sunshine?"

The next few hours, with the help of some coaxing on my part, were spent listening to Ash tell me stories about the crisis center and her job and some guy named Rod, who I swore I'd kill until she told me he was gay. She talked about the teens she'd met so far and about the progress she'd made with a few of them. I laid silent beside her, in awe of how much she'd accomplished in the short time she'd been here.

The way her eyes lit up as she spoke, the passion in her voice, I'd say Ash had found her calling. She'd found a way to use the pain of her past to help others, which had helped her own wounds heal. Knowing how much those kids meant to her only made what I had planned for tomorrow that much harder.

Kind. Generous. Courageous. That was the real Ash. The woman I longed to hold for as long as I lived. The woman I'd prayed for...searched for...vowed I'd give up drinking for.

With Ash sleeping, safely tucked beside me, her back to my front, I continued to stroke her soft skin. It was a moment that felt like heaven, or at least how I imagined heaven would be, and one I prayed I'd have with Ash again.

My heart swelled with emotions. Running lazy strokes over her tender flesh, I whispered, "I love you, Ashlan." Because, God knew I did love her, with everything I had and then some. "I love you with all my heart, sunshine. And no matter how much you resist me, no matter how much you fight, I'm never gonna let you go."

• • • • •

Ashlan

Spencer's whispered 'I love you' had my heart racing out of control for more reason than one. He *loved* me and dammit if I didn't love him too. Only, I could never tell him. That piece of truth wouldn't set either of us free. Hell, it'd be the weight that held us under as we drowned in Val's evil plan. Nope, there would be no telling Spencer how much I'd thought about him or how much I missed him or how my heart sped up every time I even thought about him. I couldn't tell him that it was his face that haunted my dreams every night. And I most definitely couldn't tell him that he was the one I thought about when I touched myself.

As conflicted as I felt in hearing that Spencer loved me, it was his next statement that sent my mind scrambling. The fact was: it wouldn't matter how much he wanted to hold on to me. It wouldn't even matter that that's what I wanted too.

Spencer had no choice but to let me go. Val held the power to destroy me. One call from her and everything I'd done to escape the narcissistic bastard I'd spent years of my life bound to by marriage, all the sacrifices I'd made in leaving town, living in a place where I hadn't known anyone just so I could keep Spencer safe, would have been for nothing.

I couldn't let her do that. I couldn't let her destroy Spencer because I was too weak to stay away from him, or to live up to my end of the deal we'd made. She'd helped me escape, fake my own death, and even gotten me a new identity. She did exactly what she said she would. It was time for me to do the same, to hold up my end of the deal and stay away from Spencer James.

After we *made love*, Spencer and I laid in bed and talked for what felt like hours. I'm sure it wasn't actually *hours*, but it could have been. One question after another, it was like Spencer was on some sort of fact finding mission. We didn't talk about Diego or Val or anything from our pasts. He asked about my job at the Wharf and the crisis center and living in Texas.

We both laughed when I told him how awful I'd been my first day as a bartender. And by awful, I do mean I completely sucked. I don't think I mixed a single cocktail right that night, and I'm certain I spilled more beer than I actually sold. If Rod hadn't taken pity on me, that night would have been my one and only spent as a bartender.

Spencer pulled me close as I told him how hard it'd been for me when I first started volunteering at the crisis center, his warm strength encouraging me to continue. "I've got you," he whispered in my ear.

And he did.

Spencer James had me mind, body, and soul. *Oh, God, how can I let him go?*

I told him about Janine, a teenage runaway who reminded me of *me*. Abusive father, dismissive mother, no self-esteem, she'd fallen into the arms of a man who said he loved her, who treated her like she hung the moon—until she ran away with him. Just like with me and Diego, that's when the abuse started. From that very first night I was his, and he made damn sure I knew it, just as Robert had done with Janine.

It was as close to a confession of my past as I could give him without completely baring my soul and, by the time I finished telling him the story, I was certain he understood how much the crisis center had done to help with my own healing.

Lying next to Spencer, I realized I'd never felt closer to anyone before. Maybe it was the way he listened, like every word I spoke were the only words that mattered. Or maybe it was the way he held me close to his side, one arm draped protectively over my waist. Or maybe it was knowing that even with my bare breasts rubbing against his chest and his hand resting on my naked ass, he didn't have a hard on, which only proved that what I was telling him really did matter to him.

Eventually, I had to get up to pee, and when I came back to bed, Spencer quickly pulled me against him, my back to his front this time. "Rest now, sunshine," he said. "Tomorrow's a big day."

In that moment, my mind gave over to the security I felt in Spencer's arms, his slowed breathing lulling me deeper into relaxation. I closed my eyes, slowly drifting off to sleep, and that's how it happened, how I lay tucked to Spencer side, wide eyed with his confession of love running like mad through my mind.

Chapter Thirty Three
Spencer

The ringing of my cell phone had me scrambling out of bed to silence it before it woke Ash. I'd kept her up until well after sunrise, and I wanted her rested for what would come later today. From what she told me last night about her volunteer position at the crisis center, I knew the move was going to be hard on her. Working with the abuse victims there had helped some of Ash's own wounds heal. The others would take more time. We'd find another center in need of Ash's help, other teens she would be able to guide. As sad as I was to even think it, I was certain there'd be one.

Ash's wounds would heal. I'd see to that. She was *mine*, even if she wasn't ready to accept that.

I moved to the kitchen, which happened to be the furthest point from the sleeping woman I was trying not to wake, the paper thin walls of her rundown apartment making the job even harder. Quietly, I answered. "Hello."

"Good, you're up," Dane said in hurried tone. "Our flight leaves in an hour. Be ready in thirty." With that, the line went dead.

Well, fuck, there went my plan for Ash to be well-rested. All I could do was pray she'd understand when I told her I was leaving and she was coming with me. That was one bit of information I kept to myself last night.

I'd planned on telling her at first, but damn if I was going to deny the woman I loved sex after she'd demanded it. It was that fierce, sexy look in her eyes that had me forgetting everything I needed to tell her. Damn if I didn't want to keep that look of confidence and lust plastered to her face for the rest of her life.

After we'd made love last night, she'd shared so much of herself, opened up to me in a way she never had before. By the time she finished telling me about Janine, one of the teen runaways she'd helped at the center, tremors rocked her body. From what I knew about Ashlan's past, she could've been telling her own story as she filled me in about Janine's bastard of a father, or the man she ran away with, the one who'd swept her off her feet and whisked her away with promises of rainbows and unicorns. Hell, maybe that's why she'd chosen *that* story to tell, because she'd believed the fantasy Diego sold her once, too.

Realization gripped me like a damn vice. Last night, Ash had trusted me enough to bare her soul to me. And what's the first thing I was going to do with that trust?

Break her fucking heart.

Sitting on the edge of the bed next to her still sleeping form, I gently stroked the silky soft skin on her cheek. "Good afternoon, sunshine," I said as she stirred.

"Afternoon?" she said sleepily while rubbing her eyes. "What time is it?"

Seeing her naked breasts pushed out toward me, her pink nipples tight from arousal—or maybe it was the cooler air now that she was no longer covered by the blanket—as she arched her back in a full-on stretch had me wanting to climb back into bed beside her. The feel of her heart beating against my chest called to me in a way I didn't know was possible. This, however, wasn't the time.

Dane would be here soon and I still had to break the news that we were leaving. "There's no easy way to say this, Ash." Holding her gaze, I broke the news as softly as I could. "It's time to go."

The pink flush of her cheeks that she'd woke up with was gone in an instant, leaving behind a blank stare. She'd heard what I said, alright.

Wanting to give Ash the space she needed to process what was happening, I stood up. Spinning on my heels, I took the two steps to her dresser and began digging around through her clothes.

When I glanced back at her, I noticed she hadn't moved. Pulling a pair of yoga pants and a t-shirt from the drawer, I said, "We have to go, Ash. It isn't safe for you here."

Sitting back down beside her on the bed, cupping her face in my hands, I waited for her eyes to find mine. "Val knows where you're at, sunshine. It isn't safe here anymore."

"It isn't safe for you," she whispered, trying but failing to hold back the tears that had filled her eyes. "She'll kill you if she knows you're here."

Gone was the confident woman I'd spent the night with. In her place sat the scared little girl she'd tried to hide when I first met her at the club. That, I wouldn't stand for.

I wiped the tears from Ash's cheeks. "It isn't safe for either of us here. That's why we're leaving. Together." Before she could object, I added, "This has nothing to do with you, sunshine. It's me Val's mad at. It's me she wants to see suffer." I kissed her lips softly. It was a kiss meant to soothe and might've been more for me than for her. "She doesn't care who else gets hurt in the process. That's why we have to get you out of here."

I didn't want to scare Ashlan, but she had to know the danger she was in. "That night at the house, the night you saw the ambulance. Val had broken in. She drugged Izzy and attacked her, all to get back at me." I intentionally left out the part about her sleeping with Drew. That wasn't a detail I was ready to admit was true. "Val knows your new identity. She knows where you live, where you work, about the crisis center. She knows it all." Desperation filled the air, my words a plea to her heart. Ash had to come with me. She'd never be safe if she stayed, and I couldn't bear to live without her again.

"Spencer, I can't—"

"I'm not about to let you stay here and get hurt, Ash. What part of that don't you understand?"

Pressing my lips to hers, I kissed her like my life depended on it. Because hell if it didn't.

When I pulled away, all the question in my voice had faded. When I spoke next, I didn't ask, I commanded. "We're leaving. Now."

Ash looked down, the submissive inside her refusing to hold my stare any longer. "I can't just leave," she said, her voice barely a whisper. "The crisis center, the restaurant, they depend on me."

Tucking a finger under her chin, I lifted her head until her eyes met mine. Seeing the pain that rested there tugged so hard at my heart strings, I was surprised it didn't just rip right out of my chest the second I saw the anguish on her face. There was nothing I wanted more than to give Ash everything her heart desired. Her safety, though, that came first and was non-negotiable. Even if it killed me knowing I was breaking her heart.

"I know this is hard, Ash, and I'm sorry." I placed a kiss to her forehead before delivering the final blow. "But we don't have a choice. We have to go."

Without another word, I handed her the clothes I'd pulled out of the dresser. "Get dressed. Dane will be here in about ten minutes. You can call the restaurant and crisis center when we're safely out of town."

"But—"

"Enough!" my inner Dom snapped. It was my only defense against that pouty look on her face. "We're leaving in ten minutes. Get dressed or you'll be travelling nude."

I left her room before she could even try to argue with me. Any resistance and I'd surely crack. Hurt, disappointment, those were emotions I hoped to never see in Ash's eyes again and, after today, I'd do everything in my power to make sure I didn't.

Frustration, anger, now those emotions seemed unavoidable considering the fireball that was headed straight toward me. "I'm not leaving without saying goodbye, no matter how growly your voice gets!" Ash yelled.

She stood in front of me, her tiny fists resting on narrow hips. "For the first time in my life, I'm surrounded by people who care about me. I won't abandon them, Spencer James, and don't you dare try and make me." She closed the gap between us, her thin finger jabbing at my chest. "I'm not that scared little girl anymore, and I'm not afraid to fight!"

The heel of my boot connected with my shin in an attempt to suppress the smile that desperately wanted to break free. From the hard set of her jaw to the narrow slit in her eyes, Ash exuded confidence. She'd found her voice. Who was I to squash that? Especially considering how adorable she was when she was mad. If saying goodbye to the friends she'd made here important enough for her to fight me for, then damn if I wouldn't let her. I'd charter a plane, rent a car, do whatever I needed to do to give that to her. After years of being conditioned to take whatever shit was handed out, I was so proud of Ash for standing up for what she *wanted*, for what was important to *her*.

"Fine," I finally said. "You can say goodbye, but do it fast."

I stepped outside in a mock huff. While I was happy Ash had found her strength, I couldn't have her thinking I'd softened. Besides, I needed to call Dane.

• • • • •

Ashlan

Adrenaline coursed through my veins, igniting all my senses. As I stood in front of Spencer, my mind firmly set on what *I* wanted this time, I felt ten feet tall. I'd laid down the law. Told him how it was going to be. There'd be no giving in either. Not that time. No matter how long we stood there staring at each other. Through the bowels of hell, I'd found courage and strength and a side of me I was really starting to like.

I narrowed my eyes even further, pursing my lips as I did.

It was Spencer who cracked first. "Fine. You can say goodbye, but do it fast."

The door couldn't close behind him fast enough as Spencer stormed out of my apartment.

I won! I won!

I won! I chanted my victory over and over as I jumped up and down, waving my arms like an excited schoolgirl.

For the first time in my life, I stood up for myself.

And I actually won! And man, if winning didn't feel fan-fucking-tastic.

By the time I hung up the phone with the Wharf's general manager, the euphoric feeling that came with winning had faded. Oh, I'd won that battle, alright, but I sure as hell lost the war. Saying goodbye was so much harder than I remembered it to be. When I'd said my last farewell to my parents it'd been so much easier. Maybe it was in knowing I'd never have to see my father again or hear another one of mom's excuses as to why she hadn't tried to protect me.

My life was so much different now. I'd reinvented myself, found my voice, built a life here. A life I very much enjoyed and wasn't ready to leave behind.

Spencer's whispered confession last night was the only thing pushing me forward. I knew he meant what he said, and not just the part about loving me. When I ran, he'd hunted me down and found me, a feat I thought for sure was impossible. If I ran again, there was no doubt in my mind he'd come after me, and that seemed far more dangerous than letting him help me.

"I thought you were saying goodbye," Spencer said from behind me.

Quickly, I swiped the tears from my cheeks, not wanting him to see me crying. He'd been right in wanting me to wait, to put some distance between me and Galveston first before I said my final goodbyes. Only, I'd insisted on doing it my way, and look what it got me.

"I called the restaurant," I finally answered. "The rest can wait until later." After that call to my boss, I knew if I called Dawn or Rod, I'd never be able to get on the plane.

Spencer pulled me into him, his strong arms wrapping around my back. "I've got you," he whispered. "Everything's going to be okay."

All I could do was pray he was right.

Chapter Thirty Four
Spencer

Bringing Ash back to my house was risky, even with the kids off doing their own thing for the summer. It's what Ash needed, though. One month in that hotel suite and she'd had all she could take. She wasn't sleeping. Every bite of food she consumed was a battle I'd had to fight. Ash needed to resume a normal life. Hell, we both did. The financials for James' Industries were showing the effects of their absent leader. Sales in every division were down to their lowest in years. If I didn't get back to work soon, I'd have a whole other problem to deal with.

Not wanting to give up a single second of the time I had with Ashlan, I'd delayed the inevitable as long as I could. Unfortunately, the time for delay had ended. While I wasn't going back to work until Monday, it was time I put my past in the past so I could move forward.

And that meant breaking Izzy's heart all over again.

Fuck. I hated that what I had to tell my ex-wife was going to hurt her even more than I already had.

Meeting with Izzy was Ashlan's idea. She'd said *this* was definitely the kind of conversation you had in person. "You had sex with her best friend. That's not something you say in a phone call or text, jackass," she'd scolded.

Yes—scolded—and cursed, at *me*.

It didn't bother me, really, mainly because she was right, but also because she was cute as hell when she narrowed her eyes at me—that button nose of hers scrunching. Of course, that night ended with her bent over the pool table in my *man cave* as Ash liked to call the space that was once Izzy's office. While I found Ash's sass adorable, I couldn't let her get away with shit like that. Giving her too much power might prove to be dangerous and wasn't worth the risk.

Ash had told me all along she thought Izzy had a right to know her best friend wasn't loyal. At the time, I hadn't understood why Ashlan wasn't harder on me for what I'd done. I mean, I wasn't what you'd call loyal either, yet Ash had never come down on me for my part in what Val and I had done. After learning about Ash's past, I finally understood. How could she condemn me for being unfaithful when she had been doing the same thing?

The last time I saw Izzy, I was drunk. It was after graduation, not long after I saw Val. *After Val had given my son a blowjob backstage.* Chills ran through me at the mere thought of how wrong that was.

While I don't remember much about what happened that night, I do remember it included Izzy running away from me in tears and her new *friend*, Alec Payne, putting me in my place. But that was all part of the past I was leaving behind. It'd been over a month since I had a drop of alcohol. It wasn't a lot of time, but it gave me enough distance to see what an ass I'd been.

Drinking had clouded my senses and turned me into the man I swore I'd never be: a lying, cheating bastard.

There was nothing I could do to change my past. I'd made my choices, and I had to live with the consequences. I just wished they didn't include hurting

Izzy. Even the thought of hurting her again had my skin crawling.

On so many levels, what I was about to do was even worse than what I'd already done. Izzy was a kind, caring, amazing woman who deserved so much more than the shit I put her through, but Ash was right. Izzy needed to know the truth. And she deserved to hear it from me—face-to-face.

If one good thing came out of all of this for Izzy, it was that she'd found Alec. The way he looked at her—as if she were the only woman alive—said it all. He had it bad. Izzy too. As soon as I saw that picture of them from the paper, I knew. Never once in all the time we were together had Izzy looked at me with such longing.

Thank God Alec was a stand-up guy, which I knew from the background check and every other piece of data I'd been able to dig up, because I wouldn't have been able to handle it if Izzy were with someone who wasn't. She deserved to be treated like she hung the moon and, from what I'd seen so far, Alec did just that. God, I was thankful for him. One day I'd even tell him that.

The new me didn't drink or sneak around or keep secrets from the woman he loved. And that was a version of me I was proud of. I held on to that thought as I finished getting ready to meet Izzy. She'd been avoiding me for the past three weeks, so when she finally called me back and said she was staying nearby in Pensacola Beach, I jumped on the opportunity to finally put this deception behind us so we could both heal.

Val may have gotten past my security system in the past but, with the improvements my team made the past month, she wouldn't stand a chance if she tried again. The iron fence now extended along the full perimeter, complete with pressure sensors on the top rail and infrared security cleverly disguised as fence posts. Sixteen beams of light crisscrossing from one sensor to the next, and Ash was safer than the Hope Diamond.

So why was I finding it so hard to leave her here?

I tried telling myself it was only for a couple of hours and that, even with her lack of sleep, Ash was stronger than she'd ever been inside, but that did nothing to calm my anxiety. In that moment, I would have given almost anything for a drink.

Almost.

Thirty five days of sobriety, and I knew one drink would never be enough. One drink would lead to two and, before I knew what had happened, all control would be lost. I was smart enough to know that if I let that happen, I could say goodbye to Ashlan.

And *she* was one thing I'd never give up.

Doing the only other thing I knew would calm my nerves, I pulled Ash close to me. "Promise me you'll stay inside until I get back," I said as Ash wrapped her arms around my back.

"For the gazillionth time, Spencer, yes, I promise. Now stop asking and just go already."

These past few weeks, Ash's sassy new attitude had grown stronger and stronger to the point she was testing the outer edges of my patience. She'd been pushing me to scene with her, but I wasn't ready to go there. And that was something Ashlan had been working hard to change.

Taking her by the arms, I moved her away from me, my nostrils flaring as I inhaled deep breaths into my lungs.

When my narrowed eyes met hers, she folded. "Ya know...so you're not late. You don't want to keep Izzy waiting, right?"

"I know what you're doing, Ashlan, and it's not going to work." Cupping her face in my hands, I leaned in, our lips almost close enough to touch. "Stop pushing me or you'll never get what you're after."

"Ugh," she sighed, a sound I heard a lot from her lately. Definitely not a sound I enjoyed hearing, but what choice did I have? There was no way I could tie her up and whip her, not after seeing what Diego had done to her.

Surprising me, Ash reached up and placed her hand on my cheek. "How many times do I have to tell you, Spencer? I'm fine." She kissed me, a quick peck on the lips. "Totally." Another kiss. "Completely."

When she leaned in to kiss me again, I fisted my hand in her hair. Pulling her head back, I sealed my lips over hers and stole the kiss right out of her mouth. Ash was right, she was so much stronger than before. Unfortunately for her, I wasn't. Seeing those images of Ash—broken, bruised...

A shiver ran down my spine just thinking about how many times her tiny body had been abused at the hands of a man she'd trusted. Reading the medical reports had only made it worse. Seeing her words in black and white, all the lies she told to hide the truth, hadn't helped either. It broke something inside me.

Something I wasn't sure I'd ever be able to fix.

Keep your shit together, asshole.

I pulled away, finally breaking our kiss. I'd wanted Ash to remember who was in control in our relationship, not die of suffocation. With a stern look, I said, "I have to go." I couldn't let that emotional shit derail my plans. Telling Izzy that Val and I betrayed her was going to be hard enough without images of Ash's injuries in my head.

"Fine, but this isn't over. I'm not some delicate flower you should be afraid to bruise. You knew who I was when you fell in love with me, so I suggest you figure this shit out."

Damn it. Her boldness was really starting to turn me on. One long stride and I closed the gap she'd put between us. "Keep it up, Ashlan. I said I wouldn't take you back into a scene, I never said I wouldn't punish you."

She threw her hands in the air. "Hallelujah," she shouted. "It's about damn time!"

Boldness, yes.

Yelling at me? Hell. No.

Pulling her close, I fisted my hand in her hair tight enough to send a message. "Is that what you want, sunshine. You want me to punish you?"

Her knees buckled, and I had to tighten my grip to keep her upright. "Yes," she said on an exhale.

My nostrils flared. If punishment was what she wanted, I'd give it to her. "Okay. If that's what it's gonna take to get you to drop this shit. I'll punish you." I tightened my hold on her hair, pulling her head back far enough so she was staring right into my eyes. "No orgasms for a week."

Just like that, I released her hair and took a step back, putting space between us. She'd demanded to be punished, and now that she had been: I couldn't offer comfort.

"That's not fair! That's not what I meant, and you know it!"

Which is exactly why I chose it as your punishment, sunshine.

"Careful what you ask for, Ash. The next time I might not be so generous."

"Generous? Is that what you call a week without sex?"

The smile on my face grew wider. "Oh, baby, I never said anything about withholding sex. This is *your* punishment, not mine." Her eyebrows narrowed into a thin line, her bottom lip protruding, which I quickly took into my mouth.

She didn't resist as my tongue parted her lips. Holding her head firmly, I claimed every inch of her mouth. When I pulled away, her ragged breathing told me everything I needed to know. It wouldn't take long to bring her to the edge of orgasm. I'd have her begging for a release.

A release she wouldn't get tonight.

Hopefully, she'd think twice before she demanded anything from me again.

My fingers dug into her ass as I lifted her into the air. "Wrap your legs around me," I said in that low register that had her immediately complying. She didn't question my order this time.

With her back firmly pressed against the wall, I thrust my hips forward, the hardness of my erection grinding against her clit.

"Ahhhhh," she moaned, her nails digging into my shoulder.

Oh yeah, this was going to be quick. Sliding my hands along the delicate curves of her body, I took her wrists in my hands, gently kissing each one before pinning them to the wall above her head.

Harder, faster, I continued to grind against her.

"Ohhhh, ahhhh, ohmygod, yes," she cried out.

One more thrust of my hips got me what I was looking for. "Please, sir?"

Trailing kisses along the edge of her jaw, I made my way to her ear. She could beg all night, she still wouldn't get that high she was chasing. Topping from the bottom, fuck that.

"Please, sir," she said again. The urgency in her voice told me she'd reached the edge.

Three little words. One command and she'd be flying. Too bad she'd insisted I punish her.

Quickly, without warning, I let go of Ash's arms, pried her legs from the death grip they had on my waist, and returned her feet to the ground.

"Sorry, sunshine, not today."

Chapter Thirty Five
Ashlan

Dammit, dammit, dammit! I'm such an idiot. I should have known Master Spence would come up with a punishment that totally sucked. Not that I could really blame him. I had been pushing pretty hard lately.

Don't get me wrong, I was thankful for the time with Spencer, all the talking, cuddling, *making love.* As awkward as those words still felt to me, that's what it'd been. Every thrust of his Spencer's hips, every movement of his cock inside me, every *ohhh* and *ahhh* and *ohmygod yes,* connected us in a way I never knew was possible. It was a side of Spencer I loved.

It's just, well, I missed Master Spence. The command of his voice. The kiss of his whip followed by the tenderness of his touch.

Oh, God, *his* touch, those strong hands exploring every inch of my body.

Pain.

Pleasure.

Pain.

Pleasure.

That was our dance, a dance more exotic than the tango.

Just thinking about my Dom had my sex quivering. *Dammit!* A week without orgasms was gonna suck even more than spending a month in that damn hotel suite had.

God! I'm such an idiot!

Walking around Spencer's house half nude still felt wrong, which was why I'd waited until I was outside by the pool before removing the shorts and tank top I'd worn over my bikini. I was well aware of the fact that I'd promised Spencer I wouldn't go outside but, technically, the pool wasn't *outside*. Spencer had a birdcage installed over the pool as an added safety precaution before we checked out of the hotel. And since Spencer hadn't said I couldn't swim, I didn't feel too bad about my decision.

Besides, no one was getting past that iron monstrosity he had erected around the property, so I didn't see what all the fuss was about. What Spencer failed to realize was I'd never felt safer in my entire life, even with him off to see his ex-wife.

Actually, I'd never *been* safer.

I was thankful Spencer finally went to talk to Izzy. He owed her the truth but, more than that, he owed it to himself. He'd spent most of his marriage hiding, sneaking around, having kinky sex in clubs. That's what his life had become, one lie to cover the last, all the while pretending to be someone he wasn't. What he and Val did to Izzy, betraying that level of trust, was more than wrong. It was time for him to stop living that lie, to tell the truth so they could both start to heal.

Five weeks alone with Spencer and I didn't understand how he'd managed to keep his lifestyle a secret. Spencer may have been a lot of things, but vanilla wasn't one of them. Even outside of a scene, the way the fucked...*oh, God*...yeah, definitely not vanilla.

Spencer and I had spent almost every second together since he hunted me down in Galveston. "When I'm with you, I know you're safe," he'd said. He made no apologies about it either, not caring that my privacy had become a thing of the past, you know, with Spencer practically glued to my side and all.

Three weeks ago, we'd had dinner in the hotel restaurant. I'd tried to excuse myself from the table so I could use the ladies room but ended up with an escort instead.

Yes, *escorted*.

Me, a grown ass woman having her hand held so she could pee in a public restroom.

To my utter shock and horror, Spencer's protection hadn't ended there, either. Nope, he'd gone into the bathroom, ordered everyone out, double checking every stall to make sure it was empty, and then stood guard outside the bathroom door so no one could come in until I was done. Needless to say, that was the last time we ate out. No way was I looking for a repeat of *that*. Until Val was caught, ordering in would have to do.

To say Spencer's meeting with Izzy couldn't have come at a better time would be an understatement. If I hadn't gotten a break from all his overprotectiveness soon, I probably would've lost it. Don't get me wrong. I love Spencer more than I ever thought possible.

There was no denying the chemistry between us either. When we came together, the earth shook. Well, not literally, but it sure felt like that to me.

It's just...I needed to be alone so I could process everything that'd happened in recent months, time alone to wrap my head around my new reality. A reality that Spencer made sure I understood included him.

Really, I didn't know if I could make it without Spencer anymore. I'd gotten used to waking up in his arms—that warm, seductive smile of his leaving me a pile of goo beside him with a ridiculous grin on my face, a smile that seemed never ending. Spencer had spoiled me with his kisses. The way the man kissed, he stole the breath right out of my lungs.

I'd gotten used to the little things, too. The smell of his body wash at breakfast, the way his forehead wrinkled when he read the paper, the little noises he made whenever he watched a sporting event, the way he laughed at the most unexpected things. I'd come to look forward to them all, so how could I live without him?

Spencer left no room for doubt when it came to his love for me. Every day, he'd taken the time to prove the words he'd said in Galveston were true.

He loved me.

And I loved him too. It just wasn't as easy for me to show it. As hard as I tried to give myself over to Spencer truly and completely, to open up and be honest about everything in my life, there were things I just wasn't ready to share.

The fact that I'd seen Drew and Val together in a scene happened to be one of those things. Guilt tugged at my heart every time I got near the downstairs bedroom where I saw them together, playing.

My heart warred with my mind. With all my sanctimonious bullshit about how some things weren't meant to be kept secret, how could I keep this from him? Didn't *he* have a right to know Val and Drew were together? Especially considering all the shit she'd pulled?

Every day, Spencer went out of his way to earn my trust. He lavished me with love and attention and too many gifts to count. And how did I repay him?

By hiding the truth of my past. By holding onto the pain and refusing to let it go. By keeping things from Spencer that had the potential to destroy him.

God, I didn't deserve that man. I didn't deserve his love or trust or understanding. And I certainly didn't deserve all his gifts.

When I left Galveston, my entire wardrobe fit into an overnight bag. Here, I had a closet full of clothes and shoes and everything else I could possible want—and then some. I'd tried objecting to him spending so much money on me. I'd tried refusing the gifts. I even tried getting mad at him.

Nothing worked.

Every single morning we woke up at the hotel, Spencer surprised me with something new. The gifts always included at least one new piece of lingerie. At the end of our month there, I had enough lacy bras and panties to fill an entire chest, a fact that was proven when he moved me to his house. And when I'd objected to having my underwear in the same chest where Izzy had kept hers, wouldn't you know, Spencer bought me one of my own.

After the first week of daily gift giving, I told Spencer he wasn't allowed to give me any more presents without a reason. The next week, every package included a card stating why he'd bought me the gift.

Because I love you.

Because you're sexy.

Because you're strong.

After that, I said he wasn't allowed to get me any more gifts—period. From that point forward, the packages always had his name on them. That had been the end of the argument, his latest move making his point crystal clear. He bought me gifts because *he* wanted me to have those things, and he had no intention of stopping.

It wasn't like I minded the presents. Actually, I loved all of them. I just wasn't used to receiving things for no reason. Spoiling me had definitely not been something Diego did often. When he gave me a gift, it was either to make himself look good or atone for my latest hospital stay.

Maybe that's why Spencer continued to buy me things, because he wanted me to know how different he was from Diego, that he spoiled me because he wanted to. Now, *that* was a comparison I'd never make. Spencer was *nothing* like the evil bastard I had been married to. Well, technically, I guess I *was still* married to.

Hearing Spencer talk about moving forward was a reminder of my own past. Maybe that was the real reason I'd insisted he make things right between him and Izzy, because I knew I'd never get that closure myself.

You'd think reading my own obituary would have helped me put my marriage behind me, and it had, to a point. In the back of my mind though, I knew I was still legally bound to Diego. Sure, the state of California had declared me dead, but that was just a technicality. And knowing *that* was enough to plant a seed of doubt in my mind about the kind of future Spencer and I could possibly have together.

An hour in the pool and I was beyond exhausted. The hotel bed had been surprisingly comfortable, but I still hadn't slept well, not even with Spencer lying next to me. All the stress of running, the emotional turmoil, not to mention all the sex...*oh, God, the sex*...had taken its toll on me: mind, body, and soul.

As much as I hated to get out of the water, I climbed out anyway. I wasn't about to end up drowning in a swimming pool after I'd risked my life to live.

Hell. No.

Drowning definitely wasn't appealing, but neither was going back inside the house. I'd been trapped indoors for so long, it was a wonder my skin hadn't paled.

I kicked myself for promising Spencer I'd stay inside. The evening sun was just starting to set. Less than an hour and the sky would be dark with night, but right now, standing at the door to the lanai, it was filled with amazing shades of red and orange and yellow.

The sun's heat called to me, the promise of her warmth prickling my skin.

Would Spencer even know if I sat in the soft sand? Or let the water tickle my toes?

Or let the sun's rays warm my soul?

Every minute that passed, the sun seemed to dip lower. Before long it'd be gone, pulled to the other side of the earth—leaving me cold and alone until Spencer got home.

Without another thought and before I changed my mind, I grabbed the towel I'd brought outside with me and took off toward the beach to watch the sunset. Spencer wouldn't be happy I'd broken my promise and especially not that I went outside alone, but once he saw I was okay, I knew he'd forgive me.

Chapter Thirty Six
Spencer

I called from the tiki bar by the hotel pool to let Izzy know I'd arrived. She'd suggested the spot, and I hadn't argued, even though being surrounded by the temptation of alcohol still wasn't easy. Right now, my comfort meant nothing. My focus was on one thing and one thing only: Izzy. Her sun kissed skin glistened in the early evening light, appearing to glow. God, she looked good. A little thin if you asked me, but she hadn't, and I certainly wouldn't comment on it.

Izzy's eyes ran right over me as she searched the bar. Clearly, she hadn't recognized me, but that wasn't a big surprise. Hell, it'd been almost three months since my last haircut, and lately I'd been testing out a goatee. "Izzy, I'm over here."

Turning toward my voice, she said, "Spencer?"

Her shock at my appearance didn't go unnoticed, but it didn't bother me either. I opened my arms for a hug, closing them around her as she pressed her body against mine.

Izzy's white gardenia scent was familiar and soothing in a way I hadn't expected. Part of me didn't want to let her go, that small part that would always love her, that would always want the best for her, but the rest of me knew it was wrong to hold on any longer than necessary so, when she pulled away, I didn't resist.

"You look great, Izzy."

She hesitated before answering. "You too."

The waiter approached soon after Izzy sat down. Relief washed over me when she ordered a Coke. I hadn't mentioned my sobriety, mostly because Izzy had been avoiding my calls for weeks, but even if I had, it's not like I deserved relief.

"Is that a new drink?" she asked as I lifted my glass for a quick sip to soothe my suddenly dry throat.

"Actually, it is," I said. "It's called water."

Dammit. That came out wrong. I hadn't meant to sound like a dick. I knew I was the asshole in this equation. Izzy didn't deserve my shit, and from her body language, it was clear she wasn't going to put up with it, either.

And *that* made me smile.

To see her back to the strong, fierce Isabella Jones I'd met in college, the woman she'd been before I almost destroyed her, warmed my heart.

She shook her head, the smile on her face growing too. "What's going on, Spencer?"

I took a deep breath to steady the nervous energy inside me. "Izzy, um… I don't know where to start." I stared down at the bar looking for the strength to get through the next few minutes then verbally slapped myself for even thinking about ordering the one thing that would instantly destroy the new life Ash and I were building.

Izzy reached out and touched my shoulder. It was a whisper of a touch, as if she wanted to offer comfort but wasn't sure she should.

Fuck, this was going to be hard on her.

"From the beginning," she said.

From the beginning...

With another deep breath, I blurted out, "I'm an alcoholic, Izzy." Her eyes widened in surprise, but she stayed silent, so I continued. "I made some terrible decisions. I let alcohol control my life. I hurt you. I hurt my family." The truth of my confession was the hot knife in the gut I deserved. Diverting my eyes, I finished with a whispered "I hurt us."

We spent the next several minutes talking about the program I'd started to help with my drinking problem. Then I spent an obscene amount of time apologizing for hurting her. Our conversation felt casual and light, which was a complete contrast to the information I needed to tell her.

Izzy reached for my hand, her eyes finding mine. "Look," she said, gently. "I'm not going to say what you've done is okay, because it damn sure isn't, but I forgive you. I've moved on, Spencer, and I hope you can too."

Her strength and courage in the face of what I'd done amazed me. She wasn't hiding from life, she'd embraced it. Alec had done wonders for her, although the tired look in her eyes was somewhat worrisome. Then again, meeting today had probably been hard on her, too.

It was time for me to stop stalling. I sucked in a deep breath then said, "The woman in the pictures, Izzy..." my voice trailed off as I searched for the right words to lessen the blow.

"We don't have to talk about her," she said, quickly. "You were right, who she is really isn't important."

"No," I drawled, garnering the last ounce of courage I could find. "I have to tell you." I took another deep breath. "Izzy, there's no easy way to say this. The woman in the pictures, the woman I had the affair with…it's Valerie."

Coke spewed from Izzy's lips onto the bar the second Val's name left my mouth. "Valerie who?" she demanded.

"You know who I'm talking about, Bella."

Damn it, why had I said that? She hated it when I called her by her childhood nickname. I'd started to say baby, but when I thought better of it, it just came out Bella.

Jesus. Couldn't I get anything right where Izzy was concerned?

After a long pause, Izzy finally broke the silence. "You're the man she cheated on Cody with."

Her declaration had been whispered, but I'd caught what she said. It was clear from that statement she knew Val had cheated on her husband. *Fuck.* I'd been sure Val would stay away from Izzy after I found her in Atlantic City and promised to ruin her if she didn't. Although, after finding out she'd seduced my son, I should've known she would never keep her word.

When the waiter walked by, Izzy all but shouted, "I'll have a Corona now, please, and a shot of tequila." Her words had been rushed, and I knew she was fighting to maintain control. I'd just split that wound she'd fought to repair wide open.

Izzy slammed the shot back first then took a long drink of her beer, draining at least a third of the clear glass bottle before setting it down on the bar. I didn't say a word at first, knowing Izzy needed the alcohol to soothe her nerves.

"Izzy, I'm sorry." Lame, I know, but I had to at least try to make her feel better.

"Don't, Spencer," she snapped. "You cheated on me with my best friend!"

Anger.

274

Good. Anger was better than sadness.

"I didn't mean for it to happen," I said truthfully, offering the only comfort I could in this situation. "I ran into her when I was on a business trip. We got drunk, and it just happened."

She took another long drink. "It just happened. That's the best you've got!"

"What do you want me to say? I screwed up. I know. Nothing will ever change that."

The pain on Izzy's face fucking killed me. I looked away, burying my face in my hands.

I couldn't help but kick myself in the shin. *I'm such a dick.*

"Why are you telling me this? Why now?"

"Keeping it from you was killing me. Plus, you have a right to know."

"You're concerned about my rights all of a sudden?" She chugged the rest of her beer and ordered another one. "You should've told me earlier if you were that concerned about me," she shouted, her voice getting louder with every swallow of liquid courage. "I feel like such a fool. I just spent the weekend hanging out with the woman who was fucking my husband!"

What did she say? Val was here? *Fuck, this is bad.*

I looked up just as she was standing to leave, her beer firmly clutched in her hand. I grabbed her arm. "She was here?"

"Yes, she left this afternoon," she said suddenly, no doubt surprised by my aggressive move.

I ran my free hand over my face to center myself then looked her in the eye so she could see how serious I was. "She's bad news, Izzy. You should stay away from her."

"That's the pot calling the kettle black, now isn't it, Spencer." She pulled free from my grip and moved away before I could reach her again.

Dammit. I'd hoped she'd stay, scream, yell at me, hit me...almost anything other than storm off, ready to drink her pain away. I'd been down that road and knew the dangers of being seduced by alcohol.

Dropping more than enough money to cover the tab onto the bar, I headed for my truck. Izzy needed space and, as much as I wanted to follow her to make sure she was okay, that wasn't my place anymore. She had Alec. But there *was* one thing I could do. Val had spent the weekend at the hotel, which meant they'd have video of her. With any luck at all, the video would lead me right to her.

Hacking into the hotel's security system was easier than I'd expected, a point I noted for my sales team as this hotel wasn't one of our accounts. Izzy hadn't said what room she was staying in, so it took me a while to find her. I traced her from the back entrance, the one I'd seen her enter, then down a few hallways.

Letting out a sigh of relief that Izzy made it safely back to her room, I started the tedious task of combing through the videos I had access to, which appeared to only be about a day's worth. *Fuck.*

My exhaustive search for clues on where Val might have gone turned up nothing. She'd disappeared in the parking garage where the security camera coverage sucked.

Frustration took over, and I pulled out my phone to call Val. *Fucking voicemail!* "I told Izzy about us. You got what you wanted. Now stay the hell away from my family, you crazy bitch."

Fuuuuuck! I wanted to scream and yell.

And drink away the pain?

"No!" I shouted, not caring that my windows were down and the parking lot was full of people coming and going. *This* was definitely not the time to lose my shit and go off the deep end, but I couldn't let myself succumb to the seduction alcohol offered either.

Switching back to the live video feed, I turned my attention back to the task at hand. The hotel had dozens of cameras, so I knew the facial scan would take a while longer. In the meantime, I'd make sure Val hadn't returned—

"What the fuck?" Pulling out my phone, I called up my newest contact and dialed.

"Detective Rux," he answered on the first ring.

"I found her," I spit out. "Valerie. Russell. She's at the Margaritaville."

"Are you sure it's her?"

"Positive. How fast can you get here?"

"It'll take me at least half an hour to get there from my office. I'll call the local P.D., have them send a team to the hotel now."

While I appreciated his action, it wasn't good enough. Val was inside Izzy's room. They needed to be there now. "Izzy's in danger," I said. "Tell them I'm going in." I ended the call before he had a chance to tell me not to. Divorced or not, I couldn't stand by and wait when Izzy could be in trouble. Stuffing my phone in my pocket, I raced toward the hotel.

Hotel security was at Izzy's door when I got there. According to one of the men, they'd been called in on a suspicious noise complaint. That's all I needed to hear. I ripped the master keycard out of the other man's hand and opened the door.

What I found dropped me to my knees. *Oh my god, Izzy.*

Chapter Thirty Seven
Ashlan

Watching the sunset, surrounded by the peacefulness of the private beach alcove and warm summer sand, I couldn't help but reflect on everything that had happened in my relatively short life. Born into abuse, destined to live a life of pain and fear, separated from friends and family and everything that brought joy, denied the life I'd spent years dreaming of—until now. Through it all—every punch, every kick, every trip to the hospital—I'd survived. All the hate and verbal abuse and thinking I was nothing, through it all I'd come out whole.

And strong.

And dare I say, *happy?*

Spencer offered me that life I'd spent years praying for but knew I'd never have: an opportunity to live life on my terms, to love and be loved, *to have a family.* Not in the traditional sense, of course, Diego made sure of that a long time ago, but a family just the same. It was the life I'd always wanted, and now that it was in front of me, now that Spencer was offering me everything I could possibly want and then some, only there was one thing was holding me back.

One thing that stood in the way between me and the life I knew deep down in the depths of my soul I deserved.

The lie I told.

A lie so big an innocent man was sitting behind bars.

Oh, Diego was guilty of many things, of that I was certain, and none of them included being a decent human being. But he was innocent of the charges against him, and I couldn't live with knowing he'd do jail time for a crime he didn't commit.

Plus, how could I build a solid future with Spencer when, technically, I wasn't even alive?

Since finding me in Galveston, Spencer had taken every step possible to earn my trust, to prove he wasn't the man he'd been when he cheated on his wife. Yeah, well, I wasn't the same person I used to be, either. I wasn't afraid to stand up for myself, or too scared to fight for what I wanted. And, as scary as it sounded, the more I thought about it, the more I knew what *I wanted* included telling the district attorney the truth. I wanted Diego to pay for what he'd done to me, but that was in God's hands. Letting any man rot in jail for a crime he didn't commit would eat at my soul and only end up destroying *me*.

And I deserved better than that.

Spencer deserved better than that, too. He'd recognized where he went wrong and then set out to fix the mistakes he'd made, to change himself for the better.

And change he had. I'd been doing everything I could think of to get Spencer to take me back into a scene. Damn it if he ignored all my bratty behavior. Not even yelling at him had earned me the sensual pain I was after. It'd been months since I'd found the kind of freedom only submission could bring. I craved the touch of Master

Spence, the caress of his command as it washed over me, enveloping me in his deep, sensual tone. I'd begged to feel the kiss of his whip or flogger or his hand...I wasn't picky.

Only, he wouldn't budge.

Of course, I knew why he was refusing and, I guess on some level, I understood his position. When he thought about taking the flogger to me, even though it was clear that's what we both craved, he saw those awful photos, the ones of my worst injuries, and he'd change directions.

He'd changed in other ways, too. Some differences were subtle, like the way his eyes smiled all the time now. The tension lines I'd thought were a permanent fixture on his otherwise smooth face had faded, too. Other changes were a lot more noticeable, as was the case with his overgrown hair and goatee. But the biggest change had to be his sobriety. Spencer hadn't touched a single drop of alcohol since we'd been back together, and *that* had helped to mend his relationship with Drew.

Drew hadn't hesitated to accept me when Spencer first introduced us. I'm pretty sure the fact that his mother had moved on and was head-over-heels in love as he called it, helped my case immensely. Drew was every bit as protective as his dad, and I had no doubts that if Izzy were unhappy, I'd be his sworn enemy for what Spencer and I had done at the club.

When I allowed myself to think about what I saw that night between Drew and Val, it made me all kinds of uncomfortable, so I did my best not to go there, because, dammit, I was enjoying getting to know Spencer's kids. Drew had quickly proven himself every bit as funny and charming as his father, and I imagined Anna's soft, sweet nature came from her mother. I mean, not that Spencer wasn't sweet or anything, it's just...well, Anna's kind of sweet softened even him.

Lying back on the towel I'd laid out, I watched in silence as the sun dipped below the earth's surface, too low to be seen. Only the orange hues remained as day gave way to the darkness of night. Closing my eyes, I allowed the peacefulness to fill my mind.

• • • • •

Spencer

As soon as the ambulance sped away, I called Alec. I had no idea he wasn't at the hotel with Izzy.

Goddammit! Why hadn't I asked? Izzy had said she'd spent the weekend with that fucking bitch, Val, and I hadn't even thought to ask if Alec had come with her.

He answered on the second ring. "Payne."

"Izzy's hurt," I blurted out in a single breath, but that's all it took.

"I'm on my way. Where is she? How bad is it?"

After giving Alec the name of the hospital and as many details as I had, I hung up to call Ashlan. Seeing Izzy's injuries had me more than worried that I'd left Ash home alone for so long. Val wanted to hurt me. What better way than by hurting the mother of my children *and* the woman I was in love with?

A cold shiver rocked my body when Ash's voicemail picked up. *Fuck.* I hung up without leaving a message, immediately trying the call again.

Racing through the city streets, I sped toward home, every unanswered call only increasing my need to get there faster. Why wasn't she answering?

Oh, God. What if I'd been wrong? What if Val had gotten past my security system undetected?

At that moment, I swear my heart was beating faster than the truck was moving. Seconds felt like minutes, and minutes felt like hours.

Oh, God, please let her be okay.

Why wasn't she answering the damn phone?

I called so many times I lost count. Even if Ash were sleeping, surely the constant ringing from my calls would've woken her up by now. There was only one reason I could think of as to why she wasn't answering my calls.

She couldn't.

Merging onto the highway, I mashed the gas pedal to the floorboard as hard as I could, pushing the truck as fast as it would go as I barreled down the long stretch of road that would take me from Pensacola back to Ft. Walton Beach, all the while praying I would get there in time. Izzy was hurt, wasn't that enough pain to atone for what I'd done?

Please, God, let Ash be okay.

By the time I finally made it home nothing appeared out of the ordinary. I'd found the gate closed and locked, as it should have been. The garage was closed, the door leading into the house locked, and the security system was actively monitoring, as indicated by the control panel near the front door. But where the hell was Ashlan?

I ran upstairs, calling to her. "Ash? Sunshine, where are you?"

No answer.

I ran back downstairs, feeling more frantic by the second. "Ashlan! Ash, where are you?"

Dammit. Still no answer.

A check of the pool deck had my senses tingling. Ash's clothes lay in a pile on one of the lounge chairs. I was certain they hadn't been there when I left earlier. I'd checked the locks on the lanai doors twice and would've noticed the brightly colored, purple tank top.

My eyes panned left, and I caught sight of Ash's phone, causing my heart to skip a beat. "Asshhhhlan!" I screamed. It was a desperate, mangled cry that was two parts fear, one part pissed off Dom. I'd told her not to leave the house, made her promise me over and over again that she wouldn't, but she did it anyway.

And now she's fucking gone!

Chapter Thirty Eight
Ashlan

"Asshhhhlan!" The mangled cry ripped me from the deep sleep I'd apparently been in, considering I hadn't noticed it was pitch black out, or that I was freezing cold.

I stood up, dusting the sand off the best I could. Spencer must've sensed my movement, because as soon as I was upright the door to the lanai came flying open.

Light from inside the house only illuminated part of the yard, but that was plenty of light for me to see the tension in his steps as he stalked toward me.

Like a deer in headlights, I didn't move.

I was stuck. Frozen in place by the angry Dom headed my way.

Tremors rocked my body, and it had nothing to do with the night air.

To my surprise—and disappointment—Spencer pulled me into his body, his arms closing around me in a death grip. "I was so worried," he said, sounding rattled. "I called and called, but you didn't answer. I drove as fast as I could. I'd thought something happened to you."

My phone.

Dammit. I'd left it in the lanai, never intending to be out there long enough for me to need it. "I'm sorry," I said, feeling like a jerk for making him worry, even if he'd pulled me in for a hug instead of sending me to my knees to be punished. "I guess I fell asleep." His deep groan told me he wasn't thrilled, but he hadn't loosened his grip, either. "It's okay. Spencer, look," I pushed away from him so I could see his face. "I'm fine. I probably shouldn't have lain on the beach. It's just...the sky was so gorgeous..."

The more I spoke, the more his nostrils flared, yet I couldn't seem to shut up. "And I'm so pale."

Spencer's head tilted, regarding me intently before he said, "Let me get this straight, sunshine. You ignored my orders to stay inside where I knew you would be safe, because you're *pale*?" The way he spit the last word out had my mouth glued shut. At my slow nod, he continued. "And if you'd..." He cleared his throat. "If something had happened to you, how pale do you think you would you look then?"

When I didn't answer, Spencer's eyes narrowed even further.

"You're right, okay," I blurted out. "I said I was sorry."

"Oh no, not this time, Ashlan. I told you, when it comes to your safety, my orders are non-negotiable." His hand closed around my wrist. "We're going inside."

Ripping my hand from his grip, I challenged. "And what if I don't want to go inside? What then, Spencer? What are you planning to do about it? Another week without orgasms?" I knew I was poking the bear, because I meant to. He needed to push past his fears about hurting me so he could finally give me the scene we both deserved.

Spencer took half a step and closed the distance between us, his eyes narrowing to tiny slits, nostrils flaring with every inhale. Oh, God, Master Spence was here.

And he was pissed.

"You wanted a scene, sunshine. Well guess what, you're about to get one. Now, move your ass."

How could I argue with that?

· · · · ·

Spencer

I ordered Ashlan upstairs to rinse off and then soak in an *extremely warm* tub until further notice, knowing the heat of the water would warm her skin, giving her a more intense sensation later. Plus, she was covered in sand from her fucking nap on the beach, and I didn't want that gritty shit tearing me up when took her over my knee. Ash wanted a scene? Well, she was going to get one, just as soon as I put my head on straight.

"Detective Rux," the man answered on the first ring.

"Have you found her?"

"Not yet, Mr. James. Several witnesses saw her fleeing in a white sports coupe, a Merce—"

"Mercedes E350?" I supplied.

"That's right. And how exactly did you know that?"

"She's in Izzy's car, which has a GPS tracker. Hold on." I ran to my man cave and fired up my laptop. "Give me a minute, I'm just booting up."

"Mr. James, I'm in the middle of an active investigation. I need to get someone on this. I don't have time to hold."

"Two more minutes, Detective, I'll have what you need." His grunt said he didn't really believe I could offer anything useful, but he'd hold, at least a little while longer.

As soon as the James' Security tracking program was up and running, I began the search for Izzy's car.

"Okay, time's up."

The sonofabitch didn't think I could track her. Yeah, well...he'd see.

"Goodbye, Mr. James."

"Wait, I found her," I blurted out. "Shit! She's over the state line." I rattled off the address in Mobile, Alabama where I tracked Izzy's car then listened to the detective ramble on about jurisdiction.

Dammit. Couldn't I catch a break in finding this crazy bitch?

It'd already been at least two hours since Val disappeared from the hotel. She'd had plenty of time to ditch the car, and who the hell knew what else.

The bad news was, Detective Rux couldn't just send police chasing into Alabama after her. He had to call the state police first, and who the hell knew how long that would take?

The good news? Val wasn't in Florida, which meant, if at least for one night, I didn't have to worry about her breaking into the house to carry out her insane vendetta.

My call to Alec had been more optimistic. Izzy was in stable but critical condition, which he said meant she wasn't in immediate danger but also wasn't out of the woods yet. He'd sent his bodyguard to a hotel with Drew and Anna when they moved Izzy into the ICU, which had been pretty soon after the ambulance delivered her to the hospital. Since Val had drugged Izzy at least once before, the doctors knew what to look for. They caught the toxin early and Alec said the doctors were hopeful she'd make a full recovery.

Considering it was me Val was after, Alec and I both agreed it was best if I stayed away from the hospital until the police had more information on her whereabouts. He gave me the hotel information so I could check in on the kids in the morning, promised to call if Izzy's condition worsened, then said goodbye. Things were far from perfect, but they were a hell of a lot better than they could've been. Izzy was in good hands. There was nothing else any of us could do tonight.

With those thoughts in mind, I checked all the locks on the doors and windows downstairs, double checked that the alarm was active, and headed upstairs to deal with my bratty sub.

• • • • •

"On your knees." I issued the order as soon as Ash stepped out of the tub. Skin wet and overheated from her long soak in the warm water, she'd soon prickle in the air-conditioned room, further sensitizing her skin. She wanted a scene? I'd give her one. Not that intense shit she was after, but after months outside the lifestyle, I bet she'd still be feeling the sting of my hand across her ass tomorrow morning.

In light of the stunt Ash pulled, she should consider herself lucky *this* was the only punishment I had in mind. After tonight, she'd understand how serious I was about keeping her out of harm's way.

She'd also understand that when it came to her safety, I would never negotiate again.

Circling her ever so slowly, I trailed a finger over Ash's shoulders, eliciting a delicious shiver. In what?

Anticipation?

Desire?

Lust?

"You pushed and you pushed to get this scene, didn't you, sunshine?"

Her answer came quickly, the excitement in her voice clear. "Yes, sir."

"And earlier today, when you *demanded* I punish you, you wanted me to take you into a scene then, yes?"

"Yes, sir."

I stepped in front of her, my bare feet slapping against the marble floor, increasing the rise and fall of her chest. "Eyes to me." As soon as she obeyed, I confirmed the smile in her eyes, proving she knew the difference between what Diego had done to her and what *I* was about to do. Fear didn't live in Ash's eyes anymore, a fact I fucking loved.

"And when I punished you earlier, you wanted me to use the whip?"

She shifted on the hard floor but didn't break her pose. "Yes, sir."

With a fistful of her hair, I titled her head back further. "You want me to whip you now, sunshine?"

She pulled her head forward then flinched as she remembered my tight hold. "Yes, sir. Please," she begged.

"Up, now." I helped her to her feet, leaning into her personal space, further increasing her discomfort. While I didn't want her to fear my punishments, I didn't want her that excited about the possibility, either. Besides, as punishments were used to deter certain behaviors, a little discomfort would be expected.

Pressing my lips to hers with a feather light touch, I said, "Whips are for good girls, Ash. And you weren't a good girl, were you?" The hitch in her breath told me she was catching on. She wouldn't be getting what she wanted, but she'd sure as hell get what she needed.

"No, sir," she said, finally.

Without another word, I sealed my lips over hers, running my tongue against the seam. It was an urgent demand for her to open, which she immediately obeyed. My tongue sought hers, circling, twisting, commanding her through our kiss. I had to make sure Ash knew how much I loved her before I reddened her *pale* skin.

"I love you, Ashlan," I said when I finally pulled away.

"I love you too, sir."

There were no more words spoken until after we were positioned, me sitting on the edge of the storage bench at the foot of the master bed, Ash laying across my lap, her bare ass right where I wanted it.

Whack...Whack...Whack... I delivered three solid swats, one on top of the other, to her right butt cheek. Ash wanted to be punished? Well, good thing, because after disobeying my repeated orders to stay inside where I knew she'd be safe, she needed a good, old-fashioned spanking.

"Who's job is it to keep you safe, sunshine?"

Whack. That swat landed on her left cheek. I wanted to get my point across, not actually hurt her. Well, not too bad anyway.

"You, sir."

"Who will do anything to keep you safe?" *Whack.* "Who would die if something happened to you?" *Whack.* "Who loves you more than life itself?" *Whack, whack, whack.*

"You, sir," she rasped out, her voice dripping with heat.

"Who risked her safety today?"

Whack. Whack.

"Me, sir."

Without a second thought, I began moving my hand over the marks I'd left. Soft, slow circles that tugged at my heart—then a spark of possession jolted me back to the task at hand.

Ash was mine.

Mine to hold. Mine to love. And mine to protect. I couldn't let her get away with jeopardizing her safety.

"Who broke her promise to me?"

"Me, sir."

"Who needs to be punished, Ash?"

"Me, sir."

"That's right, Ash. You."

I finished off with five hard swats to her already red bottom. *Whack, whack, whack, whack, whack.*

"Who loves you more than anything, Ashlan?"

Her breath hitched when she answered. "You, sir."

I lifted her to her feet slowly before pulling her onto my lap. "That's right, sunshine. I do."

With that one statement, I vowed more than my love. She owned me, mind, body, and soul, and I planned to spend the rest of my life making it worth her while.

Epilogue
Spencer

As soon as Izzy was strong enough to travel, Alec took her back to the safety of the beach house they'd been living in. An overly priced house on Siesta key that my sources told me he recently purchased—in her name. Not long after that, he'd called to tell me he was taking her out of the country for the rest of the summer. The timing of the trip in relation to his new real estate acquisition seemed somewhat suspicious, but I hadn't called him on it. Izzy needed time away from the dangers Val still presented and, from the strain I heard in Alec's voice, I'd say he did too.

Despite everything that had happened between me and Izzy, she'd made time to call me when she and Alec arrived in Spain. She'd made peace with the things I'd done. I imagined her being madly in love with Alec probably had something to do with that.

Drew headed back to campus to wrap up his summer courses and start preseason training with his new team as soon as we found out Izzy would be okay. Anna left a couple days after that to get settled into her new apartment before her fall classes started. Ash had been sad to see each of them go. It touched my heart to see how much she cared for my kids. They both seemed to like her, too. I'd been worried at first, given the circumstances of how Ash and I met. To my surprise, Drew and Anna had welcomed Ashlan with little reservation. And, actually, they all seemed to get along great.

Ashlan unveiled her *set the record straight* plan a few days after I took her over my knee. She'd said she came to the decision as she was lying on the beach that night I went to see Izzy but had decided to wait to tell me until after her butt had time to completely recover. And while I'd appreciated her honesty, I hadn't been able to let that slide.

"When you can sit without flinching, if talking to the DA is still what you want to do, then we'll look in to it," I'd said, fully expecting her to change her mind. Only, she hadn't. Which was how we ended up sitting across the table from one pissed off assistant district attorney.

As soon as the younger man opened his mouth, I knew he had been planning on using this case to advance his career. Well, too bad for him Ash's conscious refused to let her stay quiet. Over a month of her badgering and my insisting *looking in to it* took time, and she never once wavered in her resolve.

"Do you have any idea how much money you've cost the State of California, Mrs. Rivera?"

Fuck. Hearing her referred to by that bastard's name had me ready to put my fist through the wall. If I was still drinking, I might have done just that.

"Yes, and I'm sorry."

God. I hated it even more that she was apologizing for keeping herself safe. Something the police weren't able to do. Why should Ash feel guilty for saving her damn life?

"I should throw the book at you for all the trouble you've caused." He narrowed his eyes, a look that may have rattled a weaker woman, but not my Ash. She was done being intimidated. "Lucky for you," he continued, "your stunt exposed a crack in your husband's organization, a crack so big it's already led to the arrest of dozens of people in his distribution network and turned up mountains of evidence against him for other crimes. With everything we've collected, Diego will be going away for a very long time."

Thank God for that.

"That being said, I could still press charges for all the damage you did to the Bixby Bridge and for stealing a cadaver."

Fisting my hands on top of the table, I looked over at Blake Everett, the attorney I hired to handle the mess we were dealing with.

Nobody stole the damn body.

One of Val's ex-husbands bought it, but Ashlan refused to give up his name, so Blake said it'd be better to just say she stole it. While his advice to her pissed me off, it hadn't surprised me. If Ash told the DA the whole truth, she'd have no choice but to tell them who her accomplice was—or risk jail time.

There wasn't a chance in hell I was going to let Ash spend one second in jail over what happened.

Whatever expression Blake saw in my face had him shutting the other man down immediately. "I'd say Ms. Parks has been through enough torment without your threats, wouldn't you?" He stood to leave, gathering the papers back into his briefcase. "Send me a bill for the damages if you need to. We're done here."

That was the confirmation I'd been waiting for to get Ash the hell out of there and as far away from her past has possible. Taking Ash's hand in mine, I rose from the table then escorted her out of the small conference room, relieved the whole nerve-racking event was behind us.

Blake had already spoken with the man's boss, so I knew there wouldn't be any charges filed, but that hadn't made the meeting much easier. Hearing Ash relive her painful past gutted me, every last second of abuse she suffered at the hands of that motherfucker.

It'd taken every ounce of willpower I could muster to keep from flying out of my chair to put a stop to the whole damn video recorded statement. The only thing that allowed me to keep my cool was the knowledge that after today's meeting this whole nightmare would be over.

Blake stopped us in the lobby. "You two go on without me, I have a meeting with the DA so we can wrap up the fine points of the details, but he's already agreed to drop the murder charge against Diego because of a technicality—most likely having to do with the chain-of-evidence or something—to help protect your identity."

"So what does all that mean to me? I mean, what do I call myself? Ashlan Parks? Ashlan Rivera?"

"Ashlan James?" My heart answered before I could filter the comment. Ash's teary eyed expression told me she hadn't minded.

"Pick whatever name you want," Blake said. "The judge isn't going to care what name we put on your new identification documents."

Pulling Ash into my arms, I kissed her on the lips. "How about it, Ashlan? Are you ready to make it official?"

"Really? I mean, are you sure? After everything you just heard in there? You still—"

I sealed my lips over hers before she could finish her statement. I wouldn't allow her to go one more second thinking that she didn't deserve love because of what that bastard did to her. Hell, I was the one who didn't deserve *her*. I'd lied and cheated and betrayed my wife, but somehow, through all my flaws, Ashlan loved me. Together, we picked up the pieces of our shattered dreams, and our love held them together.

"There's nothing I want more, sunshine."

Contact HD Kelley at:

Email: me@authorhdkelley.com

Website: www.authorhdkelley.com

Facebook:
https://www.facebook.com/AuthorHDKelley/

Twitter:
@HDKelley

OTHER BOOKS BY HD KELLEY

Betrayed by Love Series
Scattered Thoughts
Broken Promises (Winter 2016)

USF College Series (Coming Soon)

www.greenwaypublishing.com